D0783219

Dare to Stay

Georgia Beers

Dare to Stay

THIS TRADE PAPERBACK ORIGINAL IS PUBLISHED BY BRISK PRESS, BRIELLE NEW JERSEY, 08730

EDITED BY LYNDA SANDOVAL
COPY EDITED BY HEATHER FLOURNOY
COVER DESIGN BY ANN MCMAN
FIRST PRINTING: DECEMBER 2016

ISBN-13: 978-099667746-2

By Georgia Beers

Novels

Finding Home

Mine

Fresh Tracks

Too Close to Touch

Thy Neighbor's Wife

Turning the Page

Starting From Scratch

96 Hours

Slices of Life

Snow Globe

Olive Oil and White Bread

Zero Visibility

A Little Bit of Spice

Rescued Heart

Run to You

Dare to Stay

Anthologies

Outsiders

www.georgiabeers.com

Acknowledgements

Writing a series is much harder than I anticipated, but as I reach out to put the final volume of my trilogy into your hands, I have nothing but fierce pride. I hope you enjoy these people as much as I did.

Thank you to Carrie and Susan at Brisk Press. I say the same thing every time, but it still holds true: they make a process that could be tedious and stressful easy and painless. This author is very lucky to have them.

My editors are the best. Lynda Sandoval and Heather Flournoy, I'm keeping you guys. You've been warned.

I'd have thrown myself out a window long ago if not for Melissa, Nikki, and Rachel. You three remind me every day of who I am and what I'm capable of accomplishing. And you never let me slack off. I owe you big for that and for your friendship. Thank you from the bottom of my heart.

This series may be over, but my love of animals—dogs especially—will never end. Love and thanks to all the canines who have touched my life and my heart, and all of those I still have yet to meet.

Thank you to Bonnie. For everything and so much more.

Last but never least, thank you, as always, to my readers. It is because of you—your support, your messages, your emails—that I can keep doing this weird, wonderful, crazy, awesome job of mine. You keep reading, I'll keep writing, deal?

Dedication

To everybody who has ever loved or been loved by an animal.

CHAPTER ONE

THIS WILL NEVER FUCKING WORK.

Change was not something Jessica Barstow handled well, as was evidenced by the paperwork in front of her. The annual telethon to raise money for Junebug Farms Animal Shelter was less than two months away, but as Jessica stared at the headshot of the new reporter Channel Six was sending to replace the retired one, the one who'd hosted the telethon for the past several years and the one Jessica was comfortable with, the same phrase kept echoing through her head over and over and over.

This will never fucking work.

Elbows propped on her desk, Jessica let her weary head drop into her hands as she groaned. She needed to relax, damn it, or she was going to completely stress herself out and she usually saved that for when the telethon was closer. She couldn't dissolve into a blubbering mess of anxiety just yet. It was way too soon.

Rubbing her palms roughly up and down her face a couple times, Jessica did her best to shake off the feeling of dread she always got when some big shake-up hit her life. At least she wasn't *quite* freaking the hell out. Yet.

A couple of gentle raps at her door yanked her attention away from her misery, thank God. Catherine Gardner stood in the doorway, eyeglasses dangling from one hand, and cocked her attractive head to the side.

"Well. Meltdown has commenced, I see. You look like crap."

"Gee, thanks."

"I just call 'em like I see 'em, ma'am." Catherine entered the room and sat regally in one of the two chairs situated in front of

Jessica's desk. She casually crossed her legs and studied her friend's face. "Talk to me. What's got you all weirded out?"

Jessica blew out a big breath, picked up the headshot, and handed it across the desk to Catherine.

"Wow," Catherine said, eyebrows rising up into her hairline as she slid on the glasses. "She's *gorgeous*." Jessica didn't need to look any more; she'd memorized the face. Dark hair a bit past her shoulders—tousled just enough to look sexy, but not enough to seem messy—mesmerizingly deep, blue-green eyes, amazing facial structure with cheekbones any model would kill for. "Seriously. It should be illegal to be this good looking."

Jessica allowed a chuckle. As Catherine herself was so stunning, such comments from her seemed ironic. "She's fine."

"She's fine?" Catherine looked up and studied her. "I know this whole shift in hosts is hard for you, but has it screwed up your eyesight, too? What's that tone about?" She handed the photo back.

"I don't have a tone."

"You do, and you know it."

Jessica sighed in defeat and looked away. They'd been friends for years and Catherine knew her well; she'd see right through her.

"Are you nervous?" Catherine asked.

"About what?"

Catherine shook her head with a grin. "Why do you fight me? You know I'll get to the bottom of this. If you'd just tell me what's going on, I can offer you my very wise, very sage advice and then get out of your hair, save us both a lot of work."

Jessica couldn't help but laugh, as Catherine was exactly right. "You don't want to do our usual dance?"

"Listen, I love to dance with you, but I don't have time today. My boss is a slave driver and I have nearly a dozen donors to contact before I go home."

"As said boss, I take offense to that."

"Ha. What's going on, Jess? Talk to me."

Jessica sighed and sat back in her chair. A glance out the window told her how busy Junebug Farms was on any given day, as her office was in the front of the building and looked out onto the large parking lot. It was a Monday, late morning, and therefore rather quiet, the lot peppered with only a handful of cars. Returning her gaze to Catherine, she said, "You're right. I'm just nervous. I've been in charge of the telethon for more than five years now and I feel like we finally had it running like a well-oiled machine, you know?"

"And having new television talent might throw a wrench in the gears, so to speak?"

"Exactly. Why did Janet have to retire?" Jessica whined, referring to the local, beloved television anchor who'd always done the Junebug Farms annual telethon.

"Because she's in her sixties, worked hard her whole life, and wants to spend time with her family now?"

"Stop trying to confuse me with logic."

"Let me ask you this: does your worrying and freaking out about the new talent do anything to help? Does it make it better?"

Jessica made a face at her. "No, Miss Know-It-All. It doesn't."

Catherine shrugged. "Well, there you go."

"You know, having sex on a regular basis hasn't made you any more pleasant."

"That's because you're jealous."

"Shut up. I hate you."

3

"I know."

They sat grinning at each other across the desk until a knock at the office door interrupted the friendly teasing and Anna St. John, head of public relations at Junebug Farms, stuck her head in.

The first thing Jessica noticed was the utter lack of reaction from Catherine, which was new. It was as if Catherine had a button in her head that said *Pleasantly Neutral Face*, pushed it, and all expression just slid right off. She and Anna were exes from nearly a year ago. Catherine had broken up with Anna, and Anna took every opportunity she had to launch digs at her. Over the past few months, though, Catherine had begun seeing Emily Breckenridge, whose family was one of the largest donors to Junebug Farms, and one the animal shelter depended on to survive. Jessica had initially been less than thrilled by the pairing. She worried about the implications, and what might happen to the donations if the couple went belly up. But Emily had shocked her by transferring to a different department in her company so she could continue to see Catherine without raising eyebrows. Jessica had never seen her friend so happy, as evidenced by the fact that she didn't stiffen up or invent a reason to leave as she used to do whenever Anna walked into the room. She simply remained seated and looked impartial.

"Hey," Anna said as she entered the room and approached Jessica. "Sorry to interrupt." Like most days, she sported her usual jeans, green polo shirt with the Junebug Farms logo, and her blond hair was pulled back in a ponytail. She glanced quickly at Catherine, then down at the open folder on the desk as she said to Jessica, "You wanted to touch base about the next newsletter and e-mail blast and—oh, my God, what's this?" She picked up the headshot.

"That's the new talent Channel Six is sending us for the telethon since Janet's retired." Jessica tried not to sound childish and bitter, but she was pretty sure she failed.

"Isn't she pretty?" Catherine asked, clearly to stress what she thought Jessica was missing.

"Um, yeah. She's also a hell of a kisser." Anna looked smug as she tossed the photo back onto Jessica's desk.

"I'm sorry, what?" Jessica said.

"Yeah." Anna looked up at Catherine, a self-satisfied smirk on her face. "I met her about, what? Two months ago? Three? At Sling. She totally picked me up."

Jessica made eye contact with Catherine, knowing that Anna's story—true or not—was told for her benefit. Catherine didn't roll her eyes, but Jessica was certain she wanted to.

"You're sure it's the same woman?" Jessica asked.

"Would you forget that face?" Anna bumped Jessica's chair with her hip. "She was alone at the bar, so I struck up a conversation. She seemed nice enough, but I think she was there for something…specific. Know what I mean?" Anna glanced toward Catherine and winked. Jessica rolled her lips and bit down, smothering a chuckle at the unimpressed expression Catherine now sported, the *Pleasantly Neutral Face* setting obviously malfunctioning. "We ended up making out in that back hallway near the bathroom," Anna went on.

"You didn't take her home?" Catherine asked, the sugar-coated innocence in her voice almost cartoonish.

"She decided she needed to go. Which was a bummer." Anna shrugged. "What're you gonna do, right?"

Catherine returned the shrug, complete with wide eyes and a slow headshake that almost made Jessica lose her composure, but she held on.

"Well, I certainly hope that little tryst won't affect you working with her when the time comes." Jessica said it matter-of-factly, but the idea made her stomach churn a little bit. Running a business in the age of social media was no easy feat. Running a *nonprofit* was even more difficult. She was still recovering from the Catherine/Emily close call that had kept her up nights; she wasn't ready for another one. When she took over the animal shelter after her grandmother died, she'd never expected that part of her job would be policing the love lives of her employees.

"Of course it won't," Anna said, a tiny note of hurt in her voice. "You know me better than that."

So many retorts ran through Jessica's head then about just exactly how well she *did* know Anna, but she decided to take the high road. "Oh, good. Well." She shut the folder on the stunning 8x10 of one Sydney Taylor. "She'll be here late next week with her producer to meet with us, go over some details, all that fun stuff."

"I look forward to it," Anna said. With a quick glance in Catherine's direction, she stood, bid them goodbye and left the room.

When the door had clicked shut, Jessica held Catherine's gaze until Catherine finally looked skyward and said loudly, "I don't know!" It was her stock answer to the question Jessica mentally posed every time they had any kind of interaction with Anna: *what the hell were you thinking?*

"She's a piece of work," Jessica said.

"She's a piece of something," Catherine agreed, pushing herself to her feet.

"Well, she's an excellent public relations rep, so I'm keeping her."

"Fair enough. Okay. Work to do." And Catherine was gone.

Jessica's gaze was pulled out the window as she sat back in her soft, black, leather chair. She was very careful to make sure the shelter didn't spend money in the wrong places, so their office furniture was all secondhand, their computers refurbished. But Jessica had splurged on her chair, figuring if she was going to spend more time in that one seat than any place else in her life—including her bed—she deserved to be comfortable. Granted, it didn't really match the industrial metal desk or the neutral beige of the steel filing cabinets along the walls, but she could sit there for hours and not end up with an aching spine, so she considered it money well spent.

Returning her attention to the folder on her desk, she opened it again, stared into the mesmerizing blue-green eyes of Sydney Taylor. It was no wonder she was in television; she certainly had the face for it. Brad Hyland had known Jessica for a while now, and he knew how nervous she was to do the telethon without Janet Dobson. "We need to skew younger," he'd told her. "That's why we hired Sydney, as well as a handful of younger producers and writers. They'll hopefully help us reach a younger audience." Jessica let out a snort. Sydney Taylor couldn't be more than twenty-six or twenty-seven, judging from the photo. How in the world was she going to do what Janet Dobson had perfected over the course of several years?

They were streaming online as well as on TV, a full six hours, and Brad actually seemed kind of psyched about all the changes, which did help Jessica feel a *tiny* bit better. Under the 8x10 glossy of Ms. Taylor was a list of past adopters from Junebug Farms. She'd compiled it at Brad's request, and it was one of the many things they'd go over when they met on Thursday. The adopter testimonials were also the thing that, as far as Jessica was concerned, brought in the most in donations and were the catalyst for the majority of adoptions that took place during and after the telethon. Listening to somebody's story about finding their soul mate in an abandoned dog or knowing as soon as they looked at the elderly cat that they had to have her, those were the most touching moments, the things that squeezed hearts and pushed people who were teetering on the edge of "do I or don't I want a pet," or "should I or shouldn't I donate some money," right off the cliff. And not only were they heartwarming, they were success stories. Because, as much as people wanted to think of Junebug Farms as this adorable farm that housed a bunch of sweet animals, Jessica had no choice but to look at it as a business. Her grandmother, the woman who'd started the shelter after she'd retired from her job as a fourth-grade teacher, had taught her that. She would never say so out loud—and neither would Jessica—but when it came right down to it, there was product to move. And product that stayed around too long was bad for business.

Janet Dobson had understood that.

It would be interesting to see if Sydney Taylor would.

CHAPTER TWO

"SO? HOW IS IT?"

Sydney Taylor sighed softly at the question, torn between telling the truth and pacifying her best friend. Laura's voice was curious and cheerful, with a tinge of wistfulness. She was still in Pennsylvania and, though she understood Sydney's job would take her possibly all over the country, as she told Sydney often: she didn't have to like it. "It's fine. It's a nice apartment. It's not big, but it has hardwood floors and a huge clawfoot tub. And the windows are big, so it's pretty bright in here. There's that."

"Well, that sounds nice. I'm glad you found something that'll work. Are you unpacked?"

"Not yet." Sydney looked around the room, at the small collection of boxes stacked against a wall, and her desire to open them, to fish out what meager belongings she'd chosen to bring, was all but nonexistent. "I will."

"You start on Monday?"

"Yeah. I'll go in, get introduced to my fellow newbies 'cause my boss told me they'd hired a handful of new, younger employees."

"I'd think they'd have to. Television news must be getting trounced by the Internet."

"It is. But the problem there is, you can't always believe what's online. You really need to investigate and fact-check. People believe whatever you tell them or whatever they read on whatever website they happen to find, which is just irritating."

"So you've told me," Laura said with a chuckle. "About fifteen hundred times."

Sydney gave a half-hearted laugh as well. Laura was right. They'd had this discussion over and over, as it was a sticking point for Sydney that Americans were too lazy to double-check the authenticity of what they read online.

"Did you check in with your parents?"

"I sent a text. They'll see it eventually. I think they're in the middle of the Caribbean right now."

"Again? Didn't they just go on a cruise?"

"A couple months ago, yeah. They loved it, so they're off again. They left earlier this week." Sydney could almost hear Laura shaking her head in disapproval, but she made no comment. This was not new territory. For either of them. Sydney was used to her parents doing their own thing, and since her father had retired at fifty-five, they'd been even less present. And while Sydney, their only child, pretended it never bothered her, Laura gave voice to enough indignation for the both of them.

But not today.

Today, she simply let it lie, and for that, Sydney was grateful.

"All right," Laura said after a beat. "I'll let you get to unpacking. Keep me posted on how things are going there, okay? And get out and explore your neighborhood."

"I will."

"I've met you, remember? You won't unless I prod you about it. Consider yourself prodded. There's more to come."

"I can hardly wait," Sydney said, feigning annoyance, but in reality was touched by Laura's concern.

They hung up and Sydney tossed her iPhone onto the coffee table and flopped back onto the couch, which seemed to almost hug her, it was that worn and soft. It was slate blue, the fabric some distant cousin of microfiber, the cushions shaped with age.

It had started in her parents' basement rec room. They'd given it to Sydney when she got her first apartment away from home after college. Now, it had traveled with her to upstate New York, to a small city she wasn't thrilled about. At all.

Too small. Too far north. Too boring.

All the things she'd concluded about the small city that had been last on her list of options she thought she'd had coming off her last job near home in Pennsylvania. She'd wanted a *mid-sized* city. Austin. Raleigh. Chattanooga. Someplace warmer than Pennsylvania. And not tiny. Instead, the Universe had given her upstate New York. Cold, small, boring upstate New York, super close to Canada, with average highs in the 80s and average lows in the teens, depending on the month you looked at.

Sydney groaned in frustration for the four hundredth time over her relocation, but then told herself that Laura was right, that her boxes weren't going to unpack themselves. With what seemed like Herculean effort, she pushed herself up and went into the small kitchen to unpack her dishes. A glance at the small counter reminded her that the landlord was nice and had left her a bottle of wine to welcome her and a stack of menus and information on local establishments. A well-timed rumble of her stomach told her she'd forgotten to eat today.

"A pizza sounds good right about now," she said aloud, picking up a menu. She made the call, testing out how her new address sounded, then continued to unpack.

An hour later, she sat on her couch, her stomach uncomfortably full of pizza, a half-empty wineglass on the coffee table, and her laptop open in front of her. With no cable yet, her television was useless, so she plugged in her mobile hot spot, checked e-mail, scanned Facebook, skipped through Tumblr, and told herself that was the last time she was going to be able to gorge herself like a teenage boy. She couldn't go on the air looking like a bloated version of herself.

Channel Six was going to put her on human interest to start out with. To "get her feet wet" was how Brad Hyland, the GM of the station, had phrased it. He "wanted to see what she could do," is what he'd said. Sydney'd had to bite her tongue to keep from asking, *wasn't that what my clips were for? To show you what I could do?*

Human interest. Ugh.

She so did not want to be here.

Turning on the couch, she stretched to the end so she could get a close-up view of the small fish tank on the table against the wall. Marge and Homer swam around languidly, Homer's rounder, puffier body the only way Sydney could tell the goldfish apart. They'd made the trip all the way from Pennsylvania in the car with her and she was disturbingly happy about it, given that they were…well, *fish*.

"I guess I need to quit the complaining for now, huh?" she said to the glass as she reached for the lamp nearby and clicked it on. The filter in the tank hummed quietly, sending tiny bubbles through the water and helping keep things clean for her finned companions. "What do you think, Marge? You're the reasonable one here." The fish actually seemed to look at her, its tiny mouth opening and closing in a little O. "Yeah, I see your point. That's kind of what I thought, too. Put my head down, do my job and do it well, and in the meantime, keep adding to my reel, sending it out to bigger stations. Somebody will bite. No pun intended." She nodded and reached for the remainder of her wine. "Yeah. That sounds like a plan. Thanks, Marge." She gently tapped the edge of her glass to the glass of the tank. "You're the best."

Sydney hadn't been lying to Laura. The apartment *was* really nice. Small, but modern. And small was fine with Sydney, as she wasn't home all that often and didn't have a lot of stuff. She'd learned early on that television news was a tricky business, and you could be called on to up and go at any time. Being tied down—to people, places, or things—never worked in this world. Channel Six in upstate New York was her fourth stop since college graduation, and there would be more. She was sure of it. So she limited her belongings to the necessities: clothes—her wardrobe was of utmost importance—kitchen essentials, basic furnishings, and a car. That was pretty much it. Aside from Homer and Marge, and a box of books, she had no knickknacks, no dust-collecting sentimentalities. There was one framed photo of her with her parents and one of her and Laura from their college graduation. That was enough. She didn't need attachments.

The other benefit of having so little was that unpacking in a new place was a pretty quick job. One day was enough time. She looked around now, happy with her surroundings. The windows all came with mini-blinds, so she felt no need to go buy curtains—a blessing, as she'd rather set her own hair on fire than have to shop for window dressings. The neutral off-white of the walls was just fine with her. No need to paint. The hardwood floors were a light oak, polished to shiny perfection and kept the small space bright and sunny. Tilting her head to the side as she studied, she came to the conclusion that an area rug for the living room and another for the bedroom might make sense. Hardwood was cold on bare feet and she spent almost all her time at home shoeless, thanks to her love/hate relationship with her work heels. She'd have to think about it, though. Spending the money on such things might prove to be senseless if she moved again as soon as she hoped to.

Tomorrow was Sunday, and she planned to spend the day exploring to begin looking for some ideas to pitch to her boss for stories. She needed to prepare a bit for her meeting with him about that animal shelter—the name of which escaped her at the moment—and the possibility of her hosting their telethon. Maybe she could find the place while she was out wandering.

A quick glance at her phone told her it was after ten. While she was used to keeping odd, late hours, the excitement of the day had caught up with her and with no television to lull her into couch potato comfort, she decided to shower off the moving dirt and turn in early. Tomorrow was the first day of her short—hopefully *very* short—stay here. She was ready.

CHAPTER THREE

SYDNEY WAS JUST SHOULDERING her bag to leave her apartment, on Thursday morning of her first week at her new job, when her cell rang. Seeing the name on the screen, she grinned and answered it, despite not having a ton of time.

"Hey, you." She tossed her bag onto the couch and flopped down, waiting to hear Laura's voice.

"So? Your first week is almost over. How do you feel?"

Sydney could hear her smile, sense her concern and curiosity wrapped up in one. "I'm okay," she said honestly. If there was one person in her life she could never fool, it was Laura. She'd stopped trying after living with her for a semester. There was something about her, something about their connection and the way they related, like they were meant to be best friends from the beginning. Lying to Laura was *literally* something Sydney couldn't bring herself to do, no matter what. "The station is nicer than I thought it would be and everybody seems competent."

Laura scoffed. "Well, then. I'm so glad you're finding your new colleagues worthy of you."

Sydney heard the tease—and also the underlying rebuke. "And they've all been nice so far," she hastily added. "I got my first two assignments."

"Fantastic! Tell me about them."

"Well, the first is I have to interview the owners of a local microbrewery. They just won some major beer award or something. It's basic human-interest stuff, but it's good. I can make it work."

"Don't knock the human-interest stories, Walters," Laura admonished, using the nickname she'd given her after they'd spent their first evening together in their dorm room and Laura had told Sydney she wasn't talking to her, she was interviewing her. "The news is heavy. It's depressing. It brings people down. They look to the human-interest stories to be lifted up again, 'cause the world kinda sucks. You know?"

It wasn't the first time she'd said something similar to her. "I know. I know. And I'm glad you feel that way because the second one is pretty big."

"Yeah?"

"Brad touched on it when he first hired me, but he'd labeled it a possibility. But Monday, he told me he for sure wants me to host the annual fundraising telethon they do at this local animal shelter. I guess it's a pretty big deal. Their regular anchor used to do it, but she retired last year and they want me to help bring in a younger audience."

"Seriously? That's awesome!"

"Still human interest. Not really anything gritty, but—"

"What did I just say?"

Sydney laughed. "I know. You're right."

"I usually am. When will you just accept this as fact?"

"Probably never. What's on your agenda today?" Sydney smoothly changed the subject. "How many days until summer vacation? Because I know you're counting."

"No, I am not counting," Laura said, her voice laced with indignation. "Thirty-three."

Sydney laughed. Laura was a home economics teacher at a small school in Pennsylvania and she loved her job. Which didn't mean she didn't also love summer vacation.

"It's closing in…"

"Yeah, well, it needs to close in a little faster. I've got a couple students who might end up dead a lot sooner than thirty-three days. A lot sooner."

"They probably just have crushes on you."

"Duh."

Sydney laughed.

"Okay, Walters, I've got to run. Just wanted to check up on you. Make sure you're eating, okay? I don't want to have to drive up there and feed you, embarrass you in front of your new television colleagues."

"Oh, how I wish you would."

"Careful."

With them both chuckling, they said their goodbyes.

Sydney pushed the End button and was surprised to feel a pang of homesickness. She sat there and let it roll through her, tried to analyze it. It didn't scare her, and it didn't make her sad. Rather, she felt…melancholy, tinted with a bit of confusion because it wasn't something she'd expected. Her parents had never been the kind to hover. Helicopter parents, they were not. She'd gone to college fairly close to home, close enough to drive back on occasional weekends here and there and get anything she needed, even though nobody was there most of the time, so homesickness wasn't really something she'd been hit with. Then she'd gotten a job at a station near her hometown. Then another, a bit farther away, but still not *that* far. She wanted to travel. She want to work someplace bigger, more glamorous, and yes, farther from home. It was what she'd always intended, and with her acceptance of this job, it had begun. So this twinge, this little prick of pain, wasn't a thing she'd prepared for, as she'd never experienced it before. But she missed Laura. She even missed her parents a tiny bit. She missed home.

She turned to look at Marge and Homer, swimming around their tiny world, not a care. "Well. That was new," she said to the glass. "I don't think I've ever felt that before. Weird." Homer opened and closed his little mouth at her. She slapped a hand on her thigh. "Okay. Time for work." She stood, pushed the unfamiliar emotion into a corner, shouldered her bag once again, and headed for the door.

Sydney's apartment building had once been a very large house, and what would be considered the "hallway" was actually a grand foyer. There were three apartments on the second floor, like hers, and four on the first floor. The staircase in the middle of the foyer was wide and covered with a deep burgundy carpet, the railings polished oak. A large, twinkly chandelier hung from the center, its light enough to see by, but not so bright as to be obnoxious at night. Sydney was pretty sure it had been a gorgeously elegant one-family house in its time.

As Sydney headed down the stairs, she passed a small, elderly woman with three recyclable shopping bags. She was dragging them very slowly from step to step as she made her way up. Sydney made it all the way to the front door, actually had her hand on the handle, before her feet stopped and wouldn't move. She closed her eyes and blew out a quiet breath as she allowed instinct and manners to shoulder their way in.

Setting down her bag next to the bank of mailboxes and returning to the stairs, she asked, "Hey, can I help you with that?"

The woman looked up and seemed surprised to see her. Then she gave a self-deprecating smile. "Oh, thank you, dear. I can do it, but it's going to take me longer than I thought."

"I'm happy to give you a hand. It's no problem." Sydney looked up the stairs at the three doors. "Which is your apartment?"

"Number seven."

"Ah, lucky number seven." Sydney took two of the bags and ran them up the stairs, set them outside the door to number seven. When she returned to get the third bag, the woman had only climbed one more step. "Here. Let me help." Sydney took the bag, then held her arm out so the woman could take hold of her elbow for extra support. She wore a mid-weight raincoat and her white hair was covered by a scarf, which she'd tied under her chin. She reminded Sydney of her great-grandma Ethel, who'd passed away three years before.

"Thank you," the woman said quietly, and Sydney got the feeling—judging from her slightly pink skin and lack of eye contact—that the woman was embarrassed to need the help. They moved slowly, the woman holding Sydney's arm with one hand and the oak railing with the other.

"So, you're my neighbor, huh? I just moved into number six over the weekend."

"Oh, yes. I'd heard somebody was going in there."

Trying to ignore the woman's labored breathing, Sydney said, "My name is Sydney Taylor, by the way."

"Sydney. That was my husband's name. Is yours spelled with an I or a Y?"

"Y."

The woman nodded, silently concentrating on the next and final step before saying, "Well, it's nice to meet you, Sydney." In the upper hall, she let go of Sydney's elbow and held out a hand to her. Sydney shook it, noting the gentle softness of the papery thin skin that covered delicate bones and lines of blue veins, but surprised by the firmness of the grip. "I'm Dr. Vivian Green. Thank you for your help."

"It was my pleasure." Sydney nodded at the door. "You going to be okay now? I can take these bags in for you if you want."

"Oh, no, no." Vivian waved a dismissive hand at her. "I can take it from here."

"Okay. As long as you're sure." Sydney hesitated to leave her.

"Really, dear, it's fine. I do this all the time." Vivian Green smiled at her, but her rheumy blue eyes flashed with a sharpness that told Sydney she was tougher than she seemed.

"All right. I'm off then. It was nice to meet you."

Vivian nodded as she pulled her keys from her pocket.

❧

The morning went by quickly. Sydney made several phone calls, including to Old Red Barn Brewcrafters to set up an appointment with Rick Foster, one of the owners. She got him on the phone and they went over a few details. He seemed very gracious and accommodating, not to mention proud.

They settled on a time and Sydney popped the appointment into her online calendar just as Connor Baskin sidled up to her desk. "Ready?"

They'd met on Monday, both of them new to the station. Connor was a very small guy, maybe five four, with dark hair and black-rimmed glasses and Sydney had to bite her lip to keep from calling him Harry Potter. He seemed neat, organized, and no-nonsense, so she hoped they'd make a good team, wizardly powers or not.

"I am."

Brad had assigned an intern to drive them, since neither Sydney, nor Connor—each new to the city—knew quite where they were going. Once settled into the back seat of a company sedan, Connor pulled out a tablet and began scrolling.

"So, I did some research on Junebug Farms and Jessica Barstow, the CEO."

Sydney had done her own research, but she nodded and waited for Connor to continue, interested to see if he'd come up with anything she hadn't.

"Junebug Farms is awesome," said their driver, a young man of maybe nineteen or twenty. "My mom used to take me there all the time when I was a kid. Let me pet the goats and the horses. We got our dog, Duke, from there, too." Apparently finished, he went quiet.

"Cool," Sydney said, so as not to seem to be ignoring him.

"That is cool," Connor said and then continued with his report. "Junebug Farms. Founded in 1992 by retired schoolteacher June Pickering and her husband, Clyde, it started as a small building with a barn and room to house fifteen dogs, twenty cats, and a handful of livestock. Over the years, Mrs. Pickering got involved in the community, expanded, and became a nonprofit. In 2001, she hired her granddaughter, Jessica Barstow, to help her run the place. Ms. Barstow has a business degree from Syracuse University. When Mrs. Pickering died in 2010, the shelter was willed to Ms. Barstow, who serves as CEO and the chairwoman of the board, which consists of five other members. Incidentally, those five people also serve as various department heads and, with the addition of a janitor and a retail manager, are the only paid employees of Junebug Farms. Everybody else is a volunteer."

"How many are there altogether?" Sydney asked. "Volunteers." She'd forgotten to look up that figure.

"It varies based on time of year," Connor said, scrolling on his tablet, then pushing his glasses up by the nosepiece. "On average, close to a hundred."

"Wow."

"Right? Sometimes a little more, sometimes a little less."

"That's a lot of people working for free."

Connor scrolled some more. "The telethon is in its eighth year and this is the first time it will not be hosted by Janet Dobson." He looked up at Sydney. "She retired."

Sydney nodded, aware of everything he'd said so far. They chatted a bit more and then they were sliding into a parking space. Sydney got out of the car and smoothed her pantsuit, looked around to take it all in. The scent of manure struck her.

"Wow. Ripe," she mumbled, wrinkling her nose.

"Very." Connor pointed across an expanse of green to a large barn. "That barn currently houses four horses, a burro, a dairy cow, and two sheep," Connor informed her. There was an attached corral and she could make out what looked to be two of the horses sauntering around in the dirt. "And over here"— Connor spun and pointed in the opposite direction—"is the goat house." As if on cue, soft bleating came from the vicinity.

Sydney filed it all away, knowing she would need to become familiar with the place if she was going to host the telethon, smell and all.

Connor asked their intern to wait in the car, then they headed up the walk. Two women on their knees busily planted flowers along the front of the main building. One smiled and the other waved. Connor held the glass door open for Sydney and she entered, blinking rapidly at the sudden increase in noise. The two of them stopped on the gray industrial mat and simply stood there.

"Wow," Connor said.

"Yeah," Sydney agreed, grimacing at the decibel level.

To their right was a small gift shop. A sign above the door said it was Paws & Whiskers, and it seemed jam-packed full of anything a new pet owner might need. To their left was what seemed to be a waiting area, peppered with chairs, a box of old, beat-up children's toys in the corner. The walls there were dotted with various photos of animals, but Sydney was too far away to be more specific. A tall, thin man was mopping the floor. Dressed in dark work pants and a matching work shirt, he looked to Sydney like every creepy janitor from every creepy horror movie she'd ever watched, and when he looked up and smiled at them, his alarmingly thick glasses distorted his eyes and only solidified her wariness of him.

"Front desk," Connor muttered as he pointed to a horseshoe-shaped counter. Three women milled around behind it, all late forties or older, and the phone seemed to be ringing off the hook as Sydney and Connor approached.

"I didn't expect an animal shelter to be this busy," Sydney said quietly to Connor, her voice almost drowned out when a set of double doors opened and the sound of barking, howling dogs increased tenfold. "My God."

Connor waited until the woman on the phone hung up, then identified them. "We have an appointment with Ms. Barstow."

"Yes, she's expecting you," the woman said pleasantly, her nametag telling Sydney her name was Regina – Volunteer. "Let me show you to the conference room and I'll let her know you're here."

Once they were inside the conference room, the door shut behind them, Sydney realized—much to her dismay and surprise—that she was nervous. "I didn't expect this place to be so big and…active," she said.

Connor nodded. "I know. Me neither."

It wasn't often that Sydney felt ill-prepared for a job, and it wasn't a feeling she enjoyed. "I researched a lot, but I didn't have a chance to actually watch one of the telethons. I need to do that." She was speaking more to herself, but Connor nodded again in agreement.

Regina the Volunteer came in with coffee for both of them and informed them that Jessica Barstow was on her way.

Sydney took a sip of the coffee (strong!) and had only just begun to look around the conference room, to notice the various photographs on the walls and the way the décor was neat and tidy, but inexpensive, possibly secondhand, when the door opened again and a ridiculously attractive woman walked in. Auburn hair in a ponytail, clothed in jeans and a lightweight, hooded green sweater, ballet flats on her feet, she emanated the perfect combination of casually dressy and comfortably in charge.

"Hi there," she said with a huge smile that crinkled the skin around her blue eyes and held out a hand. "You must be Sydney Taylor. Jessica Barstow. I've heard so much about you. I'm pleased to finally meet you."

Sydney stood and grasped the hand, feeling strength, warmth, and softness all at once before mentally shaking herself. "Same here. This is my producer, Connor Baskin."

An expression of surprise zipped across Jessica Barstow's face as she shook his hand as well. It was gone quickly, but was obvious enough for somebody who didn't know her well to recognize it. "Oh. A new producer, too. Brad didn't tell me."

To his credit, Connor didn't stumble or stutter, but took things in stride. "Sorry about that. You've had"—he consulted his tablet—"Jack Preston in the past."

Jessica nodded as she pulled out a chair and dropped the folder she'd brought with her on the table. "For years, yes." The friendly happiness on her face dimmed considerably.

"Well, I assure you, I'm good at my job." Connor smiled. "I'll do my best to make sure you don't miss him."

Jessica let half a beat go by before she nodded and took a seat. "Fair enough." She clasped her hands together in front of her and set them on the table. "Where would you like to start?

I'm assuming you'll want a tour? Maybe brainstorm a bit about ideas?" She opened the folder. "I brought the contact information for the adopters Brad asked for."

Sydney took the sheet Jessica slid her way and passed it to Connor. "Can you e-mail me this as well? I'm not much of a hard copy person, and I don't want to lose it." She fished in her bag and pulled out a business card, the first one she'd handed out since her arrival. "My address is at the bottom."

"Of course." Jessica nodded and Sydney noticed her chewing on the inside of her lip. "Why don't we start with a tour. You should know what you're dealing with here. Then we'll sit with our PR head and go from there."

They stood, and when Jessica pulled the conference room door open, Sydney immediately missed the muffled quiet it had afforded her. The noise increased, and somehow, in the twenty minutes they'd been in the conference room, half a dozen more people had entered the main lobby.

"Wow, does it get loud in here," Sydney said, a hint of awe in her voice.

Jessica smiled, but it didn't reach her eyes. "We'll start with the dog wing."

Sydney followed Jessica. Connor followed Sydney, whose shoes clicked loudly on the faux-marble floor, adding to the cacophony of the place. And when Jessica pulled open one of the double doors leading to the dog wing, the noise quadrupled. Barking. Howling. Whining. All of it, and it was endless. Jessica didn't wait for them, but kept walking down the aisle, past kennel upon kennel on either side, until she stopped at a desk with an empty chair about halfway down.

"This is where Lisa Drakemore, our intake and adoption head, sits," Jessica said, raising her voice to be heard over the canine symphony. "At capacity, we can house around thirty dogs, maybe a few more. We don't like to have that many, obviously, but we're a no-kill shelter, so we make room where we can, sometimes doubling up in the kennels and calling on our foster parents."

Sydney watched Jessica's mouth moving, but her voice seemed to fade away until all Sydney could hear were dogs. Abandoned, abused, neglected dogs. All around her. Everywhere she looked there was a pair of sad brown eyes looking back at her from behind a mesh fence. Her heart rate picked up speed and she had trouble taking a full breath. Jessica was still talking. At least she thought she was. She couldn't hear her voice. At all. Stars filled the edges of her vision and suddenly, she had no choice but to get out of there. With a muttered, "excuse me," she turned and hurried up the aisle, back the way they'd come, out the double doors, across the lobby as fast as her now-rubbery legs could carry her in high heels, out the front door, and into the open, into the blessed fresh air. She stopped on the front sidewalk and bent at the waist, hands braced on her knees as she sucked in as much oxygen as she could. "What the hell," she muttered, waiting for her vision to clear.

"Ma'am? You okay?" The gravelly male voice startled her, but not as much as the appearance of the janitor when she lifted her head. He was *huge*. Without forethought, she gasped and stepped away from him. Her hand lifted of its own volition, palm out, as if warding him off.

"I'm fine," she said, painfully aware of her own overreaction, of how breathless she sounded. The janitor took a step toward her with his hand out, but Connor burst through the front door just then.

"Sydney. You okay?" He laid a hand on her arm.

Jessica Barstow came out next, her face an obvious mix of concern and irritation. She looked to the janitor, who simply shrugged.

"She looked like she needed some help," he said quietly, eyes wide, voice gentle.

"Thanks, Bill," Jessica said warmly and squeezed his arm. "I think we're good."

He nodded and went inside.

"Are you okay?" Jessica asked, her deep blue eyes catching Sydney's and holding them. "Regina's bringing some water."

"I'm fine," Sydney said. "Just embarrassed." She stood up and cleared her throat, trying to shake off any remaining weirdness and return to her stoic, professional self...which proved harder than she expected. "I'm sorry if I was rude to your...guy." She gestured in the direction the janitor had gone, her heart still beating like a hummingbird's. "I didn't mean to be. He just...startled me." *And he's huge*, she thought.

The doors opened and Regina the Volunteer came out with a paper cup of water. "Here you go," she said. "Did you have a panic attack? I used to get those all the time. They're awful."

Sydney took the cup with a nod of thanks but didn't answer, as it wasn't something she wanted to discuss with a complete stranger. And frankly, she was surrounded by them. She downed the water, then inhaled slowly and deeply, let it out gradually. "I think I'm okay now."

"You look really pale," Connor said. "Maybe we should reschedule."

It was the last thing Sydney wanted to do, but the jelly-like weakness in her knees made her doubt how far she could walk. After a quick internal debate, she gave a slight, reluctant nod of assent. "Okay." Turning to look at Jessica, whose expression was now unreadable, she said, "I'm really sorry. I'm not sure what happened."

Jessica shrugged. "It's fine. Can we meet tomorrow?"

They set up a time for the afternoon, Sydney vowing to eat a good lunch before showing up. Maybe her blood sugar was low. Then they bid their goodbyes, Sydney apologized once more, and headed for the car where the intern stood next to the driver's side door, obviously wondering why they were done so soon.

CHAPTER FOUR

"AND THEN I DON'T know what the hell happened. All the color drained from her face and she just…ran." Jessica shook her head, annoyed all over again, and took a sip of her wine. "Let me tell you, she certainly didn't make me feel better about all these changes."

Catherine and Emily exchanged glances.

Jessica glared at them. "Stop that."

"Stop what?" Catherine asked, all wide-eyed innocence.

"Stop looking at each other like I'm overreacting. I'm not."

It was a gorgeous spring evening and the three of them sat on Emily's sixth-floor balcony watching the pedestrians wander and the light traffic roll by.

"Are you sure you're not?" Catherine asked. "I mean, you know how the first visit to the dog wing can be. It's overwhelming and heartbreaking and shockingly loud. Are you sure you're not giving her the benefit of the doubt because you're mad Janet's gone?"

Catherine had a point about the dog wing. That was true. Walking in there for the first time, the smell a combination of dog, feces, urine, rain, and dog food, could be devastating. And the sound. The employees of Junebug were obviously used to it and could almost tune it out. But for somebody who'd never been exposed to that kind of endless noise—not to mention the reality of what they were looking at—it was a lot. "Well…maybe she just had trouble with it. But she wasn't nice to Bill."

"What do you mean?"

"She gave him a look." Jessica sipped again. "Like...all judgey."

"Aw, really? Bill's sweet." Catherine grimaced

Emily held up a hand. "Okay, I know I'm fairly new at the shelter and I don't mean any disrespect at all here, but...at first glance, Bill kind of looks like a serial killer. If I didn't know he was a super nice guy, he might scare me, too."

Jessica sighed loudly, purposely omitting the fact that Sydney had apologized. "Why can't you two just let me hate this woman?"

Catherine grinned at her. "When she gives you a good reason, we will."

"Well." Jessica looked at Catherine and waggled her eyebrows. "There is *one* reason."

Emily looked from one woman to the other. "There is? What? What is it?"

"You didn't tell her?" Jessica asked Catherine, incredulous, as they shared just about everything.

Catherine shook her head. "I'd actually forgotten, to be honest."

"Tell me what?" Emily looked expectant. Jessica deferred to Catherine with a wave of her hand.

With a big sigh, Catherine said, "Apparently, new telethon host Sydney Taylor was here a couple months ago and picked up Anna in a bar."

"No!" Emily's eyes went wide.

"Yes. According to Anna. So do with that what you will." Catherine reached for a slab of cheese, put it on a cracker, and popped it into her mouth.

"Would she lie about that kind of thing?" Emily asked.

Jessica shrugged. "She might embellish, but I don't think she'd make it up."

Catherine made a face that said she agreed.

"Wow." Emily sat back in her chair.

"What does that mean?" Catherine asked, squinting at her.

"It means I'm pleasantly surprised that Ms. Taylor plays on our team. Aren't you?"

Jessica laughed. "Yeah, there is that. Point for her."

"She has abhorrent taste in women," Catherine added.

"And, point deducted," Jessica said, making Catherine laugh out loud.

The three of them sat in companionable silence for a few moments, simply enjoying the evening, the mild late-spring air, each other's company.

"So, how are things with you guys?" Jessica asked. "With your families?" She knew that Emily's mother hadn't been thrilled to learn that her daughter had fallen for the accountant at the animal shelter to which their well-known charitable foundation donated significantly, and she knew how hard that had been for Catherine.

Emily looked at Catherine and her face held such reverence that Jessica had to look away, felt as if she was intruding on a private moment. "It's been really good lately," Emily said and Catherine smiled in agreement. "My mother comes around. She just needs to have all the facts before she passes judgment and the facts here are simple: Catherine is amazing and I love her. End of story." She leaned forward and kissed Catherine chastely on the mouth.

"Ugh," Jessica said, making a mock gagging noise. "The cuteness of you two is going to send me into a sugar coma."

Their evening ended not long after that, as Jessica was anxious to get home. Though she'd never admit it to Catherine, there were times—only sporadic ones—when she found herself almost painfully envious of the relationship Catherine and Emily had. She wasn't jealous; she had known Catherine for a very long time, loved her dearly, and was thrilled to see her so happy. And most of the time, Jessica was just fine with her life the way it was. But once in a while…once every so often…she'd see the way Emily looked at Catherine or the way they reached for one another's hands, entwined their fingers together without even looking, and she got a pain in her chest so sharp, it yanked the breath right out of her lungs.

Once home, she felt a zillion times better. Two places in the world that made her feel relaxed and like she belonged: Junebug Farms and her top two-floor apartment in the center of the city. Leafing through the mail as she walked through the living room to the kitchen, she felt her three cats weaving in and around her legs. How they managed to a) not trip her and b) not get kicked or stepped on was beyond her, but they avoided both every time. Jessica tossed the mail onto the counter and reached down to swoop Shaggy up into her arms, buried her nose in his gray and white fur. From the floor, Fred and Scooby looked up at her and blinked their large green eyes in anticipation of dinner, which she quickly prepared.

Cats munching away happily, Jessica went into her bedroom and changed out of her work clothes. While she didn't feel the need to dress as professionally as Catherine tended to, Jessica was the owner and CEO and tried to at least always look neat and tidy. She wanted to look approachable, but also like she was competent to run the place. Once in her blue-and-white striped lounge pants and a matching blue V-neck T-shirt, she returned to the living room. It was late—nearly midnight—but she never went to bed without giving her cats some love and attention. So, she flopped onto the couch, pushed buttons on her remote until her list of DVR'd shows came up, and chose last week's episode of *Chopped*. In no time at all, she was besieged by cats, as if she'd sprinkled catnip all over herself. Shaggy took his place in her lap. Fred lounged along the back of the couch, occasionally tapping Jessica's head with a paw to remind her he was there. Scooby stretched out on the cushion next to her, his back along her thigh, his tail flicking languidly while she watched the chefs come up with a dish based around Gummi Bears and Dijon mustard.

It was after 2 a.m. when she woke up and sleepily trudged to her bedroom, three cats following in her wake.

❧

In the wee hours of the morning as dawn broke, the sky went gorgeously from black to deep indigo to purple to crimson. As Friday morning gradually made its entry, Sydney saw every one of those colors out her bedroom window as she lay in her bed, wide awake since after two. Three glasses of wine were way beyond her usual, but her panic attack at Junebug on Thursday afternoon had shaken her. It had scared her. Most of all, it had embarrassed her. Connor had tried his best to cheer her up, to reassure her that it was no big deal, but his attempts to make her feel better only made her feel worse, and she hadn't been able to shake the discomfort and uncertainty. Not to mention the overwhelming pissed-offedness.

Getting dizzy. Running away like a scared child. Ugh! How ridiculous. How embarrassingly unprofessional. Those thoughts had spun around and around in Sydney's head like a load of dirty laundry for the remainder of the day and into the night. The third glass of wine had helped her fall asleep, but—as she should have known it would—had caused her eyes to pop open at 1:47 a.m., and the spin cycle had started up again.

At 5:33, she gave up trying to relax, got her workout clothes on, and headed to the gym. It was one of the first things she'd located during her apartment search a few months back. Not only did it keep her in shape physically, but if she went too long without exercising, she began to feel mentally sluggish. She didn't enjoy working out, but she enjoyed the results.

She usually listened to music while she ran on the treadmill, but when it was early morning, she watched the news. Plugging her earbuds into the jack, she changed channels on the TV in front of her treadmill until she got to Channel Six. The anchors at 6 a.m. were Rob Kensington—painfully good looking…like David Muir with blond hair, and Josie Westfield—very pretty, but with a barely detectable lisp that drove Sydney crazy. They smiled and bantered playfully. Sydney had only met them a couple times, but they seemed nice enough, if not terribly conversational, which was how it tended to be in the news business. Everybody was friendly, but nobody got all that close because you could be transferred/hired/let go at any time. And the last thing you wanted to do was give somebody else the leg-up that you'd hoped for.

She watched the screen, watched as Rob kept a serious face and tone of voice while he reported on a house fire overnight. Then he teased the weather and threw it to commercial.

Sydney recognized the exterior of Junebug Farms immediately. The ad was short and to the point, but very well done. Lots of adorable dogs, kittens, and goats appeared. Kids hugging animals. People smiling and buying things in the gift shop. A shot of a dog-training class. All in quick succession, but all positive. According to the commercial, Junebug Farms was a shiny, happy place.

So why had Sydney bolted out the door like she was being chased?

The dogs.

She knew it then and she knew it now, she just hadn't wanted to admit it. The dogs had broken her heart.

Sydney Taylor came across to most people who met her as no-nonsense. Driven. Somewhat aloof. Maybe even a little cold. What they didn't know was that she could feel things deeply. More deeply than many, and for some reason, dogs were her Kryptonite. Dogs could get to her in a way nothing and no one else could.

She blamed Rufus.

Lovingly.

She lovingly blamed him.

Rufus was a Maltese-terrier mix of some kind. Nobody seemed to know for sure. Her parents got him for her from the pound when she was six years old. Rufus was a puppy and he was hers and, as being an only child could be devastatingly lonely, she loved him with every fiber of her being. The best part of having a small dog—and maybe the worst part as well—was that they could live for quite a long time. As Rufus had. He'd stayed with her until he was nearly seventeen years old and honestly, after being around for so long, Sydney had almost convinced herself that he was never going to leave her. She went to elementary school, and Rufus was waiting when she got home. During high school, he stayed next to her into the wee hours as she studied for her finals. While in college, she would sometimes make a trip home for the weekend, not to see her parents, but simply to cuddle with Rufus. It was after graduation, that summer of her twenty-second birthday, that he'd finally had enough. His body was old, his fur matted, his eyes cloudy. He could hardly hear anymore. He slept close to twenty hours a day and pushing himself to a standing position was difficult and painful. But still, Sydney cuddled him every night. She gave him his pills. She carried him outside so he could relieve himself. She bathed him gently when she didn't get him outside quickly enough. They spooned like sibling babies and—Sydney was thankful now, but hadn't been then—he'd simply passed away in his sleep, his back tight to her stomach, as she slept on.

Even now, nearly nine years later, it brought tears to her eyes, and she squeezed them tightly shut as she ran, ordering the memories, the tears, to back the hell off. At least it was clear now, though. Something about the dog wing at Junebug Farms—the smell maybe?—had triggered a memory for her that she did her best to keep buried. The thought of all those lonely dogs, locked in kennels for God knew how long, simply broke her heart.

So she ran on the treadmill until she could leave the thoughts, images, and memories of lost dogs behind her. It took a while, and by the time she got back to her apartment, her early start to the morning had all but evaporated. The rest of her day went similarly, and before she knew it, it was after noon and time to head back to Junebug Farms. Connor met her at the back door; they ended up with the same intern driving them in the same sedan, and for a moment, Sydney thought of it as a weird *Groundhog Day* sort of do-over, that she was doomed to relive the same day again and again until she got it right.

"You going to be okay?" Connor asked once they were more than halfway there. There'd been no information exchange, no background or history this time. Just silence.

"Yeah, I'll be fine," Sydney said with a nod as she gazed out the window. She watched as they moved from city to suburbs to country, all within about thirty minutes. When they pulled into the exact same parking spot as before, she almost laughed out loud. They got out of the car and she caught Connor shooting her a look of concern. "Seriously. I'm fine. That was just a fluke, some weird thing that won't happen again. Don't worry." She kept it friendly, though she would bet Connor was more concerned about the embarrassment and his own reputation than actually worried about her. But she didn't know him well at all, so forced herself to try not to judge.

Today's volunteer was Judy, and Sydney felt herself blow out a breath of relief that at least *something* was different. The sound was still overwhelming and the smell hadn't changed, but there were fewer people and the atmosphere felt a little more…relaxed was the only word she could come up with. *Maybe because it's Friday?* She wasn't going to question it; she just did her best to focus on her job.

Jessica Barstow looked gorgeous today. It wasn't something to be argued. If you didn't think so, you were obviously blind. She wore jeans again, and for the first time, Sydney found herself paying attention to the figure underneath them. *Wow. Nice.* Uncertain why she was surprised, she did a quick scan. The denim was dark, which made the jeans seem slightly less casual. Jessica's shirt was a light blue waffle-weave Henley with a feminine cut and the Junebug Farms logo embroidered tastefully small on the left side of the placket. Her auburn hair was again pulled back in a ponytail and silver hoops decorated her ears. She was a very pleasing blend of neatly casual with only the slightest bit of makeup. A little mascara and not much else.

"You came back," she said with what seemed a genuine smile as she held her hand out to Sydney.

"I did," Sydney replied, shaking hands and again noting the warmth, the soft strength of Jessica's grip. "I'm really sorry about yesterday."

"No worries. I just hoped you weren't coming down with something."

"I feel absolutely fine today." Sydney pasted on her camera smile, the one that said every single thing was as it should be, even if it wasn't. "How about showing us what we missed yesterday?" She worded it that way on purpose and Jessica, thank God, took it as it was meant—*we already saw the dog wing…we don't need to go there again*—and directed them toward the front doors.

"Let's go outside." But Jessica stopped short as her eyes took in Sydney's three-inch heels. "Um…will you be okay in those? The path is gravel and dirt."

With a glance down at her feet, Sydney gave a nod. "Shouldn't be a problem," she said with a confident smile, though she knew the possibility of rolling an ankle on a piece of gravel was pretty realistic.

With a shrug, Jessica led the way in her flats, talking as she walked toward the large barn, giving them the history of the shelter, which both Sydney and Connor already knew from their research.

"The grounds are beautiful," Sydney commented, and she meant it, even as she tried to be subtle about how carefully she was stepping. The grass was thick and lush, the petunias planted along the brick front of the building blooming in all shades of pinks and purples.

Jessica smiled with pride. "We have volunteers who take care of a lot of those types of things." She gestured to the flowers and Sydney remembered there'd been a woman working on them yesterday. "They mow the lawn, plant the flowers, help muck the stalls in the barn, walk the dogs, play with the cats, answer the phones, run the front desk. We'd never survive without all the amazing people who donate their time here."

Sydney opened the Notes app on her phone and typed in *Volunteers*, thinking it might be another good thing to focus on for one of the many stories they'd need to fill six hours of live television in a few weeks. "How many do you think you have altogether?"

"It varies all the time, but I'd say on average, probably close to a hundred or so."

Connor gave Sydney a wink and subtle thumbs-up as his research was confirmed.

The barn smelled exactly like one, the strong scents of hay and manure wafting through the air so thickly, Sydney was surprised they couldn't see it, like smoke or vapor. Jessica glanced down at Sydney's feet a second time, at the heels that went so well with her skirt and jacket, but not so well with the terrain of a farm and said, "We don't have to go all the way in, but this is where our livestock reside. Currently, we've got four horses, a burro, a dairy cow, and two sheep."

"How do you end up with livestock?" Sydney asked.

"They tend to come in as abuse cases or cases of neglect. Often, Animal Control is called to a farm or an expanse of land where there have been reports of animals not being properly cared for." She gestured at Sydney and Connor. "Step in a bit," she said. "We won't go trudging through, but you should see this guy."

Sydney moved carefully and a few feet inside the barn, she could see into a couple of the stalls. One held a horse, but its appearance brought tears to Sydney's eyes almost immediately that she blinked rapidly to try and dispel. He was more skeleton of a horse with sagging skin hanging over it. He watched them carefully with his huge brown eyes as Jessica inched closer, talking quietly, soothingly. She held out a hand to him and, ever so slowly, he stepped toward her. Little by little. Inch by inch.

"Hey there, handsome," Jessica said very softly. She cooed to him and her tone was gentle, relaxing, and Sydney was mesmerized. "This is Jock," Jessica then said, this time to Sydney and Connor. She carefully slid her hand along his snout. "As you can see, he was not getting nearly enough food. Or attention." She talked to him a bit more and Sydney was touched again by the gentleness, the tenderness in her voice. "You'd think this was a case of abuse, but it really wasn't. Jock's owner was a very elderly man who was suffering from the onset of dementia. So he didn't intentionally not feed Jock. He simply…forgot sometimes. A lot of times. Luckily, a concerned neighbor called 911. They sent Animal Control, who then contacted us. We had room and Jock is slowly but surely regaining his strength." As if he understood her words, the horse blew at them, his lips making the sound of a raspberry. The trio laughed and Sydney felt herself transfixed.

"Can I pet him?" she asked quietly, surprising herself with the question. Surprising Jessica, too, judging by the expression of mild disbelief on her face.

"We can try, sure," Jessica said, with a nod. "Come here." Sydney stepped toward the stall, catching herself as her heel hit a chunk of…something…and Jessica shifted her stance until she stood alarmingly close, her front slowly pressed against Sydney's back. "Give me your hand," she said, her voice startlingly near Sydney's ear. Sydney obeyed and Jessica linked their hands. "He's a little skittish with strangers, but he trusts me, so let's do this together." She reached out her hand—and by extension, Sydney's hand—and stroked the horse's snout. Sydney's hand was on the bottom and she felt her breath hitch the slightest bit, hoped Jessica hadn't noticed. Whether it was from how shockingly soft the horse's velvety nose was or how comforting and warm Jessica's hand was, she couldn't tell. So instead, she caught her bottom lip between her teeth and did her best to focus on the horse for the next few moments.

When Jessica finally, gently, pulled their hands back from the horse, Sydney reclaimed her own and quickly stepped forward, away from Jessica and toward Connor, who caught her by the elbow to keep her from toppling. When she looked at him, he'd already let go and was furiously jotting notes on his tablet, one corner of his mouth tugged up in a grin. She glanced back at Jessica, whose face had tinted a soft pink as she cleared her throat and looked away.

"Goats?" Jessica asked, seemingly out of nowhere, snapping them all to attention. She led them out the door and back to the gravel trail. "This way."

Connor looked at Sydney, who shrugged, and they both fell into step behind Jessica.

≈

What the hell was that?

Jessica's pace was fast. Too fast, and she knew it. The TV people had to scurry to keep up with her, and she was pretty sure scurrying wasn't easy in those heels Sydney Taylor was wearing. But seriously, who wears heels to an animal shelter? Especially when you know you're getting a tour? If she rolled an ankle, it would serve her right. Janet Dobson would never have worn such inappropriate footwear.

Sydney's hand under Jessica's had felt good. Really good. Unexpectedly good. Soft and warm and soft and strong and soft. It had been a long time since Jessica's skin had touched another woman's, and she'd found herself enjoying it a little too much. Obviously.

That's definitely enough of that.

She shook herself mentally and led the two across the property. At the goat pen, she launched into a robotic explanation of the shelter, how they cared for the goats, where they'd come from. It was all burned into her memory because she'd given this tour a zillion times. And it was good that she didn't have to think about what she was saying, because she couldn't get the image of her hand guiding Sydney's along the lines of the horse out of her head. It was disturbingly sensual, their forearms parallel, their fingers almost entwined...

So, Sydney Taylor was pretty. So what? That wasn't news. So her hair was shiny and smelled great, and was probably really soft. Who cared? And her eyes were ridiculously hypnotizing and her body was—

Stop it!

Jessica did her best to banish the visions from her head.

"And that's about it," she said—too loudly she thought. "You saw the dogs. We can check out the cat wall inside, but essentially, that's the whole shebang." Her eyes darted from Sydney to Connor and back, and then she set off toward the front doors of the main building.

Once inside, Jessica felt a little better, like she'd been underwater and had finally broken the surface. She inhaled deeply as Sydney and Connor caught up with her.

"The cats are here," she said as she finally slowed her pace and allowed herself to relax a bit. She strolled in the direction of the cat enclosures housed directly across from the front desk. "This is affectionately dubbed the Cat Wall. We can house about fifty at one time and we can squeeze in a few more if need be." She gestured at the wall of glass cubicles like she was Vanna White. It was a wall like a tic-tac-toe board of windows. Each one held a cat. Some held more than one. Today was a good day; Jessica counted nine that were empty.

"Hi there. Am I too late for the tour?"

The voice pulled Jessica back from her counting of the cat cubbies and she met the twinkling brown eyes of Anna St. John. *Here we go*, Jessica thought as she pasted on a smile. "Afraid so." Resigned to playing the game Anna had forced her into, she turned toward her guests. "Anna St. John is our public relations director. Anna, this is Sydney Taylor and Connor Baskin of Channel Six. They'll be working on the telethon in a few weeks."

Anna shook Connor's hand first, then held on to Sydney's. "Well, hello there. Good to see you again."

Jessica watched the different emotions play out on Sydney's face. Confusion was first, like she couldn't place Anna. Then a glimmer of recognition. Then her eyes widened for such a short flash that Jessica would never have noticed if she hadn't been specifically looking. Then Sydney's cheeks reddened just a touch, she gave a nod and muttered, "Likewise," and looked like she actually pulled her hand from Anna's. Jessica had a very short zap of sympathy for her, but that went away pretty quickly.

Heels at an animal shelter and hooking up with Anna: two reasons to question Ms. Sydney Taylor's judgment. Already.

Two reasons were all she needed. Two reasons were more than enough.

"So," Jessica said, clapping her hands together once, which caused Sydney to flinch. "Is there anything else you need from me?" She was all business again, that silliness from the horse barn driven right out of her brain by the subtly lascivious expression on Anna's face.

Sydney cleared her throat. "Um. No. No, I think we're good. Connor?" She looked to her producer for obvious help and he stepped right up.

"That should do it for now," he said with a smile. "I've taken a lot of notes. I've got some terrific ideas. Let us go back to the station and bat some things around and we'll get back to you, okay?"

Jessica nodded once and took Connor's outstretched hand, shook it. "Excellent. I'll wait to hear from you. And we'll meet with Anna as well next time." When she grasped Sydney's hand, the flash of being back at the barn, stroking Jock's soft head in tandem, hit her so hard she felt light-headed, and she let go as if Sydney had burned her.

Sydney didn't seem to notice, and Jessica assumed maybe she was too busy mentally kicking herself for her tryst with Anna. Her discomfort was obvious.

"Thanks for the tour," Connor said, then looked to his talent. "Ready?"

Sydney nodded, met Jessica's eyes one more time, then turned to follow Connor out the door.

Jessica and Anna stood side by side and watched as they left.

"Damn. She's even sexier in the daylight," Anna said, then bumped Jessica with her hip like they were old school pals who shared a secret.

Jessica simply shook her head and walked away.

CHAPTER FIVE

"WELL, I CAN HEAR your voice, which means you're alive, which means you've definitely survived your whole first week in the new job. Yes?"

Sydney couldn't help but grin. "Yes. I survived."

"You sound less than thrilled, but I am ignoring that, because surviving is infinitely better than not surviving. I, for one, am glad you survived. I'd miss you if you hadn't." Her voice was full of its usual cheer and positive energy, and Sydney could hear the sounds of the kitchen in the background: dishes, pots, things clanging.

"Am I on speaker? What are you making?"

"You are on speaker, hot stuff, as I am trying a new recipe to see if my class can handle it." Not a lot of schools continued to offer the home ec courses that Laura taught, but the one in Pennsylvania where she worked did. She taught several different ages and the students loved her. She actually had a waiting list for her classes.

"Brownies? Cookies?"

"Cupcakes," Laura answered.

"Chocolate? Please say yes."

"Yes. I wanted to try something more creative in my dessert chapter, but we'll start simple."

"There is no need for any other flavor of cupcake," Sydney said. "Chocolate is life. Also, I want one of them. Right now."

"But what of your girlish television news figure? You can't be eating cupcakes."

Sydney sighed and glanced at the salad she'd grabbed on her way home. "I know. You're right. Damn it."

"So tell me about your week again." Laura was good at that, at cutting to the chase, and Sydney was again reminded of how straightforward she always was with her. She was also the first person Sydney had come out to, in their dorm room one night, after Sydney had struggled, denied, and bargained with herself for almost two years before finally accepting her homosexuality. Laura was her conscience, her voice of reason.

"It's been…interesting."

"Well, that's cryptic. Elaborate, please." The sound of an egg cracking came over the speaker.

Sydney gave her the rundown repeating some stuff like meeting the other staff members, getting to know the station, exploring the city a little, her assignment on the local brewery, and meeting Connor, who would be producing the telethon she was hosting.

"You like him?" Laura asked. Despite their very different careers, Laura paid close attention to the details of Sydney's and always asked the right questions.

"I do. He seems to know his stuff. After our meeting today at the animal shelter, he had some great ideas for interviews and extra stuff, new features to jazz things up, bring it into the social media age instead of letting it stay stuck in the past, you know? We'll run things by the head of the shelter next week."

"Is it a nice place?" Laura was stirring or mixing something now. Sydney could hear the spoon against the metal bowl.

"It's actually *really* nice. Big. They've got livestock, which surprised me. And goats. Not just the typical cats and dogs that most shelters have."

"Really? That's cool. How's the staff there? Lots of volunteers?"

"Yeah, quite a few. And some paid staff, but not many, I don't think. Oh!" Sydney gave up on her salad, pushed it across the coffee table and turned sideways on her couch, propping her feet on a throw pillow. "You're not going to believe this. Remember when I visited here back in March? To explore and find an apartment?"

"I do."

"Remember that I found a gay bar and went out one night?"

"Mm hmm. I also remember you hooked up with some girl there."

"Hey, I didn't hook up with her. We made out. That was all."

"Semantics," Laura said, with a scoff.

"Yeah, well, that girl? She works at the shelter."

"Oh, no."

"Yeah. I met her today and it was *so* weird."

"I told you to be careful about hooking up with random strangers." Laura had adopted her schoolteacher voice, which Sydney found both endearing and annoying. "Serves you right."

"You make me sound like a slut," Sydney said, using a laugh to try to cover the fact that she was a little stung. "I don't hook up with random strangers."

"You know what I mean."

"Are you done scolding me, Ms. DiSalvo?"

"Maybe." There was a beat and Sydney used it to let the hurt roll off. "How weird was it?"

Sydney blew out a breath. "Just...awkward. I don't think Jessica—she's the CEO and was giving me the tour before she introduced us to Anna, the girl from the bar—knew that we'd already met. But..." She flashed back to Anna's smug smile, her extra-long handshake, her a little-too-firm grip. "I don't know. She's...I don't know."

"She won't make trouble for you, will she?" Laura asked, the scolding tone replaced with concern.

Sydney shrugged, even though Laura couldn't see her. "I have no idea. I'm not really sure she could. I mean, I don't broadcast my sexuality, but I don't hide it. My boss knows I'm gay. Come on, it's 2016. There are many more exciting things in the world to make a big deal out of besides who I sleep with. And I didn't sleep with Anna, so…"

"Yeah, well, still. I'd watch my step around her."

"It's funny, when we were making out that night in the back hall of the bar, there was just…something about her that suddenly turned me off. I mean, she was cute and into me and it was fun, but there came a point where…I don't even know how to describe it." Sydney had spent many hours later that week trying to put a finger on exactly what it was about Anna that had precipitously given her pause. She remembered kissing her—that it was nice—but after a few minutes, she was weirdly overcome by a feeling of…warning. She'd pulled away and made a lame excuse about needing to get up early the next morning. Then she'd picked up her jacket and bag, went back to her hotel, and didn't return to the bar for the remainder of her trip. "It was like a red flag went up and I just…stepped away."

"Instinct is a good thing. Imagine if you'd actually slept with her and then met her today."

Sydney grimaced. "Yeah, that would have been all kinds of worse."

"The Universe was looking out for you."

"Apparently."

"I'm kind of shocked you paid attention."

"Hey!" Sydney said with great mock indignation, then laughed. "I pay attention."

"Rarely."

"That's why I have you. So you can make me pay attention."

"If only you'd listen to me when I talk."

They laughed together, and for the first time since shaking hands with Anna, Sydney felt a little bit better. That night had been really poor judgment on Sydney's part and she knew it. She had also felt a little bad about the way she'd run off from Anna that night in the bar, but after today, she knew she'd done the right thing. She hoped not to get tangled up with Anna in any way, shape, or form during the telethon, but knew that Anna, as the head of public relations, was bound to be front and center. Sydney wondered if she needed to address things with Anna or if Anna would be good with the let's-never-mention-it-again form of closure. *I guess we'll find out.*

"Tell me about the city. What do you think? I know you're less than thrilled to be there."

Sydney hadn't actually said that to Laura, so it was yet another testament to how well her ex-roommate knew her. Sydney sighed, ran her fingers through her hair as she gazed toward the window of her small living room. "It's fine. I did a little exploring last weekend, but haven't had a lot of time since. I know I'm pretty close to the Shopwalk District, which is a nice, walkable part of town that has a lot of restaurants and shops and stuff, so I think I'll take a stroll tomorrow and check it out."

"Make any new friends?" The sound of a spoon against a metal bowl told Sydney Laura was at the scoop-the-batter-into-the-cupcake-tins part of her project.

"Does the old lady in my building count?"

"Absolutely."

"Does helping her get her groceries up the stairs count as friendship?"

"Totally."

"Oh, good. Then yes." She told Laura the story of Dr. Vivian Green, how they'd met, where she lived.

"Aww, cute," Laura said. "What's she a doctor of?"

"I didn't have a chance to ask. I was on my way to work."

"Well, you've done your good deed for the week, but your next assignment is to make some friends closer to your own age. I know you don't plan on staying there, but you are going to be there for a little while."

"I know." Sydney sighed.

The sound of the oven opening and closing came over the phone before Laura continued. "You're not an island, Syd. You'll get lonely. I mean, I know nobody there will compare to me, but still…"

Sydney chuckled. "I know," she said again. "You're right."

"Promise me you'll put yourself out there." When Sydney didn't respond right away, Laura's voice got stern. "Promise me."

"Fine. I promise."

"Good. Thank you."

They talked for a while longer, Laura talking about her students, which were her favorites, which drove her to drink at the end of the day. When they'd said their goodbyes, Sydney set her phone on the coffee table and twisted on the couch so she could see her fish swimming around in their tiny world.

"You guys. Laura says I have to find friends. What do you think?"

Marge swam up to the glass, opened and closed her little O-shaped mouth, and stared at Sydney for a moment before she turned away.

"Great. Thanks for the advice." She righted herself so she was on her back, looking up at the ceiling of her apartment and wondering why she hadn't mentioned the horse-petting incident to Laura. She'd certainly have had some guidance, an opinion, something to make Sydney feel better about it. She was pretty sure she wanted to just blow it off, and Laura would have inevitably helped her to do that. But…

"Hmm," she said to the empty room.

Maybe she wanted to hold onto it a little longer, let it be just hers before she pulled it out, shared it, and tossed it away like a paper towel. Jessica Barstow was tough. That was obvious. She couldn't have gotten where she had without being so. She was no-nonsense. And she'd made it fairly clear she wasn't thrilled with Sydney's presence around the telethon. Whether it was because she was new, or because she was younger than the previous host, or because she wasn't a local, or a combination of all three things, Sydney wasn't sure. But the horse-petting moment, that had felt almost…intimate. Jessica's voice had been low and gentle and dangerously close to her ear, her hand was soft and strong, but so feminine. Sydney remembered now simply staring at it, at the neatly filed nails devoid of polish, the obvious strength coupled with the actual softness, blue veins trailing lightly under pale skin. Then there was the body heat. Jessica had stood so close, right up behind her. *Talk about intimate!* Sydney could still feel Jessica's breasts pressed into her back, could still feel the tickle of Jessica's breath on her neck as she spoke in an almost-whisper to the horse.

The chill that ran up her spine—the good kind of chill—caused goose bumps to break out on her bare arms and visions to show up in her brain that she just did not want to deal with. Jessica Barstow was pretty, yes. That was a fact.

"Okay, she's sexy as well. I can admit that." Sydney spoke out loud again. "But so what? Lots of women are pretty. Lots of them are sexy. Means nothing. And"—she grabbed the remote from the coffee table and pointed it at her TV, which was newly hooked up to the cable—"I'm not going to think about it anymore. I'm a professional, damn it."

Literally shaking her head, she flipped through channels quickly, forcing herself to focus on her choice of shows rather than the very attractive, rather brusque, super sexy head of the animal shelter she was hosting a telethon for.

The one with the warm, soft hands and husky whisper of a voice…

᭬

Jessica glanced at the clock and instantly understood why her eyelids felt like there was sandpaper on the insides. 9:47 p.m. on a Saturday. She'd been at the shelter since six that morning, and in her office doing paperwork since about seven that night. Her stomach chose that moment for a well-placed growl to remind her she hadn't eaten since lunch.

She dropped her pen onto the desk and reached her arms over her head, stretching her spine as she raised one arm and shoulder up, then the other, hearing a couple of alarming pops as her vertebrae protested being in the same position for so long. With a sigh, she powered down her laptop, stacked some papers into a neat pile, slipped the computer into a bag, and headed out of her office.

Some people might think of Junebug Farms as creepy at night, like an empty and dark high school, but Jessica loved it. This was her favorite time. Even Bill Tracey had gone home; she knew because only the nighttime lights were left on. He shut off the rest when he left for the night, and now there was a gentle glow from dim lights around the gift shop, behind the front desk, and along the baseboards. It wasn't silent—it was never silent. There was always at least a small amount of sound coming from the dog wing. Occasional barks. Some soft whining or even a mournful howl. They never all slept at once. It wasn't unlike Jessica to go into the dog wing late at night and sit with a dog that was having a hard time. Lisa had discovered her more than once in the morning, sleeping on the floor of a kennel, spooning or holding an upset dog, both of them fast asleep. This place was in her blood, but it was also in her soul. A scared, trembling dog could break her heart just as easily now as it could the very first year she'd worked here as a regular when she'd been sixteen and her grandmother was just beginning to make a name for the place. If she could make its stay any easier by cuddling, petting, cooing to an animal, she'd happily spend hours doing just that. She needed them to know they were safe, especially those that came from abuse or neglect situations. Those poor animals carried so much baggage and Jessica, like her grandmother before her, did everything she could to make them understand that it was okay, that they were going to be safe and warm for the rest of their lives.

The dog wing was fairly quiet, and Jessica was slightly ashamed of her relief. She was tired and hungry and just wanted to go home, so she stealthily set the alarm and headed out to her car.

Don't get so caught up by things here on earth that you forget to look up once in a while.

Her grandmother's voice sounded in her head as clearly as if she'd been standing next to her, and Jessica obeyed, stopping next to her car and looking up. The night was clear and crisp, and this far out of the city, the stars were a glowing mass of sparkles against the deep indigo background of the sky, like tiny diamonds on a velvet pillow. She inhaled deeply, filling her lungs with fresh air, then let it out slowly and climbed into her car.

Most people drove out of the city after work, but for Jessica, it was the opposite and she liked it that way. The shelter was several miles outside the city limits, technically in the suburbs, but it felt like the country. Her home, however, was in the city, her apartment the entire top two floors of an old Victorian house in the Shopwalk District of downtown. She had a renter in the apartment on the first floor, and she owned the house outright, thanks to her grandparents. She didn't make a huge income at the shelter—she preferred to put the money back into it when she could—so having the house as an investment was helpful.

Also helpful was its proximity to Bucky's Bar and Grill. The thought of Javier's cream of mushroom soup sent Jessica's stomach growling again as she slid her car into her designated spot in the three-car garage behind her house. Knowing if she went inside, she'd get too comfortable to leave again—and also knowing there was no food in there for her to whip up something quickly—she transferred her laptop bag to the trunk of her car, grabbed her purse, and walked the block and a half to Bucky's.

The bar was busy, unsurprising for 10:30 on a Saturday night. Tucked in the back corner was Velvet Jazz, a local band that featured three men on instruments and a woman who sounded *almost* like Diana Krall if you closed your eyes. They were closing in on the end of "Cry Me a River" when Jessica made eye contact with Henry Buck, bartender, owner, and friend of Jessica's since she was twelve.

"Jessie," he called as he rimmed a glass with a lemon and slid it in front of a customer.

Jessica grinned and waved. Nobody else had ever called her Jessie except her grandmother, so there was something warm and comforting about this silver-haired man who knew her so well referring to her by that name. There was an empty barstool in the very corner of the bar and she took it, hanging her bag on the hook underneath and making herself comfortable. Before she even finished settling in, a dirty vodka martini with three olives appeared like magic.

"Aw, you know just how to make a girl feel good, Uncle Henry," she said with a grin.

"You look like you could use it," Henry said, his voice gentle even over the sound of the band. "You eat?"

Jessica shook her head and Henry looked unsurprised.

"Soup?"

"Love some."

Henry knocked on the bar, gave her a wink, and went to his computer where he punched in some instructions. Jessica knew Javier, the chef, would receive the order in the kitchen in the back. Henry might have been in his seventies, but he made sure to keep Bucky's up to date with the latest in bar and restaurant equipment, a computer system to manage his sales, and a state-of-the-art sound system. There was a reason he'd been in business for nearly forty years. Jessica watched with love as Henry sidled around Kim, the other bartender working tonight.

Jessica took a sip of her martini, felt the gentle burn as the alcohol coursed down her throat, felt the warmth as it coated her stomach. Immediately, she began to relax, not realizing she'd been a little wound up until that very moment. Summer was fast approaching, the busiest time of year for them next to Christmas. The telethon would be upon them before she knew it, and she was more nervous than usual, given all the changes. The kennels weren't full, but they were fuller than she liked to see them, and the telethon brought in their biggest chunk of money the whole year, so she was having a love/hate relationship with it right now.

Shaking the work thoughts out of her head, she looked around the bar, subtly bopping her head to the original song Velvet Jazz was playing now. The lighting was dim except for over the band, but Jessica could make out some of the regulars. Bucky's drew an interesting mix of people. Some were older, friends of Henry's who'd been coming here for decades. Some were younger professionals who appreciated going to a bar that wasn't blasting rap or classic rock, a bar that wasn't full of college-age kids drinking cheap beer as quickly as possible. Bucky's was a classy joint, as Henry used to tell her when she was a kid, and he was right. It still was.

Henry slid a paper placemat under her drink and gave her a rolled-up napkin with silverware in it, left, then returned with a big, steaming bowl of Javier's famous cream of mushroom soup. The aroma wafted up from the bowl, enveloping Jessica in one of the smells of her childhood. Javier had worked for Henry ever since Jessica could remember and she'd eaten his soup just as long.

The first spoonful was like an elixir of peace and instantly, she felt better. She spooned in a second bite, picked up her napkin, and dabbed at the corner of her mouth as she glanced down the bar to the opposite end from where she sat.

And locked eyes with Sydney Taylor.

The whole bar seemed to fade away for a moment so that all Jessica could see were those eyes. Even though she was too far away to see the color, her memory filled in the blanks and that deep-sea blue-green held her gaze for a long moment until Sydney raised her beer glass in a silent salute.

"Damn it," Jessica muttered, refocusing on her soup. What was Sydney Taylor doing here? In her neighborhood? In her bar, for God's sake? She continued to eat, but knew it would be rude not to acknowledge Sydney any further. When she looked back up, Sydney was no longer watching her. Instead, she was engaged in a conversation with a good-looking bald man. Judging by the way three other men at a table several yards away were watching, Jessica guessed there was a bet in place. Or a challenge. Sydney was on television and was most likely recognized often. She watched, amused, and worked on her soup. The bald guy leaned close, said something near Sydney's ear, and she threw her head back and laughed. Jessica couldn't pull her eyes away from that delicate expanse of throat. Even in the dim lighting, she could see enough to make her swallow hard, reach for her glass, and finish off her drink.

Concentrating on eating her food, she didn't look up again until she'd finished all the soup, and at that point, Sydney's seat had been vacated, the bald man back with his posse, sans new date. She sighed, unable to decide if she was disappointed or relieved, then picked up the large plastic pick from her empty glass, put it between her teeth, and pulled the last olive free.

"Come here often?"

Jessica stopped mid-chew as the timbre of Sydney's voice registered much too close to her ear, and her brain tossed her the image of standing close to her, their hands linked, their bodies pressed together as they pet a horse. She finished the olive, swallowed, and turned to meet those eyes with her own.

"I didn't want to leave without saying hello," Sydney added, her smile warm and seemingly genuine.

"Hello," Jessica said, forcing a smile in return. "I didn't expect to see you here." Which was as close as she could come to saying "what the hell are you doing in my favorite place?" without being a bitch.

"This is my first time, but I really like it." Sydney looked around the bar as if maintaining eye contact with Jessica was uncomfortable. "My apartment is only two blocks away, so I walked. I was sort of exploring the area this afternoon and saw this place. I decided I'd grab a drink." She glanced at Jessica's empty bowl. "A little late for dinner, don't you think?"

Her tone was gently teasing, and Jessica felt her own fake smile soften into something less artificial. "Occupational hazard. I tend to lose track of time at work."

"You were at the shelter this late?" Sydney's beautiful eyes widened.

"Happens all the time," came a deeper voice, and they both looked up to see Henry clearing away Jessica's place setting. "She works way too hard." He gave her a look that had Jessica blushing and Sydney grinning.

"Your dad?" Sydney asked as Henry winked.

"Not technically, but close enough." Jessica raised her voice on the last three words and saw Henry chuckle as he walked away with her dishes. He was replaced with Kim, who asked them if they wanted another round.

"Oh, no," Sydney said before Jessica could answer. "I'm on my way out. I just wanted to make sure I said hi." She laid a warm hand on Jessica's upper arm and gave it a gentle squeeze, and Jessica felt as if it left a heated imprint on her skin, a glowing pink outline of Sydney's hand. "It was nice to see you."

"You, too," Jessica said, a little surprised that she now meant it.

With a smile, Sydney turned away and left the bar. Jessica watched her go and when she turned back to the bar, Kim was still standing there. She lifted her brows expectantly.

"Yes," Jessica said with a nod, trying to get her bearings and having no idea where they'd gone. "I'll take another. Please."

ॐ

Once out in the night air, Sydney blew out a breath, only then realizing she'd been tensed up and doing her best to stay aloof and professional. Seeing Jessica Barstow across the bar had thrown her and she didn't like that. It was pretty obvious from Jessica's less-than-warm hello that she didn't like it either. Seemed like she might be a regular there, the way the staff appeared to know her so well, so Sydney wondered if she should steer clear of Bucky's from now on.

The Shopwalk's streets were busy, bustling with the young crowd that tends to be out and about on a Saturday night after eleven. Sydney pulled herself together, turned to her left, and started walking, enjoying the sights of brightly lit bars and restaurants, the sounds of various live bands and jukeboxes coming out open doorways, and the smells of food from the kitchens that remained open at this hour. Her thoughts returned to Bucky's. And Jessica. Sydney liked the bar. She liked the feel of it, the atmosphere, the cleanliness, how the staff was friendly and kind, not brusque or hurried. She'd only been hit on once and the guy was very nice, very gracious when she gently shot him down. Though not terribly familiar with jazz, she'd always enjoyed the rhythm of it, so the live music was a bonus. And the crowd there seemed a bit more…sophisticated than bars she'd experienced in the past with people her age, ones filled with drunken men and overly made-up women, each trying unsuccessfully to flirt with the other. It was so not Sydney's speed, something her friends endlessly teased her about. Laura liked to tell her she was an old soul. Sometimes, Sydney enjoyed that moniker. Other times, she found it insulting.

Sidling past a group of laughing twenty-somethings, Sydney located her street sign and turned down her block, and her mind—annoyingly—took her back to the subject of Jessica Barstow. Sydney had watched her for a long time before Jessica noticed her. And she'd enjoyed it. Jessica, relaxed and comfortable, was really nice to watch. It told Sydney that maybe—*maybe*—there was more to her than abruptness and a cool demeanor. Watching her smile—really smile—when she talked to the older guy bartending was kind of a surprise. It was a different kind of smile than Sydney had seen so far. It was soft and tender and genuine. And it reached her eyes, crinkled them at the corners a bit, made her entire face seem to relax into contentedness. It wasn't businesslike and brittle like the smiles she'd been on the receiving end of.

At the front steps of her house, Sydney made a scoffing sound. Why was she agonizing over the way a business contact smiled around her? *I mean, that's what you do in business. You act like a business professional.* She trudged up the lobby stairs, the entire house quiet, much to her delight, and only then did she realize that she'd never actually run into a business acquaintance outside of work. That must be what had thrown her off a bit. She slid her key into the lock and pushed the door open.

Yeah. That must be it.

CHAPTER SIX

A GLANCE AT THE CLOCK on her office wall told Jessica it was quarter to eight in the evening. She was bone tired, so exhausted she was pretty sure if she put her head down on her desk, she'd be out like a light in mere seconds. But that wasn't going to happen because she had one more appointment.

"Damn it," she muttered under her breath as she pushed herself up from her desk and headed out to the front doors. The earlier phone conversation had not gone as she'd expected.

"Sydney? It's Jessica Barstow at Junebug. I'm afraid I need to reschedule our one o'clock today. I apologize. It's been totally chaotic here, and I have to take care of some unexpected issues immediately."

"That's no problem at all." Sydney's voice was professional and Jessica found herself thinking back to Saturday night in Bucky's when she'd been so much more relaxed. *"When's a good time?"*

"You know, I'm going to be here for a while tonight, if you're interested in coming after hours. Otherwise, Thursday would work for me." If you're interested in coming after hours? Why did I say that?

"Television news has no office hours." Sydney's reply came with a gentle chuckle and Jessica found herself smiling. *"I could do eight, no problem. I think Connor's got something tonight, though, so it would just be me. Is that okay?"*

"That's fine. Anna will be gone as well, so it'll just be the two of us. The doors will be locked, as we close at six on Tuesdays, so just text me when you get here. Okay?"

"Sounds great. See you tonight."

They'd hung up and Jessica had sat staring at the phone in her hand, wondering who had body snatched her and had that conversation with Sydney Taylor. Unfortunately (or maybe fortunately) there hadn't been time to dwell on it, as Animal Control was bringing them six dogs seized from a suspected dogfighting ring. Always dicey—and sometimes dangerous—it took all hands on deck much of the time to get these types of dogs settled in and calmed. Today had been no exception and she felt emotionally drained from the ordeal. Lisa had only headed home fifteen minutes ago and she looked just as wrung out as Jessica felt.

Through the front doors, she saw Sydney Taylor get out of her car and head toward her, a messenger bag slung over her shoulder and a paper bag in her hand. Her heels clicked loudly in the quiet of the parking lot. Jessica pushed the door open for her and held it. "Thank you for meeting me," she said, her voice sounding more tired than she meant.

"It's no problem," Sydney said, her usual, cool smile in place.

"You could have changed into more comfortable clothes," Jessica commented, taking in the red skirt, black-and-white silk top, and heels, hoping she wasn't staring, but enjoying the outfit in a big way. "Not that you don't look great, but it's just us." She shifted her gaze to the door, irritated with herself for letting that slip. *What the hell, Jess?* She turned the lock and the deadbolt on the front door snapped home.

"Oh, no, I'm still working, so I'm still wearing my work clothes," Sydney replied, her voice matter-of-fact.

Jessica gave a subtle nod and indicated Sydney should follow her. *Suit yourself,* she thought, happy in her jeans.

"I haven't seen this office," Sydney commented as they went down a small hall into Jessica's private office.

"Welcome to the Inner Sanctum," Jessica said, waving her arms like one of the models on *The Price is Right*. "I don't usually meet with people here—that's what the conference room is for—but I'm so tired tonight, I need my chair. I hope that's okay."

"You're the boss," Sydney said, looking around.

Jessica watched as, rather than sit, Sydney set her bags down, then went to the far wall where six 9x12 frames were lined up, each showcasing a letter Jessica had received from a client or customer or child thanking her for whatever animal they took home. Some were drawn in crayon.

"Wow," Sydney said, then her glance dropped to the table below the frames to the pile of additional letters. "Are these all thank yous?" she asked, those gorgeous eyes wide on Jessica's face.

Jessica felt her face warm and she shrugged and sat behind her desk. "Regina comes in and switches them up every month or so. She thinks it's good for me."

"To know how grateful other people are for what you do?"

Jessica nodded.

"I agree with Regina." Sydney cocked her head as she studied Jessica. "Does that embarrass you?"

"No."

"The current color of your face says differently." Sydney said it lightly, though. Gently. Kindly enough that it didn't make Jessica feel weird. Or exposed.

"Well. It's just my job."

"Your job makes people ridiculously happy, you know. That's a pretty amazing thing."

Had her brain just completely short-circuited from the day? Jessica wondered this because she had no words. No comeback. Nothing to counter what this very hot young woman in front of her was saying. She simply…looked at her. *Come on, brain. Make words. Make. Words.*

"Hey, are you okay?" Sydney asked, approaching the desk. She braced her hands on the surface and looked closely at Jessica's face. "You look…worn out."

"Oh," Jessica said. "Well. Thanks for that."

Sydney laughed. "Maybe I can help." She crossed the room to the chair and picked up the paper bag. "I brought dinner. I hope that's okay. I haven't eaten and you sounded a little frazzled on the phone, so I took a wild guess that you hadn't either." She proceeded to pull out two wrapped sub sandwiches from Marletto's Italian Deli. "I've got tuna and turkey. I hope you like at least one of them." She looked up then, snagged Jessica's gaze with those mesmerizing blue-green eyes of hers, and smiled hesitantly.

"You brought me dinner?" Jessica watched her nod slowly. "I haven't eaten since breakfast." She snatched up the tuna sub, unwrapped it, and took a bite, all in one smooth move. Holding a hand in front of her mouth as she chewed, she said, "Oh, my God. I could kiss you right now."

The only thing that made her replay that line in her mind was the slight raising of Sydney's eyebrows to go along with her lopsided grin. Jessica cleared her throat and continued to chew as Sydney unwrapped her own sub and settled in.

"Rough day?" Sydney asked, then took a bite and waited for Jessica's response.

"Brutal," Jessica replied, letting out a big breath.

"Want to talk about it?"

Jessica thought about it for a minute as she forced herself to slow down, lest she choke to death on a sandwich. "You know what? I really don't, if that's okay. But tell me about your day. Take my mind off mine."

"Well." Sydney finished the bite in her mouth, and Jessica watched in fascination as she visibly began to loosen up just the tiniest bit. "I went to a brewery today, so already, my day was way better than yours." She laughed and the sound was very cute, very feminine, and it made Jessica smile.

"A brewery? Yeah, you totally win."

"I've never been to one before. It was pretty cool. I had to interview the owners. They won a big national award recently."

"Oh, was it Old Red Barn?"

"It was."

A thought occurred to Jessica then and she sat up straight, palms against the desk.

Sydney furrowed her brow and turned her head from one side to the other. "What?" she asked. "What's happening?"

Jessica held up one finger as she crossed the room to the little corner fridge, pulled the door open, and took out two bottles. She held them up for Sydney to see. "Green-Eyed Beauty from Old Red Barn. Lisa brought me some a few weeks ago. How's that for a coincidence?"

"Okay, that's a little weird," Sydney said, but with a grin.

"You up for one?"

"Absolutely." She held her hand out. "Long day."

Jessica pulled the bottle out of her reach. "You're old enough, right?" she said with a wink.

"I'll have you know that I am thirty, thank you very much."

Jessica blinked at her, surprised. "You are?"

"Mm hmm." After a beat, she added, "Do you need to see my ID?" And Jessica realized she hadn't handed over the bottle yet.

With a laugh, she did so, used a bottle opener on her own beer, then set it on her desk. Sydney held up her bottle and Jessica closed a hand over hers to brace the bottle. She kept her eyes riveted to the bottle opener even as the smooth, warm skin registered under her own fingers, and she swallowed hard. She popped the top and retreated quickly, suddenly needing space between them. Jessica sat back down behind her desk with a thud and lifted the bottle to her lips, but stopped when she heard, "Wait!" Sydney stood up and leaned toward her. "You can't sip without cheering. It's bad luck."

"Is it?"

"Absolutely. Trust me on this. My mom's family is Irish. We know the rules around alcohol." Raising her bottle, she said simply, "Here's to it," and touched her bottle to Jessica's with a soft clink.

"That's it? 'Here's to it'? I was all prepared for some wise, traditional anecdote."

"Oh, no. I said we're *Irish*, not poets. We want to drink as quickly as possible." Sydney grinned, then sipped.

"I see."

"Mm, this is really good." Sydney licked her lips while Jessica tried not to watch. And failed. *Is it getting warm in here?*

The next hour went quickly as they finished their subs, then talked about the various volunteers Sydney thought would make for the best interviews. They went through her list and discussed each individual person or family so Jessica could add some extra information she might have that wasn't in the files she made. Resistant as Jessica had been to the changing of the guards, so to speak, she had to admit that Sydney Taylor seemed to know what she was doing. She was creative and thorough and asked insightful questions. After the last one, Sydney closed her folder and smiled.

"You really know a lot about each person. There are so many; I can't believe you remember them all."

Jessica shrugged. "My grandmother taught me how important it is to actually *see* people. You know? To listen and remember. I think that's something that is, sadly, becoming lost in this day of electronics. Everybody is looking down at their phones. Nobody is making eye contact. I'm as guilty as the next guy. Nobody is noticing the people around them. The actual people, not the avatars on their devices. You know?" She took a sip of beer and watched Sydney's face. "That just made me sound super old, didn't it?"

Sydney laughed that laugh that Jessica found so pleasant, the one that was genuine, not an act of a television personality. "No. Not at all. I was just realizing that I am probably one of those people who's on her phone too much."

"Yeah?"

"Oh, God, yes. Between my job and my notes and trying to stay on top of the news and being away from my family, it's my life. It's the only way I can stay connected."

"Well. It's not the only way. People stayed connected before smart phones."

"True. But everything moves so much faster now. Let me amend that to say it's the only way I can stay *quickly* connected and therefore not get left behind by others in my field. Better?"

"Better. And it's kind of amazing, the technology of it all."

"Right? Everything is right there when you need it. And stuff has developed and grown so fast." Sydney sat forward in her chair, her eyes crackling with excitement. "I mean, online dating? Come on. Hardly anybody met that way twenty years ago. Now? Everybody meets online."

"Yeah, not sure I could do that," Jessica said. The thought of not seeing somebody live beforehand just felt…wrong to her.

"No? Are you married?" Sydney asked.

"No." Jessica shook her head and smoothly turned the conversation back to Sydney. "What about you?"

"Am I married? No. I don't really have time," Sydney said, and for some reason, Jessica felt like that was only a half-truth.

"Everybody has time for love. Come on. There's nobody who interests you? Not even Anna?" Jessica meant it to come off as a lighthearted teasing, but Sydney's face looked stricken and she immediately felt terrible. *I should probably not be around people when I'm this tired. My filters are completely gone.*

Sydney opened her mouth to speak, then closed it again before any sound came out. She opened it a second time and managed, "She mentioned that, huh?" Her cheeks flushed a deep red and Jessica had the urgent, inexplicable need to make her feel better. "I wondered when I met her here the other day."

"You know what? It's none of my business. It's really not. I'm so sorry I said anything. It's been a long, exhausting day, I'm really tired and just a little bit punchy, and my manners have evidently left for the night. That was totally out of line." Jessica grimaced. "I'm so sorry."

"No, no, it's totally okay." Sydney waved it off, but was clearly very uncomfortable. She shifted in her chair, uncrossed her legs and re-crossed them the other way, took a large swig of her beer.

"Um, so, how do you like it here so far?" Jessica asked. It was a desperate, glaringly obvious attempt to change the subject, but Jessica ran with it anyway, and so did Sydney.

"It's okay. It'll do for now." Sydney's voice was a bit clipped, though Jessica could tell she was trying to fight it. "I really wanted a bigger market, but…that's how this job works. So I'll just wait and be ready."

"For?"

"For the next job offer."

"And you'll move again?"

"Yup."

"Just like that, huh?" Jessica sipped her beer, contemplated. "I don't know if I could do that, just up and go at a moment's notice."

Sydney lifted one shoulder, seemingly still not quite comfortable with eye contact. She looked over Jessica's shoulder and out the window as she spoke. "It comes with the territory. You get into this job and you know that's one of the aspects of it if you want to develop your career."

"Couldn't you develop your career in one place? I know Janet Dobson, the woman who hosted the telethon before you, worked at Channel Six for…" Jessica gazed up at the ceiling for a beat. "Almost twenty years. She's an icon here."

"I guess, if you don't want to ever have a larger audience, that's fine. But if you do, you're going to have to move." Sydney shrugged. "So you plan on it."

"Plan on spontaneity," Jessica said. "Interesting concept."

Sydney smiled and it felt real and finally, the atmosphere in the room lightened just a touch.

"So, you don't plan on staying here then?"

"No way," Sydney said with a shake of her pretty head.

"I see." A sharp stab of disappointment poked at Jessica then, but she wasn't sure why and chose not to think about it. "That's too bad. It's a pretty cool place. Have you been able to see much of it?"

"Not really. I've only been here a short time and I got started on my job right away. My hours can be long."

"You should try to do a little exploring. You might be surprised by what my city has to offer."

"Your city?" Sydney smiled at the phrase.

"Lived here all my life."

"If I decide I want a tour guide, I'll give you a call."

There was a beat of not-quite-awkward silence and then Jessica finally said, "Well. I guess that's it for now then, right? Did you get everything you needed from me?"

Sydney nodded and crumpled up the wrappers from her sub. Jessica followed suit and the two of them cleaned up in silence. More than once, their proximity to one another was close, and neither of them did anything to put more space between them. Jessica wondered if Sydney was as aware of it as she was.

"I'll walk you out," Jessica said, and each of them packed up their belongings. At the front door, she stopped and turned to Sydney. Again, they stood very close together. Jessica could smell a pleasant scent—a spicy citrus of some sort—that seemed to radiate from Sydney's skin. Ignoring the tightening in her lower body, she asked, "So, what's next? When do we meet again?"

Sydney gazed off toward the goat house, quiet in the almost-dark, and Jessica was able to take the moment and study her face. The strong jawline that tapered into a softened chin, the angle of the shadow thrown by sharp-but-not-too-sharp cheekbones. Sydney reached up and absently tucked her hair behind her ear and Jessica saw the sparkle of a gold hoop. "It'll be a week or so," she said, looking back at Jessica and—not for the first time— surprising her with the color of her eyes, even in the dim light. "I'll do some interviews with volunteers. We'll make some rough cuts and then you can take a look and see if we're on the right track."

"That sounds great. I can fill Anna in until we can set up another time to meet."

"Perfect." Sydney's voice sounded less than enthused by the prospect, something Jessica found unexpectedly amusing.

As they walked to their respective cars, Jessica was hit by two simultaneous desires. One was to stop Sydney, to talk to her seriously, to apologize once again for bringing up the Anna thing, to somehow take away that new, slightly shuttered expression she now wore. Two was to run away as quickly as possible, get home, hug her cats, and bring this cursed and horrid day to a close, once and for all.

Number two won out.

&

Sydney gave a small wave from the driver's seat of her car as Jessica pulled away, and she breathed a quiet sigh of relief. It wasn't lost on her that she was about to be one of those people they'd discussed earlier, sitting and checking her phone while the world went by without her. In her own mind, she chalked it up to work, even though she was responding to a text from her best friend. Plus, she needed a minute to just decompress from this meeting, which felt like it had knocked her around a bit and left her head spinning.

It had turned out to be a very...interesting evening. She'd been nervous about meeting Jessica Barstow alone; the woman was intimidating, all authoritative and sexy. Yes, sexy. Sydney could admit that, and not for the first time. She was stunning, really, but a little bit aloof. Her confidence was magnetic, and without Connor to act as a buffer of some sort, Sydney worried she'd come off as less professional than she intended. She'd wavered all over the place about dinner. Was she being presumptuous? Or would Jessica think it was a nice gesture? Was there anything that could be read into it? That Sydney didn't think her smart enough to feed herself? That she was just being nice? Was she overstepping boundaries? Sydney had gone back and forth eight times before deciding to bring the dinner in…mostly because she thought she might faint from hunger if she didn't eat.

She'd made the right choice. Not only had Jessica been just as hungry, but that line about almost kissing Sydney hadn't gone unnoticed. By either of them. It was just an off-the-cuff remark, a figure of speech. Sydney knew this. But the visual it threw at her unexpectedly was…enticing, to say the least. And how many times did they end up standing much closer than normal business acquaintances usually did?

"A lot, that's how many," she said aloud. "Okay, Syd, enough with the fantasizing about your hot subject, especially since she now knows you like girls. Thanks for that, Anna." She groaned, and with a shake of her head, she finished typing her response to Laura, then reached for her key and turned it.

Nothing happened.

"What the hell?" she muttered and tried again. A click-click-click was the only sound the car made. "Noooooooo," she breathed into the empty interior and tried one more time, even as she knew the dying battery Laura's boyfriend, Zack, warned her to replace had apparently gone through its death throes while she'd been having a sub inside. She dropped her forehead to the steering wheel. "Son of a bitch."

The loud rapping on her window scared her so badly, she jumped in her seat and let out a little squeak that would embarrass her later. Her fear was not lessened by the sight of the gigantic janitor from Junebug, his large, horror-movie-slasher glasses distorting his eyes so they made him look like a cartoon villain. A *scary* cartoon villain. She hadn't realized he was still here.

"Need some help?" he asked through the glass, as Sydney couldn't bring herself to roll down the window because it was dark and she was alone and freaking herself out. Rolling down the window in a dark parking lot was what stupid women in horror flicks did right before the scary guy reached in and strangled them to death.

"I have Triple A," she replied, loudly through the closed window.

"Sounds like a dead battery. I'm happy to jump it for you."

"It's okay. Really." She held up her cell for him to see, tilted it back and forth. "I can call them."

He gave a shrug, but added, "It'll probably take them an hour or more to get here."

Sydney groaned quietly. Her phone told her it was after ten. She did *not* want to be there until midnight. She looked out the window at the guy who stood there, hands on his hips as if he had all the time in the world for her to make a decision.

"So he can murder me," she muttered. "And bury my corpse under the goat house where nobody will ever find me. Or feed me to the—stop it!" She sat there, thoughts in a flurry. She was being ridiculous. And inexplicably rude to this man—again. The guy worked for Jessica. Jessica was a smart woman and, Sydney hoped, would never hire a creepy serial killer to be around the animals she so loved. Right? Taking a deep breath and deciding to accept this line of reasoning, she turned back to him and nodded. "Okay. I'd appreciate the help."

The guy's face lit up like Charlie unwrapping his candy bar and finding the last Golden Ticket. He held up a finger and said, "Be right back." Then he disappeared into Junebug Farms.

Sydney sighed at her crappy luck, then sent another text off to Laura.

Battery dead. Don't tell Zack. Having it jumped. If you never hear from me again, look for my corpse under the goat house at Junebug Farms.

Laura's text came back just as headlights broke from around the side of the building.

You were a great friend. I'll miss u. Kinda.

Sydney grinned at the note, then looked up as a pickup truck that might have seriously been older than she was pulled so it faced her, the headlights causing her to squint until she got used to the sudden light. He hopped out, which Sydney only knew when his silhouette appeared directly in front of her.

"Pop the hood," he said loudly so she could hear him over the engine. She did, then watched as he opened his own hood, pulled jumper cables from the back of his truck, and hooked them up. She could see him through the opening between the bottom of her hood and the car, and she watched as he moved expertly. Zack would be impressed.

"Okay, give it a try."

Sydney turned the key and the car sputtered, then roared to life. She gave a small whoop of joy while the man removed the cables and closed her hood. When he came around to her window a few moments later, it was obvious he didn't expect her to roll it down.

"You should be good now," he said through the glass. "But you should have it looked at and probably replaced or it'll just keep happening."

Sydney felt silly now. Embarrassed and a little foolish. She rolled the window down "Thank you."

"You're welcome, Ms. Taylor."

She cocked her head to the side in question.

"I practically live here," he said, but with no trace of sarcasm. Just fact. "I know who you are."

"Well, then, you have me at a disadvantage, because I don't know your name."

"Bill Tracey."

Sydney stuck her hand out the window. "It's nice to officially meet you, Mr. Tracey. I owe you one."

He shook her hand and smiled, and just like that, he looked much less scary and much more like a regular, hardworking, nice guy.

Sydney made it home before eleven, let herself into her apartment, and flopped onto the couch. She was overtired and needed to unwind a bit before she tried to sleep, so she simply sat and watched Marge and Homer as they wandered aimlessly around their tiny underwater world. The tank was small, but decked out—as Sydney liked to say—with glittering blue gravel on the bottom and a scuba diver discovering a treasure chest to liven the place up a bit. The small light was on at the top, and she reached over to click off the lamp on the end table so the room was only visible by the soft, bluish light from the fish tank.

Her thoughts, unsurprisingly—because she knew herself—turned to Jessica Barstow and the evening they'd had. Sydney'd been outed, pretty much, which only served to validate her trepidation around Anna St. John. *Yeah, your brain throws up warning flags for a reason. Obviously.* And while the fact that Jessica knew something about her she hadn't shared had initially bugged her—not because Sydney was closeted, but because she felt it was her choice to tell somebody and her choice to decide when—she had to admit now that she'd been happy with Jessica's reaction. Meaning that she hadn't really had one. Sydney could count on one hand the number of people who'd shown any kind of disapproval in the handful of years she'd been gainfully employed in the very public business of television news, and those had all been very subtle signs. A slight change in facial expression, a dimming of the eyes, an almost indiscernible grimace. For the most part, though, nobody seemed to care one way or the other. It had shocked her how glad she was when

Jessica didn't blink an eye, because, for some reason, *her* disapproval would've stung—something she refused to dwell on. Not to mention, it was pretty clear that the possibility Jessica played on her team was high; Sydney couldn't have been the only one to feel the heat between them. She almost let herself flash back to the horse-petting incident, but was able to corral her thoughts just in time and shake them away.

Anyway. Whatever.

She replayed the rest of the meeting in her head, then pulled out her notes. As they'd talked and Jessica had given her a little more history about Junebug Farms, Sydney had jotted down the bare bones of an idea that she would run by Brad tomorrow, see what he thought. Much as she'd eschewed the whole "human-interest" angle she'd been saddled with, she was starting to think maybe she was better at this than she'd expected.

Sydney readied herself for bed, grabbed her laptop, and perused the websites of a couple of stations she had her eye on, had had her eye on for months. No openings currently listed, but she'd send a couple e-mails anyway and then probably her reel. Knocking on the door couldn't hurt, right? Persistence was good.

If there was one thing Sydney had learned in the past few years, it was that nobody was going to toss her desires into her lap. If she wanted something, she needed to go get it.

CHAPTER SEVEN

"YOU OKAY TODAY, BOSS?"

Bill's voice startled Jessica enough to make her flinch in her chair. She'd been staring out the window, lost in thought, and had very nearly forgotten he'd been fixing the leaking faucet on the sink in her bathroom.

"Yeah. I'm fine, Bill. Just tired. Thanks for asking."

Bill studied her for a moment, his large, thick-lensed glasses distorting his eyes just enough to make it hard to hold his gaze, and Jessica was pretty sure he didn't miss a trick. He was the custodian—had been since before her grandmother had died—and a man of few words, so people tended to overlook him, but he knew all the ins and outs of every building on the property. He was an integral part of keeping Junebug Farms running smoothly, and sometimes, Jessica wondered if she was the only one who realized it.

"I had to jump Ms. Taylor last night," he said, as he dropped a tool loudly into the metal box he'd brought in.

Jessica blinked at him, replayed his words in her head. "I'm sorry?"

"Her battery died. I had to give her a jump to get her home."

"Oh. Oh!" Jessica shook her head and chuckled. "Really? But she was okay?"

Bill waved a hand as he hauled his toolbox up off the floor. "She was fine. Needs a new battery, though."

Jessica felt a wave of guilt rush through her. She'd left pretty quickly last night, tired and embarrassed and just ready for the day to be over. "I should've waited to make sure she got off okay."

Bill shrugged it off. "It was all right."

"Well. I'm glad you were here. Thanks for helping her."

"Faucet should be good now." Bill jerked his chin back toward her bathroom. Then he was gone.

And now Sydney was on her mind again. "Oh, who am I kidding?" she muttered to the empty room. "It's not like she's been *off* my mind at all." Jessica had slept fitfully last night, probably from being overtired. She found that lately, any time she lay awake, staring at her ceiling, cats curled up all around her body, her thoughts drifted to Sydney Taylor.

She didn't understand why.

And that bothered her.

Before she could analyze it some more, there was a rap on her door and she looked up into the smiling face of Anna St. John.

"Hey, got a minute?" Anna asked, not waiting for an answer, but instead entering the office and taking a seat. In the same chair Sydney sat in last night.

"Sure. What's up?" Jessica straightened her own chair and pulled herself closer to the desk in an attempt to look like she was paying attention.

"I've got some stuff for you to sign off on." Anna handed over a bunch of papers. Jessica took them and sifted through. "Sydney Taylor was here last night, huh?"

Jessica looked up at her and squinted. "She was. Why?"

Anna shrugged, raised her eyebrows in innocence. "No reason. I heard Bill talking to Regina about having to jump her car."

Jessica grimaced. "Yeah, I should've stuck around. I assumed she was right behind me, but didn't really pay attention. I feel bad."

"I was thinking I might give her a call," Anna said.

Jessica blinked at her, surprised. "Really?"

"Yeah." Anna picked a piece of lint off her pant leg, her face the epitome of overconfidence. "We had a nice time. Maybe we can have another one. For longer." She waggled her eyebrows in such a way that Jessica just looked at her.

"Do you think that's such a good idea?"

"You don't?"

"Well," Jessica shrugged. "I don't know. I just..." Her voice trailed off, as she really had no words. And realistically, no logical reason to deter Anna from asking Sydney out. She blew out a breath. "I mean, no, sure. Go for it. She seems nice."

"And she's super hot," Anna said with a chuckle.

"She's attractive, yes." Jessica tried to focus on the papers awaiting her signature, not enjoying this conversation at all and wanting it to end. Like, now.

"It's time for me to get back out there, you know? Since Catherine..." Anna let her voice trail off and turned her gaze toward the window, which pulled Jessica's attention.

Anna and Catherine had been a mess from the start. That was clear to anybody and everybody who spent five minutes with them. And like so many lesbians tended to do, they'd stayed in the doomed pairing for much longer than they should have. While they hadn't caused anything disruptive or distracting during business hours, the tension between them had been obvious at times, hung heavy in the air, crackling. Since Catherine had started dating Emily Breckenridge, however, that strain had died down to almost nothing, much to the relief of the rest of the staff. Catherine was happy now. And Anna was obviously lonely, which Jessica definitely could sympathize with. There was no reason for Anna not to give Sydney Taylor a call.

Why that thought caused an uncomfortable ripple in Jessica's stomach, she refused to sit and think about.

Signing the last paper, she handed the sheets back to Anna. "There you go."

"Great. Thanks." Anna took the papers and stood, but hesitated. "You think it's a good idea? Calling Sydney?"

Her face told Jessica that it was an honest question. She really wanted her input. "If it'll make you happy? Sure."

Anna grinned and waved the papers. "Thanks for these. Gotta run."

Jessica watched her go and kept staring long after she was gone. Well, maybe this would be good for Anna. She could use some happiness; everybody deserved that. Anna wasn't Jessica's favorite person, but she wasn't a bad person either. She was just…volatile? Was that the right word? A mixed bag? She had the tendency to be a chameleon; she could change her habits/moods/whatever to match those of her partner, which, she supposed, could be a good thing…for a while. After that, it inevitably became the hanging thread that, once pulled, unraveled the entire relationship. That's what had happened with her and Catherine, and, though Anna seemed to date regularly, she hadn't met anybody serious since.

The idea of Sydney being the next serious one didn't sit well with Jessica, and that fact irked her to no end. Thank God her phone rang and pulled her attention in another direction because this was getting ridiculous.

❧

Sydney had set aside time that afternoon to watch recordings of previous Junebug Farms annual telethons. She wanted to get a feel for how things were done, who, of the staff at the shelter, was best on camera, and what kinds of stories they'd already done, so as not to be too repetitive. A glance at her watch told her she'd been at it for nearly five hours, watching, skipping ahead, listening, skipping ahead, and her eyes were beginning to burn. Despite the gravel that was apparently creating walkways inside her eyelids, the time hadn't been a waste at all, as she'd learned two things fairly early on.

First, the telethon definitely needed updating, something— many things, actually—to pull it into the twenty-first century. It wasn't horrible, but it was certainly not going to be snagging the attention of any Millennials. It needed streamlining, tweaks to make it slicker, more present, a faster pace. Sydney already had a list of ideas in front of her to go over with Connor.

Second—and this was the thing that had kept her in the tiny, dimly lit viewing room for more than half the day—was that Jessica was a natural in front of the camera. She came across as relaxed and poised, approachable and friendly. You watched her talk and you immediately wanted to have coffee with her. And the camera loved her. *Loved her.* That creamy smooth skin of hers, not pale but not tanned, begged for you to touch it, to run your fingertips along her jawline. Her hair caught all the lighting exactly right, especially in the segments that were shot outdoors. The red strands captured the sunlight, gave it a warm hug, and reflected it back softly out into the world for all to see and enjoy. Sydney had the almost irresistible urge to wrap a lock of it around her finger, just play with it, test its softness. She listened as Jessica talked about the shelter, how it had begun, when she'd decided to take over, what it meant to her that every abandoned or abused animal have a chance, and Sydney was enthralled. She recalled that moment a couple hours ago when she'd watched a much older segment, one where the death of Jessica's grandmother was still fairly fresh, and the way her heart had squeezed in her chest at the sight of Jessica's soft blue eyes tearing, the movement of her throat as she'd swallowed down her obvious emotion at talking about a woman she cared deeply for. Sydney had felt her own eyes well up.

"Yeah, she's a gold mine," she muttered aloud in the small room, amazed at how somebody who could be so coolly aloof in person could come across so warmly onscreen.

The door opened, startling her—

"Hey, Syd, I e-mailed you a schedule of interviews I've set up so far." The television screens that filled the room were reflected in the lenses of his glasses as he glanced up to look at her. "You looking at old telethons?" Connor Baskin always did that: began talking the instant he entered a room, completely unaware of whether or not he'd interrupted anything. Sydney was learning that he was a very focused guy, which she could appreciate.

Sydney nodded. "I thought I should. And her?" She pointed to the frozen shot of Jessica on one of the screens. "We should use her as much as we can. She really resonates."

"I thought the same thing," Connor said. "She's poised and sophisticated enough to capture the older crowd, but hip and hot enough to pull in some of the younger demographic, if we give her the right stuff to say."

"You think she's hot?"

Connor gave her a look that said, *does a bear shit in the woods?* "You don't?"

"I do. Of course." Sydney didn't like the uncertainty in her voice, so cleared her throat. "Anyway, I think we should use her more than they have in the past. Think she'd be up for that?"

Connor shrugged as he said, "Well, I think that shelter means the world to her, and if we position it so this maybe brings in more money, she'd be all for it."

Sydney looked back at the screen, at Jessica's face and the soft half-smile she was giving the camera. "What if we made her a cohost?"

She turned back to Connor, who was wearing what Sydney had come to know as his thinking face. Pursed lips, wrinkled forehead, eyes looking skyward. "It could work, if Brad agrees." He studied the still. "We'd have to polish her up a bit, keep her part simple and easy. And she might not want to. The idea might terrify her."

Sydney nodded as he spoke, listening to each statement, knowing he was right, and cataloging ideas in her brain at the same time.

"She does look great on camera," he said.

"She looks *amazing* on camera."

"We should find out." Connor gave one nod, then turned to leave, tossing over his shoulder, "We need to get some B-roll soon." And he was gone.

Sydney watched the door slowly shut, then turned back to the monitors and hit the Play button. Jessica was moving again, talking and smiling widely, occasionally raising a hand and gesturing to make her point. She was articulate; she never stuttered or stumbled over words. She was positive and likable and gorgeous to look at, and Sydney had the sudden flash of a tally board with numbers ratcheting endlessly upward. If she used that sort of incentive, she was sure she could get Jessica on board. Or...she didn't really even have to tell her. Right? She could just give her more and more things to say and do and comment on and before she knew it, she'd be cohosting alongside Sydney.

This could work.
This could work really, really well.

CHAPTER EIGHT

THE BUTTERFLIES HAD STARTED.

It happened every year when the telethon got close, but it was very specific. Jessica had been anxious for a couple of weeks now, but there hadn't been that unnerving fluttering in her stomach like there was now.

"And so it begins," she said quietly to herself as she watched out the window of her office. A white Channel Six van had pulled into the parking lot and a man was unloading some equipment and nodding while Connor Baskin talked to him, pointing in various directions around the grounds. The side door opened and Sydney Taylor slid off the passenger seat in black slacks, a royal blue sleeveless top, and her standard three-inch heels, which made Jessica roll her eyes. Sydney had called about an hour ago, told Jessica they wanted to take advantage of the sunny day to grab some B-roll—which Janet Dobson had taught Jessica was television speak for "background shots"—as yesterday had been gray and rainy. With the telethon barely three weeks away now, the pace of everything was picking up.

After making a quick intercom call to Anna letting her know Sydney had arrived, Jessica headed out to the lobby to greet her. Sydney's smile was hesitant when she saw Jessica, and she walked toward her with her hand out.

"Hey there," she said, and as Jessica shook her hand, it occurred to her that they stood eye to eye with Sydney in her heels. *If I'm five seven, that would make her about five four. Smaller than I thought.* Where those thoughts came from or why they now occupied her brain, Jessica wasn't sure, and she did her best to shake them away.

"Sydney! Good to see you." Anna's cheerful voice cut through the air before Jessica could say a word and pulled all attention her way as she scuttled across the faux marble floor, arm outstretched. The expression on Sydney's face was amusing to watch. Jessica detected very distinct emotions. Surprise followed by a quick flash of hesitation followed by resignation.

Sydney shook her hand. "Anna. Hi." She introduced her cameraman as Jeff and reintroduced Connor.

Anna clapped her hands together once. "Okay. So. B-roll. I've got some great suggestions, some spots set up, so follow me and we'll knock this all out in no time." She turned on her heel and started off toward the cat wall, obviously expecting everybody to follow her. Sydney did, but not before glancing over her shoulder at Jessica with an expression that, this time, Jessica couldn't read.

"I'll come see you when we're done," she said as she moved away.

Jessica nodded and watched Anna wave an arm in a wide arc as she talked animatedly to Jeff, her eyes never leaving Sydney. She blew out a breath and went back to her office, happy to have been excluded.

The first two years she'd run the telethon, after her grandmother had passed away, Janet Dobson had been the one to offer suggestions on what would work well for B-roll. Jessica liked to think she'd learned a thing or two, but it really wasn't her forté and it always made her a little nervous, made her feel unarguably out of her element. Once she'd hired Anna, she'd been able to—very happily and with great relief—let go of all of that and leave it in hands more capable when it came to publicity. This was the first time since then that a little part of her still wished she was participating, even as a bit player.

Which was ridiculous, as it made her stomach churn with anxiety to even think about it. She didn't enjoy the fast pace of television, and it was even more nerve-wracking for her to be in front of the camera, but Anna insisted that Jessica was "the face of Junebug Farms." So, she did it for the shelter.

It took some time, but by the time the knock on her door sounded, Jessica had become absorbed enough in her work that two and a half hours had gone by. When she looked up from her desk, Sydney stood there and she could see not Jeff, but a glimpse of his camera behind her.

"Hi," Sydney said.

"Hey."

"I was thinking…could we get some footage of you working?" She stepped into the room to allow Jeff in, and Anna pushed in after him.

"I thought it'd be a good idea to get some shots of you at your desk, you know?" Anna said, wandering the room, arms outstretched as if directing. "Maybe gazing out the window or—"

"No gazing," Sydney said, wrestling control back from Anna. "Sitting at your desk, doing what you were just doing. That'll be fine."

"Really?" Anna said, cocking her head to the side and parking a hand on her hip. "You don't think it'd make a cool shot to have her standing, like, here?" She went to the window and positioned herself near the frame, adopted a pensive expression. "Like this?"

"I think we're good," Sydney said, then looked to Connor for help.

"Sydney's right," he agreed belatedly. "At the desk is fine."

Jessica watched this whole exchange as if she were at a tennis match, her head pivoting from one side of her office to the other, keeping her opinions to herself…though she almost burst out laughing when Anna actually *pouted*.

"Okay, Jeff," Sydney said, arms out in front of her, hands forming a U. "I want you to walk in the doorway, start here on this wall. Make sure you get some of these drawings and letters. Then pan left toward the desk where Jessica will be sitting, doing…" Her voice trailed off for a moment as she looked at her. "Paperwork?"

Jessica grinned and gave a nod. "I do that."

"Perfect. We'll do a couple takes, okay?"

It didn't take long. They were finished within twenty minutes, Sydney adding a tweak or a slight change here and there, moving things on the desk, adjusting the blinds for better lighting, things like that.

"I just have to say," Sydney commented while Jeff packed up his equipment. "The camera loves you."

"Doesn't it?" Anna jumped in before Jessica could respond, though it didn't stop the blush that crept up Jessica's neck. "I've said that from the beginning. That's why we began focusing on her when I came on board. It was my idea to make her the face of Junebug Farms. It's impossible to photograph her badly."

"I completely agree with that." Sydney gave her a wink, which settled low in Jessica's body, then took a deep breath and blew it out. "Okay. I think we're done for today."

Anna glanced at her watch. "Hey, what do you all say to hitting Happy Hour?"

Jeff and Connor immediately nodded. "We got in at six a.m.," Connor said, gesturing to the cameraman. "And I'm pretty sure I speak for my friend here when I say we could both use a drink."

"I know I could," Anna said. "Sydney? What do you say?"

Much to Jessica's surprise, Sydney turned to her. "How about you, Jessica? You up for it? I am if you are."

Something about those blue-green eyes made it impossible for Jessica to say no, so she simply nodded.

"Great." Sydney turned to Anna. "You have a place in mind?"

Half an hour later, Jessica pulled her car into the parking lot of The Dove House, continually thanking the Universe that Anna hadn't chosen Sling, the local gay bar where she and Sydney had first met. The Dove House was fifteen minutes from the shelter, a suburban bar and grill, simple in its décor of dark wood and brass. Nineties pop emanated from the hidden speakers in the ceiling and the bartender was a substantial man named Mike who had a graying goatee, a neck tattoo, and who mixed a very good martini. Not Henry good, but good enough.

The five of them found a round table and took seats, Sydney situated between Anna and Jessica. Connor, Jeff, and Sydney all had beer. Anna was drinking a vodka tonic, which she lifted in toast.

"To a good day's work that's going to lead to a very successful telethon."

They all clinked their glasses together at the center of the table with various words of agreement, then sipped.

For the next hour, they joked and laughed and the bar got busier, people stopping by on their way home from work. Jessica liked this group, she realized. Jeff was sort of quiet, but really nice. While he didn't say a lot, Jessica got the impression he didn't miss much. Connor had a dry wit and would send an unexpected zinger into the middle of a conversation that had everybody cracking up within moments. Sydney was pleasant and charming, surprisingly easy to talk to, even as she did her best to politely deflect the subtle flirting Anna was doing…which was getting less subtle by the minute.

"Seriously," Anna was saying. "Have coffee with me. Just coffee. So we can get to know each other…a little better than last time."

Jessica pretended to be listening to the conversation Connor and Jeff were having about stouts versus porters, but she kept her ears tuned to her right.

"Oh, I don't know if that's a good idea," Sydney said quietly, obviously not wanting the entire table to hear.

"Come on," Anna coaxed, not at all subscribing to the same volume control. "It's just coffee. I won't bite." She paused for effect. "At first." When Sydney didn't respond, Anna softened her approach. "I promise. Just coffee. Please?"

Jessica couldn't fight it any longer; she turned to them. And made direct eye contact with Sydney. Their gazes held for a beat until Jessica pulled hers away and made a point to refocus on the guys. She could almost feel the temperature drop near her right arm and she clenched her molars together when she heard Sydney say, "You know what? Yes. Let's do it. Coffee it is."

"Fantastic," Anna said as she clapped her hands together once. "This weekend?"

"Let's bump it to next week," Sydney said, and Jessica had to commend her. Coffee on a weekday would take up much less time than on a weekend. She gave Sydney one imaginary point on the scoreboard in her head. But just one. Accepting the invitation at all had gotten her negative ten points, so she still had some recovering to do.

"Here, give me your phone." Anna took Sydney's phone from the table in front of her and began dialing. She handed it back and said, "There, now you have my number and I have yours," as her own cell began to ring. She grinned widely as she pressed Accept.

That was enough. Jessica had reached her limit and she stood, her chair sliding back loudly on the wooden floor. "I'm exhausted," she announced. "And I still have some work to get done, so I'm out of here."

"Already?" Jeff asked, then blushed as he must have realized how that had come out.

"I'm afraid so," she answered, but laid a hand on his beefy shoulder and squeezed. "Thank you for the drink." She took in the rest of the table, carefully avoiding eye contact with Sydney, and shouldered her purse. "Everybody get home safely, all right?" With a wave, she hurried toward the door, not able to move fast enough, suddenly feeling as if all the air had been sucked from the bar and she couldn't get a full breath. Once outside in the parking lot, she stopped next to her car, braced herself on the hood, and sucked in a huge lungful of air, feeling instantly better. Well. A *little* better.

By the time she got home, she felt almost like her normal self. She wasn't a stupid woman, so she didn't have to question why the evening had bothered her. She was slightly attracted to Sydney Taylor. *Slightly.* It wasn't complicated math to do. No big deal. It happened. And it probably wouldn't even ping her radar if it hadn't been for Anna's blatant fawning. But she had encouraged Anna to go after Sydney, so what was she so upset about?

"Did she have to be so freaking obvious?" Jessica asked Scooby as she held him up so they were nose to nose. "She was kind of pathetic," she told him in a baby voice. "Yes, she was. Yes, she was."

Nope. No big deal. A little bit of a crush, that was all. For God's sake, the woman was a television news reporter. Most people probably had a crush on her; Jessica was not unique. She was sure of that. She shrugged it off, made herself a cup of decaf French vanilla coffee, and settled on her couch with her laptop, intending to work and channel surf.

She was twenty minutes into *Diners, Drive-Ins, and Dives* and wondering if there was room in her backyard for a meat smoker when her phone dinged, indicating a text. It was from Anna.

Thnx for the encouragement. Coffee with Syd on Monday at 11. So psyched!

Jessica pinched the bridge of her nose for a full ten seconds, then typed back.

Good for you.

Tossing her phone to the couch cushion, Jessica stroked her hand over Fred's soft fur and realized that, for the first time ever, she wished the telethon would hurry up and get here.

So that it would be over and she'd never have to see Sydney Taylor again.

But then she picked her phone back up to check her calendar and realized that she'd see Sydney again soon. Very soon.

Like, Monday morning.

At nine.

CHAPTER NINE

MONDAY MORNING, SYDNEY FELT like she'd been run over by a steamroller. She'd hardly slept at all and when she had, it had been fitfully with weird dreams that she couldn't remember now, but knew hadn't been pleasant ones. The sound of her alarm had nearly given her a heart attack, and when she'd stumbled to the bathroom and gathered up enough courage to look at her reflection, she barely recognized the worn, haggard woman looking back at her. Coffee had helped. But not much.

The day was gray, clouds the color of an old, beat-up furnace hanging low in the sky. The forecast didn't call for rain, but the air was heavy with moisture and Sydney could actually feel her hair frizzing on her head the second she stepped out of her car in the parking lot of Junebug Farms.

Sydney had spent the weekend surfing the Internet, checking the sites of stations she was interested in. She'd come across a couple that were requesting reels from prospective reporters and, after researching details on the cities, she'd sent hers off to three places: two in California, one in Indiana. She was trying hard not to obsessively check her e-mail, as it was way too soon for a response, but she couldn't seem to help herself.

Like right now. She thumbed through the screens on her phone to give a glance to her inbox. Nothing. She blew out a breath, shouldered her bag, shut the car door, and headed into the shelter for her update meeting with Jessica Barstow.

I don't know that I'd ever get used to this, she thought as she entered the front door and had her ears assaulted by the daily noises of an animal shelter. As had become her habit, she stood still for several moments, letting her brain acclimate to the shift in sound. Barking, whining, and the hum of conversation were standard, and she just needed a moment or two to find her footing, to steady her nerves, like allowing your eyes time to adjust to the dark.

"Hi there, Ms. Taylor!" The cheerful voice came from in front of her and to the right, and Sydney saw Regina – Volunteer waving at her, that huge smile of hers splitting her plump face in two, just like always. Seriously, how could you be sad with Regina – Volunteer grinning at you like that?

Sydney smiled and waved back as she headed toward the horseshoe-shaped front desk.

"You're here for Ms. Barstow?" Regina asked her.

"I am." Sydney leaned on the counter as Regina dialed her phone and then spoke into it at a totally normal volume. Sydney wondered how Jessica even heard her.

"She said to wait in the conference room and she'll be right with you. Can I get you some coffee?"

"I would be forever indebted to you if you did," Sydney said, knowing there wasn't enough caffeine in the world to make her feel awake this morning, but she was still willing to give it a shot.

The door to the conference room was made of something heavy and it did a nice job muffling the cacophony of the lobby. Sydney sighed with relief as she sipped the coffee Regina had brought her. It was strong and sweet and could have used another creamer, but Sydney was happy just to have something that might help her feel more present. It was a big might, but it was there.

Sydney had just glanced at the clock on the wall, noted that it was nearly 9:10, when the door opened and Jessica came into the room wearing her usual perfectly fit jeans and a white button-down shirt with the sleeves rolled up to just below her elbows. The first three buttons were undone enough to entice Sydney to want to know what lay farther down. Thankfully, that was overshadowed by the fact that Jessica was followed closely by Anna, and a large, bald African-American man Sydney hadn't met before. She stood, greeted Jessica and Anna with handshakes, and pretended not to notice the lack of eye contact from Jessica, even as she held onto her hand a beat longer than necessary, tightening her fingers just slightly enough when Jessica tried to pull away to force her to look up. Their eyes held for one delicious moment and Jessica's cheeks tinted a soft pink.

"Sydney Taylor, this is David Peters," Anna said by way of introduction. "He's in charge of our fundraising, and he and I work together much of the time, so I thought he should sit in on this."

"Absolutely. Nice to meet you, David." Sydney shook his hand, watched as her own seemed to disappear in his huge palm. His grip was gently firm and his smile was warm. Sydney sat back down and opened the folder she brought, then touched her tablet so it woke up. "Okay, so this meeting is basically to update you guys and keep you in the loop as far as what we're thinking for the telethon, what kinds of hooks and stories we're working on, show you the path we're taking, and make sure it all sits well with the shelter." Nods went around the table and Sydney began her pitch, showing a list of short video stories they'd already done and more they had scheduled. Interviews with both volunteers and adopters would pepper the entire broadcast, hopefully bringing in more of each. "One of the biggest issues is that we need to skew a bit younger," Sydney explained, finding David Peters's intense eye contact and periodic nods reassuring. "That means shorter clips, a faster pace." She snapped her fingers as she spoke.

"Janet was never about that," Jessica said quietly, pulling Sydney's focus her way.

"I know," Sydney said with a nod. "I get that. But today's attention span is very short. You have mere seconds to grab somebody or they're on to the next thing, flipping the channel or leaving your stream to check their Twitter feed, so we have some ideas for that." She went down a list she'd made, showed them a few examples of things other productions had run to give them a general idea what she was thinking. Anna and David both enthusiastically jumped on board. Jessica was a different story.

Sydney finished going over things, then turned fully toward Jessica, whose beautiful face of smooth, porcelain-like skin was marred by a deep, scowling frown as she shook her head back and forth almost imperceptibly. "What is it?" Sydney asked gently.

"Janet didn't do any of this," Jessica said.

"I know that."

"Don't worry, Jessica," David said, resting a huge hand on Jessica's bare forearm. The color contrast was almost shocking. "This is good stuff. I think pulling us more into the present, the whole shooting for a younger audience thing is really smart."

"It really is," Anna agreed, her smile almost comically wide. "Sydney has great ideas. Fantastic ones."

If she hadn't been watching at that very second, Sydney might have missed Jessica's near-eye-roll at Anna's words. But she saw it. And it was irritating.

What the hell is her problem?

"You have no reason to worry," Sydney told her quietly, working hard to keep her voice steady and professional and not to show the annoyance she felt at Jessica's sudden dissatisfaction.

"Well, I am worried," Jessica said, her brow furrowed. "It's very different."

"Sometimes different is good, Jess." Anna shifted in her chair, looked from Sydney to Jessica and back.

"Listen," Sydney said, doing her best to keep her voice professional, to not sound annoyed at the sudden resistance, to not remind Jessica how freaking hard she had been working. "You don't have to worry because you'll be very involved." Sydney clicked on her tablet and went back several pages, showing some of the ideas she'd presented earlier. "This one, this one, this one, here, here, here. You will be directly involved in all of these things."

Jessica's brow furrowed further, creating a divot above the bridge of her nose that Sydney wanted to smooth away with her thumb. Which bugged her. Jessica looked at the screen in Sydney's hand.

"Also," Sydney said, pointing to the screen. "I think your tour video is great…"

From what she'd learned from Brad, Janet Dobson had had Jessica give her the basic tour of the shelter, but she'd brought a cameraman along and filmed the whole thing. At the beginning of each telethon, they played it to give viewers who might be unfamiliar, or who'd never visited, a chance to see the whole place. "I sense a 'but' coming," Jessica said, not quite stifling her sigh.

"I think it's time to update it. This is, what? Three years old?"

"Maybe four."

"Exactly. We need to snazz it up a bit. Update it."

"I think that's a great idea," David said. "Make it a little more modern. Add some music. Quicker edits. It'll help us connect to our younger demographic."

Sydney liked this guy. He got it.

"Exactly," Sydney said with a nod and a grin. Jessica avoided her gaze, which was a little frustrating and…if Sydney was going to be honest, stung a bit. But she put on her best coaxing voice.

"Look," Sydney said, softening her tone. "You're the boss here. If there's anything that's not working for you, you just say so." Sydney watched Jessica's face, watched her absorb the words. "Okay?"

For the first time since the meeting began, Jessica finally looked her in the eye. The intensity of her gaze was so heavy, Sydney literally felt it in her chest, had to force herself to hold the contact. It felt a little…weird. And unnerving. And delicious. And Sydney felt her thighs clench reflexively. *Damn it.*

"Okay," Jessica said. She nodded once. "Okay."

"Excellent," Anna said with a clap of her hands. "This is going to be so awesome."

David seemed to share Anna's excitement, and he stood. "Really great stuff, Sydney. I'm looking forward to this." He held out his hand. "Sorry to bolt, but I've got a million things going on that relate to the telethon."

"Completely understood," Sydney said with a smile. "Go." She turned to Anna, who was still grinning, and Jessica, who was gathering her things, eyes on the table. "He's great. I like him."

Anna nodded in agreement, then stepped close to Sydney. She closed a warm hand over Sydney's arm and her voice changed. It wasn't any quieter, but the tone was undeniably…familiar. "Hey, we've got half an hour before our coffee date. Should we just go now?" She arched an eyebrow at Sydney, who looked over her head long enough to see Jessica yank her own gaze away, give a half-hearted wave, and scurry out of the room like it was on fire.

"Yeah," Sydney said absently, watching Jessica's retreating form out the doorway. "Why not?"

⁀

Starbucks wasn't terribly busy at this time of morning, though Sydney knew from experience that it would pick up steadily over the next forty-five minutes. Anna insisted on buying her coffee and the second she set it in front of Sydney, her stomach churned, telling her she'd had more than enough caffeine for a while. Still, not one to forget her manners, she made a show of taking a sip.

Their table was small and had two chairs, but Anna proceeded to slide hers around so she sat closer to Sydney. And also in the aisle, forcing people to sidle around her as they went by. Sydney immediately began to calculate how long she had to stay to fulfill the politeness requirement. Settling on thirty minutes, she surreptitiously glanced at her watch and did the math in her head.

"So," Anna said, that perpetually wide smile plastered on her face. "This is nice."

"It is."

"Maybe not quite as nice as the last time we were alone together, but…" She waggled her eyebrows in a way that made Sydney swallow a grimace. "Maybe we can do that again."

"Maybe." God, why did she say that? The last thing in the world Sydney wanted to do was make out with Anna. That being said, the second to the last thing in the world Sydney wanted to do was piss off Anna. Or anybody at Junebug Farms, for that matter, as her job pretty much depended upon getting along with them; it was much too late to assign somebody else. Brad would kill her. And possibly fire her. So she smiled a smile that she could tell by feel didn't reach her eyes. Luckily, Anna didn't know her well enough to see that it was fake.

"And so?" Anna said, then took a sip of her latte. "How are you liking it here so far?"

"It's fine. It'll do for now." Sydney saw her strategy and grabbed at it.

"For now?"

"Oh, yeah, I'm not staying."

Anna's face fell. Almost literally. The corners of her mouth that had been lifted since she walked in the door, slid downward. Her eyes drooped a bit, as did her shoulders. "Why not?"

Sydney tipped her head back and forth a bit, measuring her words. "It's a bit…small for my liking."

"Really?"

"Mm hmm. I want something bigger. With more action."

"I see." Anna gazed out a nearby window and it was as if Sydney had shut down her entire line of conversation, like she needed to search her brain for a new one. Then she looked down at her coffee and her expression was so sad, Sydney felt awful.

"But, I mean, I'm here for a while, I guess." *Oh my God, shut up. You have an out. Take it!* She watched in near horror as Anna visibly cheered up.

"Silver lining," she said. "For me, at least."

Sydney smiled that artificial smile and lifted her cup to her lips.

ॐ

What the hell is the matter with me?

It was a thought Jessica couldn't shake. She had a million things to do, two more meetings, and about a dozen phone calls to make, but she couldn't seem to get out of her own head. Instead of being a productive member of the shelter, she sat in her desk chair with it faced away from the desk and gazed pensively out the window watching the comings and goings in the parking lot, trying not to think about her humiliating behavior at the meeting.

A knock on her door snagged her attention, thank God, and she slowly spun around to face Catherine Gardner, dressed to the nines as usual in a black pantsuit and an ivory shell under the jacket. Her heels clicked on the floor as she crossed the room, and she looked every bit the sleek, professional businesswoman.

"Hey, I have a new donor I'd like to discuss—" She squinted when she saw Jessica's face, then sat, set down the paper she held, and cocked her head. "What's the matter with you?" Her question was gentle, but Jessica chuckled bitterly at how it mirrored her own.

Jessica sighed loudly. "I honestly have no freaking idea."

"Well, that's ominous." Catherine folded her hands on the desk and made her listening face. "Talk to me."

Another sigh. "I'm frustrated. With myself." Jessica took a deep breath, then told Catherine about the meeting, all of it, how Sydney was laying out her ideas and Jessica pouted over them. "It's true that I am uncomfortable with all these changes she's proposing, but...I acted like a teenager. All sullen and moody." She shook her head, covered her eyes with a hand. "I embarrassed myself. And the others. David gave me an odd look when he left; he knew something was up." She let out a loud groan and when she uncovered her eyes, Catherine was grinning at her. "Stop it."

"You stop it," Catherine countered, the grin staying put. "You're fine."

"I was not fine," Jessica told her. "I was ridiculous."

"I didn't say you weren't ridiculous."

"Gee, thanks."

Catherine chuckled. "How long have I known you?"

Jessica shook her head. "That math is too complicated for me. A long time. Let's just say that."

"Fair enough. I've known you a long time. Probably longer than anybody else here. Yes?"

Jessica nodded.

"I've seen you in and out of relationships. I've seen you when you like somebody. I've seen you when you *don't* like somebody. And I've seen you in this position you're in right now."

"Which is?"

"When you have a *little* crush." Catherine held up a hand, her forefinger and thumb scant millimeters apart.

Jessica gasped. "I do *not* have a crush."

"Oh, but you do, my friend. You do. Remember Stephanie Knight?"

Jessica thought back to the volunteer they'd had several years ago. Tall, dark hair, deep brown eyes, and a voice as deep and rich as melted chocolate. Jessica had gone all stuttery any time she was around the poor woman, unable to complete a sentence, dropping things, being a general embarrassment to herself. Stephanie never seemed to notice, but Catherine had. "She was soooo pretty..."

"She was. And you had a huge crush on her. Similar behavior from you." Catherine continued to grin. "I think the one you have on Sydney is smaller, though. You haven't spilled anything on her yet, have you?"

"No," Jessica said with indignation, not liking this subject at all. "I don't even really like her. Okay, that's a lie. I kind of do. But I don't think she cares for me one way or the other. I'm certainly not giving her any reason to."

"Doesn't matter. You can still crush on somebody you don't like. It just makes it a little more...interesting. I mean, you could do worse, you know? Sydney's stunning. God. *I* might have a crush on her. I know Emily does." At Jessica's raised brows, she explained, "We watch her on the news."

"She's having coffee with Anna right now," Jessica blurted.

Catherine blinked at her. "Ah."

"Yeah." Jessica grimaced, something Catherine seemed to find amusing.

"I see. So…you have a bit of a *jealous* crush."

Jessica dropped her head to her desk and groaned some more.

Catherine laughed. "Stop that, you big drama queen."

Jessica felt a small smile tug at her mouth as she lifted her head.

Catherine leaned forward, closed a hand over Jessica's. "It's fine, Jess. *You're* fine. It's no big deal. Why are you letting it bother you? Accept it for what it is and relax. Laugh it off. You're a professional. You're in charge. You got this."

Jessica nodded, taking the words in, rolling them around, trying them on. She *was* a professional and she *was* in charge. She hadn't gotten this far in life by hiding in her office when something bugged or confused her. She was better than this worry. Being ridiculous was a choice she'd made at the meeting this morning, but she didn't have to make it again. Apparently, she just needed to hear the right words. She met Catherine's gaze and gave her a grateful smile. "You're right."

"Yeah, that's not uncommon. Besides, if she's having coffee with Anna, we know her taste is kind of…questionable."

"True, though to be fair, Anna did kind of put her on the spot by asking her in front of people."

"Oh, that's tricky."

"Right? So there's a possibility that Sydney only said yes to be polite."

"Therefore, maybe she does *not* have questionable taste." Catherine tapped a finger against her lips. "This gets more and more interesting as we go."

"Ha ha." Taking a deep breath and feeling oddly better, Jessica sat up straighter. "Okay. Moving on. Talk to me about this new donor."

So she had a little crush on a TV personality. So what? It was fine. It was unusual for her, but nothing she couldn't handle.

Right?

CHAPTER TEN

THE NEXT WEEK WAS insanely chaotic for Sydney, so much so that when she actually remembered to eat, she had to stop and congratulate herself. Connor had done a fantastic job setting up interviews with various volunteers and adopters. On Thursday afternoon, she found herself standing on the front stoop of a cute little bungalow in a suburb of the city, Jeff standing behind her with his camera and equipment. Connor was working on a few other things, so she was on her own here. Finger on the doorbell, she pushed, and the door was pulled open almost immediately.

"Hi there!" The woman who answered the door was about thirty-five, blonde, petite. Her smile was wide, creating two deep dimples in her cheeks that made her seem even more cheerful—which didn't seem possible to Sydney, as she was obviously one of those perpetually happy people you either loved or hated. Or both. "You're the TV people."

"We are. You spoke to my producer, Connor Baskin? I'm Sydney Taylor and this is my cameraman, Jeff Leiber." She held out her hand.

"Sherry Dugan. It's so great to meet you. Come in! Come in!" She pumped Sydney's hand like she was hoping for water, then stood aside so they could enter the house, the giant smile never slipping.

Sydney went inside, through the small foyer as Sherry led her to the right and into a modest but tastefully decorated living room. "Will this work?" she asked, her face telling Sydney that she might be a little bit self-conscious about her house.

Making a show of looking around, turning in a slow circle, Sydney smiled. "It will be perfect."

Sherry Dugan visibly relaxed. "Oh, good." She gestured to the cheerful floral couch of blues and corals. "Have a seat. I'll get Maddie and Rex."

"What do you think?" Jeff asked Sydney as he waved a hand at a corner of the room. "From here? And we can move that chair there around to here." He used a finger to indicate a solid blue wingback chair that nicely complemented the colors of the couch. "Set it up so you're face to face and then I can do two angles."

"Perfect," Sydney replied, scanning her tablet containing the questions and talking points she wanted to touch on when conversing with Sherry and her daughter.

A moment later, Sydney heard Sherry say, "Okay. In here, honey." She set her tablet on the coffee table and turned to take in the sight.

Maddie Dugan was thirteen years old, but didn't look any older than nine or ten. She was petite and blonde like her mother, but her blue eyes held wisdom far beyond her age, most likely due to the empty space from her knee down where the remainder of her left leg once was. Her hair was short, but hip instead of boyish, and she tossed her head to get it out of her eyes as she maneuvered into the room using a metal crutches, its band around her very thin upper arm. Limping next to her was a brindled, barrel-chested dog with sweet brown eyes, three legs, and nothing but love for her. Sydney could see it immediately, the adoration the dog had for the girl, the way he stood close to her hip and periodically gazed up at her to check in.

"So, this is my daughter, Maddie," Sherry said. "Maddie, this is Sydney Taylor. She's going to be interviewing us."

Maddie stuck out her hand and Sydney shook it. "It's nice to meet you, Maddie."

Maddie pressed her lips together in what probably passed for a smile in the world of thirteen-year-olds. "Same here," she said quietly.

"And this is Rex, I assume?" Sydney said, gesturing to the dog. "May I?" She waited for Maddie's permission before squatting down to meet the dog's gaze. "Well, hi there, Rex. It's nice to meet you as well." Rex eyed her for a beat before apparently deciding she was okay and swiping his warm tongue across her chin. Sydney laughed. "I guess I'm approved." She stood up and clasped her hands together. "Okay. I thought you two could sit on the couch. And Rex can maybe sit at your feet between you? Is it okay if we move this table?"

Sherry nodded and she and Jeff slid the rectangular coffee table out of the way. When the family was seated on the couch, Sydney took a seat in the wingback chair, crossed her legs, and scrolled on her tablet, giving Jeff time to get things set. After a few moments, she looked up at the trio, smiling at how they made a picture-perfect portrait. Two blondes, both in jeans, Sherry in a light blue blouse and Maddie in a black One Direction T-shirt, Rex sitting handsomely on the floor between Sherry's shin and Maddie's good leg.

"What grade are you in, Maddie?" Sydney asked.

"Eighth."

"Not for much longer, though, huh?"

"One week and three days."

Sydney laughed. "But who's counting, right?"

"I am. I'm counting." Maddie gave her first genuine smile, and Sydney knew she was beginning to loosen up.

"I get that. Totally. Okay, so tell me two things: your favorite subject and the subject you're best at."

"A two-part question, huh? Tricky." Maddie squinched up her face and made a show of thinking. "Well, I'm pretty good at math, but I really like Global."

"Yeah? Like history and stuff?"

"History, yeah, but also, like people. Like, different cultures and stuff."

"So, you like people."

Maddie nodded, looked to her mother for approval. Sherry nodded and smiled. "I wouldn't be surprised if she ended up in some kind of social work," she said, obviously proud of her daughter.

"And you like animals, too, yes?" Sydney asked.

Maddie's nod was enthusiastic. "I have two hamsters, a goldfish, two cats, and Rex."

"I have goldfish, too," Sydney said, by way of finding common ground.

"What are their names?" Maddie asked.

"Marge and Homer."

The girl's laugh was a shock, a barked guffaw that surprised Sydney and had everybody in the room laughing in response. Even Jeff was trying to stifle himself.

Sydney waited for things to calm down a bit before asking, "Tell me how you got Rex."

Maddie looked to Sherry, who grinned and said, "Go ahead. You tell it."

With a nod and what seemed like a moment to get her bearings, Maddie began to talk. "Well, it was a few months after my accident and I wasn't doing great. In my head. You know?"

"You were depressed?"

A quick nod. "Yeah. I kinda got stuck thinking about all the things I couldn't do anymore. I was mad all the time. I started seeing Dr. Jean—"

"Her therapist," Sherry supplied quietly. Sydney nodded her understanding.

"And she thought maybe a dog would help me. Give me something to focus on and take care of. Give me something else to think of besides my missing leg. So I talked with Mom and Dad. We just had the cats at the time. And we decided to go see what they had at Junebug Farms."

"We were just going to look," Sherry clarified with a half-grin.

"Famous last words," Sydney said. "And then what happened?"

"Well." Maddie looked at the ceiling, obviously trying to arrange her thoughts. "I wasn't really that big on the idea. I was still feeling sorry for myself and I was just mad all the time."

"Understandable," Sydney said, unable to imagine that kind of loss for a kid.

"We were in that part of the building where all the dogs are. And it was so loud. They were barking and whining and there were two other kids there with their parents and they just stared at me on my crutches." Maddie stopped and swallowed. Then she took a breath and went on. "And I told my mom I wanted to go home." Sherry was nodding, watching her daughter tell the story, her own emotion clearly written on her face. Sydney hoped Jeff was getting it. "So we turned to walk toward the door and Ms. Barstow was coming toward us."

"Jessica Barstow, the head of Junebug Farms?"

Maddie nodded. "She was walking Rex on a leash and I noticed right away that he moved kind of funny."

"And what did you think about that?" Sydney asked.

"I felt bad for him. Like, right away. I know what it's like to walk funny."

Sydney smiled, liking this kid so much already. "Then what happened?"

"It was kind of weird," Maddie said, her voice filled with uncertainty. Again, she looked up at her mom and again, her mom gave her a nod. "It was like he saw me and wanted to come to me. He started to pull at the leash, so Ms. Barstow had no choice but to follow him. He's a lot stronger than he looks. And that's when I saw that one of his back legs was missing. And when he got to me, he sniffed my stump. Then he sat down right in front of me and just looked up at me, all calm and handsome." During the story, her hand had moved to rest on Rex's big black and brown head and she stroked him absently as she spoke. "And I just knew. Isn't that weird? I always thought people who said stuff like that were just dumb. 'I just knew.' But now I get it. Because, I just knew. Rex was supposed to be mine. We were supposed to find each other." She bent forward and kissed the top of his head, then looked up at Sydney with smiling eyes.

Sydney had known within the first five minutes that the interview with Maddie was going to be gold. They talked for over an hour, and then they'd gone into the backyard so Maddie could show her some of the tricks she'd taught Rex. By the time Jeff had begun packing up his equipment, they'd been there for nearly three hours and it was well into dinner time.

"I'm sorry we stayed so long," she said to Sherry, as she gathered the last of her things and she and Jeff stopped on the front steps.

"Oh, please, don't worry," Sherry said, holding Sydney's hand in both of hers. "This was really good for her." She glanced at the stairs where Maddie and Rex had gone so Maddie could get started on her homework.

"She's an amazing kid."

"Thank you." Sherry's face glowed. "I think so, too. Listen, I wanted to say this, but not on camera because I worried it might sound made up or doctored, but..." She looked down at her white tennis shoes as if gathering the right words. "I owe Jessica Barstow so much. I found out later that she'd seen us on the security monitors when we first entered the shelter. She watched us looking at the dogs and she saw Maddie. She was on two crutches then, she hadn't mastered walking with just one yet. Rex had been rescued from a dogfighting ring and when he was brought in, his leg was so mangled, they couldn't save it. He'd been at the shelter for nearly six months, and she didn't think he'd ever get adopted, but she told me that when she saw Maddie on the security monitors, she just had this strange feeling. She wasn't even going to say anything if Rex didn't seem interested. She said she would've just kept walking right by us. But..." Her voice trailed off and Sydney watched as Sherry's eyes welled up. "He saw Maddie, and it was like he knew. He *knew* she needed him." She sniffled quietly. "Jessica Barstow is an angel, as far as I'm concerned. A guardian angel sent from heaven. Do you know she still calls every month or two just to see how things are going?"

Sydney smiled, picturing Jessica watching the security monitors, observing as Maddie hobbled her way in. "I'm not surprised," she said to Sherry, and it was the truth.

"That shelter is lucky to have her, that's all I'm saying."

"Agreed." Sydney held out her hand once more. "Well, it's time for me to get out of your hair. Thank you so much for your time. And please thank Maddie again for me."

In the van, she and Jeff rode for a few moments in silence before he spoke up.

"That was something, huh?"

Sydney blew out a breath. "It really was. I think we should see if she'd be willing to be on the telethon live. She doesn't even have to say anything, just make an appearance with Rex. It's an amazing story."

"Do you believe in that stuff?"

"In what stuff?"

"In, like, things being meant to be?"

She glanced at Jeff to see if he was being sarcastic, but his expression was serious. His dark eyes were slightly wider than usual, his thick eyebrows raised expectantly.

"You know, it's not really something I've ever given a lot of thought to. But after hearing that..." She nodded. "Makes you wonder."

"I've read that when a dog is in a shelter and you rescue it, it knows. That it's grateful and more loyal than a non-shelter dog would be."

Sydney thought about Rufus, about how devoted to her he was for so many years. "I believe that's true," she said softly. "I really, really do."

The interior of the van got quiet again and stayed that way until it pulled into the half-empty parking lot of Channel Six. Sydney slid out the passenger side and shouldered her bag.

"I won't need the footage until tomorrow morning when I meet with editing," she said to Jeff. "Okay?"

"Not a problem." He opened the side door of the van and began hauling out the stuff that needed to go inside the building.

"Can I help?" she asked, knowing he'd say no, that most videographers didn't want others touching their equipment.

"Nah. But thanks."

"All right. Don't forget, we've got to shoot the shelter tour tomorrow afternoon." She pointed at him as she backed toward the doors.

"I'll be ready," Jeff said with a smile. "I checked the forecast. Looks like we'll have some sun. That'll make the outside stuff look better."

"Definitely." Sydney pushed open the doors. "Thanks for today, Jeff."

He gave her a little salute, and she decided she really liked him. She'd worked with videographers and camera operators she didn't like. They could be condescending and smarmy, often saddling her with the stereotypically unflattering descriptions of on-air talent…snotty, hoity-toity, full of herself. But Jeff seemed real. Genuine. She liked that about him.

Once inside, she realized it was after seven and she'd been at it for more than twelve hours. Her intention had been to sit at her desk in her small cubby and organize her thoughts about her interview with Maddie Dugan, but the second she sat down, she felt like she hit the wall. She could still arrange the way she wanted the interview edited, but doing so on her couch in her cozy clothes with a glass of red wine and a slice of pizza seemed way more appealing.

An hour later, she was exactly there: in yoga pants and a worn Adidas T-shirt, bare feet, a glass of Cabernet on the end table next to Marge and Homer, her teeth sinking into that first delicious bite of pizza with cheese, mushrooms, and green peppers. She'd limit herself to this one slice for tonight, as she'd forgotten to tell them to forego the cheese—and seriously, what was pizza without mozzarella dripping from it? Her tablet lay on the coffee table, her questions to Maddie listed on the screen. Next to that was a notebook where she'd jotted observations as the interview had progressed. Sydney had a pretty clear vision of how she wanted things edited, so she wrote that information down, but she did so on autopilot, as her thoughts seemed to veer off in the direction of Jessica Barstow more often than Sydney seemed able to control.

It should've been surprising to hear that the cool, collected, somewhat aloof Ms. Barstow had a heart of gold, but it wasn't. Not to Sydney, and she had no idea why. Jessica didn't exactly exude warm fuzzies around her.

"I mean, she's not openly rude," Sydney said to Marge, who'd swum close to the glass of the tank and floated there looking at her. "She's just..." Her voice trailed off as she took another bite of pizza and chewed, searching for the proper description but coming up empty. She shook her head, glanced back at the goldfish that was in the same spot as if waiting patiently for her to continue. "I don't know. She's a lot of things, I guess. She's smart and driven. I've seen that already, a lot. She's successful. She seems to care a lot about her staff and it's obvious how much she loves the animals." Another glance at the goldfish had it still staring at her. "I feel your judgment, Marge." The fish didn't move. Sydney sighed in defeat. "Okay, okay. Fine. She's pretty. I think she's really pretty. And sexy. Okay, fine. She's hot. You happy now?" The fish took a beat, then turned fin and swam away. "Hard ass," Sydney mumbled.

A quick look at her calendar told her the telethon would air in less than two weeks, and there was still much to be done. Not a lot more she could do tonight, however. Instead, she organized her papers and notes, then hopped online to check her e-mail. She'd sent her reel to several stations and was hoping to hear something from one—or all—of them soon. Nothing today, but a station in Austin had just posted an opening and Sydney wasted no time sending her application, resume, and reel through cyberspace.

Just as she hit Send, her phone buzzed, indicating a text. It was from Anna.

Hey, sexy. Just thinking about you. You still up?

Sydney sighed. This was about the fifteenth text since their coffee date. Sydney had been parsing out her responses so Anna wouldn't get too used to hearing from her. The last two had gone unanswered, and Sydney felt guilty for not answering this one either, but Anna had offered up the perfect excuse: Sydney would say later that she'd already been asleep.

She turned the phone off with a grimace as she stood up and then clicked off the living room light. Tomorrow would be a busy day. They were going to shoot the shelter tour. She'd see Anna then.

She'd also see Jessica.

CHAPTER ELEVEN

JESSICA WAS NERVOUS.

Which was unlike her, and the unfamiliarity of it made her more nervous. She'd given this tour a hundred and fifty times, easily. More than that, actually. Many, many more. She'd been on camera more than a dozen. This was all old hat for her. No big deal. Piece of cake. She could practically do it in her sleep.

But, she was still nervous, and she wasn't sure why.

When Regina buzzed her office to let her know Sydney and her crew had arrived, Jessica felt her heart rate kick up several more notches and her stomach did a rather unpleasant flip that had her stopping in her tracks in the middle of her office and sending a worried glance toward the bathroom.

"God, get your shit together, Jessica," she whispered into the empty room. She stood still for several moments, waited for the acid in her gut to settle, and then headed out toward the lobby, index cards containing a few notes clasped in her hand.

Friday afternoons tended to be busy for the shelter. People took the day off and came by, classes had field trips here, individuals who'd been vacillating about whether or not to bring home a new pet usually decided to do so before the weekend, so they'd have time to adjust. Today was no exception; the lobby was buzzing. The yellow bus she'd seen parked outside had expelled its contents of elementary-aged children, who were talking animatedly next to the cat wall. The phones rang pretty regularly and four volunteers sat behind the front desk today. Jessica noticed Lisa exit the hallway from the other offices, wave to her as she crossed the lobby, then open the door to the dog wing, which sent the decibel levels through the roof with barking and howling for a good five seconds. Then the door closed, and the atmosphere returned to just "very loud."

Jessica's eyes landed on Sydney and she had to consciously pull her gaze away after a beat. *Because staring is rude.* She wore navy blue slacks and a powder blue, short-sleeved, summer weight sweater that was beautiful in its simplicity. A simply patterned, lightweight scarf was draped casually around her neck, the ends dangling down just past her breasts. Her hair was sleekly shiny and gorgeous, dark waves falling around her shoulders as she conversed with Connor near the front desk. When Sydney turned and made eye contact with her, Jessica felt her breath hitch as she wondered if she'd ever *not* be pleasantly startled by those eyes.

"Hey there," Sydney said as her heels clicked across the floor and she met Jessica halfway. "You look great."

"You think?" Jessica looked down at her dark jeans and seafoam green camp shirt. "The color's not too pale? Janet always told me not to wear white because it would reflect too much light and make the picture go all wonky." At Sydney's half-grin, she added, "Technical term. Wonky."

"I've heard it. But seriously, you look great. The color's perfect, plus it looks terrific on you. Complements your skin tone and hair. Which, by the way, looks amazing like that."

Jessica reached up and touched her hair self-consciously. She'd pulled some of it back with a clip and left the rest down. "I thought my usual ponytail might be too casual." She shrugged.

"Well, I love the ponytail as well, but this looks really terrific." Sydney reached out and fingered a lock of Jessica's hair, much to her surprise, and held her gaze for a beat before they were interrupted by Anna, who zipped across the lobby like she was on Rollerblades.

"Hi," she said, much too cheerfully for it to have been genuine, Jessica thought. She reached out and gave Sydney's upper arm a squeeze, her closeness forcing Jessica and Sydney to step apart from each other. Jessica clenched her jaw. "Ready to do the tour?" Anna's smile was wide and her eyes were bright and she seemed slightly bouncy, like she'd had way too much caffeine today.

"Almost," Sydney said, subtly stepping away. "Let me check with Connor, see where we're at." She turned on what looked to be a rather expensive heel.

"God, she looks good, doesn't she?" Anna said quietly to Jessica, then gave her that shoulder bump Jessica was beginning to detest.

"I guess. I hadn't really noticed," Jessica lied, feeling Anna's gaze turn toward her more than saw it.

"Seriously? Do you need glasses?"

"How's my hair?" Jessica asked, desperately needing to change the subject. "I don't wear it like this very often."

That seemed to snag Anna's attention, at least for the moment, as she furrowed her brow and studied Jessica's head. Reaching out, she moved a strand here, a hunk there, then fluffed the ends. "There. Perfect. You look terrific." She cocked her head. "Are you nervous? You seem a little…shaky."

Jessica held out her hand and they both took note of the slight tremor in her fingers. "Damn it."

"You've done this a million times." Anna rubbed a hand up and down Jessica's upper arm. "Relax. You're gonna be great." Somebody from behind the front desk called Anna, and she hurried away.

Sydney approached then, almost as if she'd waited for Anna to leave, her eyes on Jessica. Jeff followed behind her with his camera and Sydney gestured to another man, this one short, round, and balding, with an infectious grin and kind brown eyes. "This is Ron, our audio guy. He'll make sure you sound good."

He reached out to shake Jessica's hand and held up a small mic as Jeff stepped a few feet away to fiddle with his camera.

"Gotta put this on," Ron said matter-of-factly, but Sydney stepped in.

"I'll do it," she said and took the little black piece out of his hand before he could argue. He shrugged his indifference and went back to his equipment. Sydney held up the contraption, which consisted of a small microphone on a wire. The wire led to a small, rectangular box. "Okay, this will clip onto the back of your pants," Sydney said, stepping behind her. Jessica could feel Sydney's fingers sliding along the waistband of her pants, brushing her skin, tugging gently until the transmitter was in place.

Then came more.

She flinched slightly as Sydney's fingers brushed the bare skin of her waist underneath her shirt. "This has to go under and up to clip in the front," she said, very quietly and very close to Jessica's ear. Jessica turned to meet her gaze. A beat went by. Two beats. Sydney's voice was a near-whisper as she asked, "You want to do it, or should I?"

Jessica swallowed hard, could barely form words, but needed no time to think about her answer. "You," she said softly. "Please."

With a nearly imperceptible nod, Sydney turned her gaze to the task. She slipped the hand holding the tiny mic directly up under Jessica's shirt, the backs of her fingers sliding along Jessica's bare stomach. She moved to stand in front of Jessica, blocking anybody else's view as she used her other hand to dip down the front of the shirt, her fingertips inadvertently brushing against Jessica's nipple as she grabbed the mic from one hand with the other. Jessica's flesh hardened immediately and she hoped Sydney didn't notice. Then she hoped she did.

The moment was over instantly. The mic was clipped to the placket of her shirt, tucked in subtly so it could be seen, but barely.

"There." Sydney smoothed her hand over the spot, stood still for a moment before meeting Jessica's eyes finally. Hers were dark and heavy with…Jessica tried not to think it, but the word screamed into her head and wouldn't leave. *Arousal.* "You're perfect." Their eyes stayed locked for one more loaded moment before Sydney turned and walked toward another woman on her crew.

Jessica pushed out a breath, felt her own blood rushing in her ears, knew her nipple was still erect and waiting for more contact. She squeezed her eyes shut and swallowed hard as too many thoughts blew through her head, too many for her to focus on. All she could do was breathe. That was hard enough right now because she had never been so turned on in her life.

When she opened her eyes again, Sydney was on her way back, the other woman in tow. She introduced Bridget, a twenty-something makeup artist with several tattoos on her arms, jet-black hair cut in a ragged bob, and huge blue eyes. "Bridget will make sure you're not too shiny or washed out on camera."

Bridget stepped in and gathered up all of Jessica's attention, which was a good thing. She patted a sponge along Jessica's forehead, cheeks, chin, and neck. Then she swiped a coat of something on her lips. Jessica hoped it wasn't too bright. She wasn't a fan of bright lipstick. Her face must have conveyed her thoughts because Bridget smiled and said, "It's just a little gloss. Trust me, you don't need much of my help." She winked.

Jessica smiled at her and felt the blush rise in her cheeks.

"Okay," Sydney said as Ron came forward again, this time wearing headphones, and fiddled with her mic. "Here's what I'm thinking. We start here in the main lobby and you talk about the shelter itself, how it came to be, how you got here. Jeff will be on you some of the time and he might pan around a bit, so don't worry if you see the camera moving off of you. I'll ask questions to lead you if I think you're getting stuck or veering off topic, but we'll edit me out mostly. With me so far?" She caught Jessica's gaze with her own and Jessica felt her heart rate kick up a notch. *Those damn eyes.*

"Yes." Jessica nodded.

"Good. Then I thought we'd move over to the cat wall and you can tell us about that. Then we'll move into the dog wing, but I think we'll just shoot video, no audio. It's so loud in there. We can do a voiceover later. Then we'll go outside and you can give a little history of when things came about. When the goat house came along, when the barn was built. We'll wander to both places and get some good shots of all the animals *outside* of this building. I think it's important for people to see that there's more than just cats and dogs here. The old video tour I watched didn't really stress that."

Jessica watched as Sydney directed her, watched the sparkle of excitement in her eyes, the gentle lifting of the corner of her mouth when she was explaining her reasoning for something, the grand arm gesture when she encompassed the whole of the building. Her enthusiasm for this project was surprisingly contagious, and Jessica felt her own anticipation building, even as she tried *not* to focus on Sydney's hands, on the way they'd felt against her skin.

"How does all that sound?" Sydney finished her pitch, looked from Jessica to Anna, then back, and stayed on Jessica, who mentally shook herself back into the moment.

"I think it's perfect," Anna said before Jessica could even open her mouth. She tried not to be amused when she noticed a very slight bristling on Sydney's part…and that her gaze didn't leave Jessica's. "Updating the tour was a fantastic idea and it's gonna be *amazing*." Anna stepped forward and touched Sydney's arm again.

"Okay, then," Sydney said, again subtly stepping out of Anna's reach while saying something to Jeff. "Let's get started." Jeff moved back a few steps to set up his wide shot. "Hey, Anna, do you think you can get a bottle of water so we have it handy for our talent here?"

"Oh, of course. Be right back." And Anna was off.

Sydney stepped forward, closed a warm hand over her bare forearm. Jessica wet her lips, felt the gloss coating them, reveled in the heat from Sydney's grip. "Don't be nervous," Sydney said quietly, standing in Jessica's personal space and making the hair on the back of her neck tingle. "I can tell that you are, but I'm telling you not to be. You're terrific at this. I've seen it. Just take a deep breath, relax, and talk to *me*. Don't worry about the camera or anybody else. Just talk to me. Okay?"

Jessica swallowed, then nodded her head. "Okay."

"You got this." Sydney smiled just as Anna arrived with the water. She took a step back, out of Jessica's space—*thank God!*—and Jessica felt her lungs suck in air, as if she'd stopped breathing with Sydney so close.

"Here's the water," Anna was saying as she handed the bottle to Sydney and once again touched her for no reason. Jessica felt her jaw clench and couldn't seem to help it. When she glanced at Sydney, Sydney was looking right at her. Jessica quickly looked down at her notes, flipped through them without really seeing them at all.

This is getting ridiculous.

❧

"She's so good," Sydney whispered in Connor's ear as they stood and watched Jessica talking about the barn, when it had been built and why, the animals housed there, and how they'd come to be at Junebug Farms.

"She really is," Connor whispered back.

"I told you." Sydney could feel Anna's eyes on her, but didn't look her way. She was too enraptured by Junebug's charmingly attractive CEO.

Jessica hadn't stuttered once, she'd just kept on talking like she'd memorized a script, except it didn't sound that way. It sounded perfectly natural, like she was simply having a conversation with Sydney. As soon as she'd begun, the jitters Sydney had noticed seemed to vanish. Jessica spoke with authority and confidence, but remained completely likable and approachable rather than intimidating, like you'd want to go out to coffee with her after the telethon.

"She looks amazing," Connor whispered, pulling Sydney out of her thoughts and into the perfect visual of Jessica Barstow standing in the sunshine.

"I told you," Sydney repeated as she took in the image that couldn't have been more perfect if an Oscar-worthy cinematographer had set it up. The light green of Jessica's shirt was perfect against the lush darker green of the grass next to the barn. The sun glinted off her auburn hair in such a warm, inviting way, Sydney wouldn't have been surprised if somebody told her they'd chosen certain strands of it to highlight specifically. It was getting warm out, but Jessica hadn't yet broken a sweat and her lips somehow managed to stay glossy, much to Bridget's dismay as she stood nearby, letting out a quiet sigh every so often, probably feeling useless and unnecessary. Her skin tone looked perfect; she wasn't pale but wasn't too tan, and she looked so incredibly smooth and inviting. And now that Sydney had actually touched some of the skin under that shirt, she had a hard time not picturing herself doing it again, slower, taking the time to savor. She shook the thought away, not wanting to be that distracted, but also thinking she'd maybe save that image for later on…

They wrapped the whole thing in under two hours, with minimal retakes and almost no corrections. Sydney didn't hold back; she walked right up and embraced Jessica in a tight hug, which apparently surprised her at first. Sydney felt Jessica's arms wrap around her only after a beat or two, but she didn't care. She was that thrilled with the way things had gone.

"You were incredible," she said, her hands on Jessica's upper arms. "A seasoned pro."

"You think so?" Jessica's face flushed a lovely pink and Sydney decided right then that she wanted—no, *needed*—to make Jessica blush any chance she could. It was charming.

"Do I think so? I do. But let's ask the boss." She turned to Connor. "Hey, Mr. Baskin, Ms. Barstow here isn't buying my gushing over how good she was. Want to chime in?"

"I will happily chime in," Connor said, his grin wide as he pushed his glasses up his nose with one finger. "You were perfect. *Perfect.* Couldn't ask for better. We'll do some creative editing and it'll just…" He sliced his flat hand through the air like a wave. "Flow. My editor's going to think I don't need him. You watch."

Anna stepped into their little circle, stood so close to Sydney she had to take a small step to the side to keep from falling over. Anna's smile was so obviously forced it made Sydney furrow her brow in confusion. "That was great, Jess. Really great." Her voice held little inflection at all as she looked at Jessica and Jessica's jaw muscles bunched under her skin.

"Thanks," she said, but didn't elaborate.

Anna turned to Sydney, a real smile in place now and the transformation was almost a little creepy. "So. Happy Hour?"

"Oh, I don't know," Sydney said. "I should probably go back to the station and go over some of this stuff."

"Go ahead," Connor said to her. "I can take care of this. It's Friday. Go have fun. You're coming in tomorrow, so I'll catch you up then."

Sydney wanted to shoot him a death glare, but she knew he'd be clueless as to why. He was just being a nice guy, which she understood and appreciated. How could he know she didn't want to go out with Anna? She watched as Jessica stepped away from them and headed into the barn to coo over Jock. Sydney could still see her, but was pretty sure Jessica could no longer hear them. Which may have been the point.

"See?" Anna said with a triumphant expression. "I get you all to myself. Let me run inside and grab some things and we'll go. I can drive you home after." She dropped her voice and said suggestively, "Or you can come to my place."

I have no car! Damn it! Sydney's brain shrieked at the realization. She had not thought this through. At all. And now she was stuck. She tried to accept her fate as she watched Anna skitter away into the main building. Jeff and Bridget gathered up their stuff and headed toward the van in the parking lot. Ron helped relieve Jessica of her mic (Sydney frowned at that missed opportunity), then followed the other two crew members, and Connor, who was on his cell, talking to somebody. Jessica sauntered over, her eyes following Anna's retreat, the expression in them guarded.

"Hitting Happy Hour, huh?" she asked Sydney.

"I guess so," Sydney sighed. "Hey, do you want to come?" She hoped she didn't sound as desperate as she feared.

Jessica barked a sarcastic laugh. "Uh, no. No. Thank you, though."

Sydney squinted at her, studied the look on her face, analyzed the tone of her voice, noted the complete lack of eye contact. "You're sure?" She sounded as disappointed as she felt.

Jessica looked up at her then. "I am. Thank you, though." She suddenly looked a little...sad. It was the only way Sydney could describe it.

"Are you okay?" Sydney asked, reaching out to touch her arm, then thinking better of it and letting her hand drop.

"I'm fine. Just tired. In fact, if you're done with me, I think I'm going to head inside. I still have some things I need to take care of before I can go home."

"Yeah, sure," Sydney said, but Jessica was already walking away from her. She watched her go, feeling more disappointment than she even expected. She had no time to dwell, though, as Anna was on her way out within the space of a few more seconds.

"Let's go!" she said enthusiastically, waving her arm in a *come on* gesture.

Sydney was far enough away that she could groan quietly and not be heard by Anna.

So she did.

Nine more days and this will be over. Nine more days. You got this.

Concentrating on putting one foot in front of the other proved difficult, but she managed to do it, walking the path to Anna's car, resigned to her fate.

◦◦◦

"Oh, my God, this is so ridiculous."

Jessica said it aloud into the emptiness of her office, even as she sat in her desk chair facing the window and watched Sydney get into Anna's car. They sped off to have drinks and probably appetizers and probably a really good time. Her stomach flipped.

"This has to stop."

Another beat went by.

"Maybe if I just keep saying these things out loud to nobody, the world will change and things will be lovely again."

"What things?" Catherine's voice surprised her, and Jessica spun around in her chair trying not to look as freaked as she felt.

"Hey, what's up?" she asked in what felt like a normal voice. What she really wanted to shout was, "How much did you hear?!" She folded her hands on her desk and made an expression she hoped was "friendly and expectant."

Catherine squinted at her for a moment before sitting in one of the chairs opposite the desk. "Nothing. I'm heading out and wanted to see how it went."

"How what went?"

Catherine blinked once. Twice. "The filming? Of the tour? For the telethon? Which is next weekend?"

"Oh. Yeah, that. It went fine."

Catherine folded her arms and made a show of getting comfortable. "All right. What's going on?"

Jessica held both hands up like a robbery victim. "Nothing. Nothing's going on at all. I swear."

Catherine narrowed her eyes at her, studied her face for so long Jessica started to feel twitchy. Finally, she relented. "Fine. I don't believe you, but it's clear you don't want to talk about it. But seriously, Jess, you're acting so weird. Promise me you're okay."

Jessica quietly blew out a sigh of relief. "I'm fine. I promise. Just a little stressed out about the telethon. You know how I get." She forced a smile and changed the subject before Catherine could chip away any further. "What's going on tonight? Anything?"

"Emily wants to go to Sling for Happy Hour, so I'm going to meet her there."

"You hate that place," Jessica said, ignoring that Sydney and Anna were most likely there.

"I know. But she really wants to go, and if I do this now, I win enough points to get us out of there early."

"Clever."

"I can be." Catherine stood and looked down at her friend. "You want to join us?"

With a grimace, softened by a smile, Jessica said, "Absolutely not. I'm fine."

Another beat went by before Catherine said, "Okay. If you change your mind, we'll probably be there for a couple hours."

"Thanks." Jessica watched as Catherine left, then fell back in her chair and groaned.

A glance at the calendar open on her computer gave her the tiniest bit of comfort.

Nine more days and this will be over. Nine more days. You got this.

❧

Happy Hour at Sling was probably busy during the week, but not so much on a Saturday evening. The bar was fairly quiet at this early hour, but Sydney predicted it would fill up quickly with twenty-somethings ready to dance and drink their faces off come eleven o'clock that night.

Georgia Beers

She and Anna sat at the bar, and Sydney tried hard not to chug her beer in an attempt to hurry the evening along so she could bow out and go home. Not only would that be rude to Anna, but Sydney hadn't eaten and chugging a beer or two would have her fairly tipsy within the hour. She didn't want that. While the idea of numbing her brain to this whole situation sounded somewhat tempting, she didn't want to put herself in any sort of situation where she couldn't bob and weave her way around Anna's attempts to get close to her. Mentally *and* physically.

Therefore, it was with great relief that Sydney's eyes fell on Catherine from Junebug Farms and another woman as they came through the front door. She smiled like a crazy person and waved madly at them. "Hey there, Catherine. Come sit with us." Somehow, she was able to refrain from actual begging, but it was close.

Anna stiffened slightly, but said nothing as Catherine and her date, Sydney assumed, judging by the fact that they held hands, approached.

Catherine held out a hand to Sydney and they shook. "Fancy meeting you here," she said with a grin, then turned to the woman next to her. "This is my girlfriend, Emily. Emily, this is Sydney Taylor."

"I know who this is," Emily said, her face lit up like a child meeting Santa. She grabbed Sydney's hand and shook it heartily. "I'm a big fan."

"Well, thank you. That's very kind." Turning back to Catherine, Sydney couldn't help but say what she was thinking. "I had no idea you played on my team."

"It's a good team."

"What can I get you two?" Sydney asked. Anna sat on Sydney's right and Catherine and Emily took the two stools to

129

her left. Anna sat quietly as Sydney ordered a glass of wine for Catherine and a beer for Emily.

"So, the tour," Catherine said after touching her wine glass to Sydney's bottle as well as Emily's. Anna looked in the opposite direction, and Sydney squinted at her. "How'd it go?"

"Amazingly well," Sydney said, trying to remain as professional as possible rather than gush. "Jessica is really good. Much better than she gives herself credit for."

"Yeah, that's a theme for her." Catherine chuckled gently and Sydney began to understand that Catherine cared a lot about Jessica. "She's good at almost anything she sets her mind to."

"I told her she's fantastic in front of the camera."

Anna chose that moment to lean in Sydney's direction. She put a hand on Sydney's thigh as she did so, addressing the three in a volume a few notches higher than necessary. "I've been telling her that since I started working there. She's the face of Junebug Farms. It only makes sense."

Sydney noticed two things in that moment. First, Anna's hand on her thigh stayed there and seemed a bit more possessive than Sydney was comfortable with. Second, Catherine didn't look at Anna once as she talked, though Emily did, politely, her face guardedly neutral. Sydney shifted her body on the stool, hoping she made it look like she was merely changing positions and not trying to get Anna's hand off her leg.

For the next hour, things went much the same way. Sydney liked both Catherine and Emily. Catherine was intelligent, if a bit on the reserved side. Emily made up for it with a dry wit that had Sydney laughing more than once. Through the whole thing, Sydney had to subtly refute Anna's not-so-subtle attempts to show them as a couple. It wasn't an easy line to walk, and by the time she decided she'd stayed long enough and asked Anna to take her back to the station so she could get her car, she was mentally wiped out.

The drive from the bar to the television station was mercifully short, so there was little time for conversation. As Anna stopped next to Sydney's car, she asked, "Wanna come to my place?"

Sydney had to catch herself to keep from turning her down too quickly. "You know what?" she said instead. "I have to pass. I'm exhausted. It's been a really long day, and I still have a few things I need to get done before I can head home. But thank you."

Anna's disappointment was obvious, but thank God she didn't argue, and Sydney managed to extricate herself from the passenger's side before she got caught by anything as awkward as an attempt at a goodnight kiss. Bending down so she could look into the car, she thanked Anna for a nice evening, slammed the door shut, and went inside the station, where she watched out an office window until she was sure Anna was gone. Only then did she head back outside and get into her own car. Man, she wanted to be home.

How much longer could she do this?

CHAPTER TWELVE

SYDNEY WAS TIRED. THE kind of tired that made her eyes hurt. The kind of tired that made toddlers burst into wracking sobs. The kind of tired where, if she sat down on the staircase to her apartment and leaned just the right way against the banister, she'd be asleep in seconds. That kind of tired.

She wasn't complaining, though. This was news. This was the job. This was what she'd worked so hard for since she was old enough to understand what she wanted to be when she grew up. This kind of tired only made her happy with the realization that she was well on her way, that her childhood plans would come to fruition soon. She'd spent yesterday at the station. All day, from 7 a.m. until nearly 10 p.m., editing, writing, doing voiceovers. Today, she'd given herself an extra hour of sleep and went in at eight, but now it was nearly 8 p.m. on Sunday and she realized that she'd had zero weekend. With a weary sigh, she headed up the stairs.

"Well, don't you look like you got run over by a train." It wasn't a question posed by Dr. Vivian Green. It was a statement of fact.

"I'm sure I do," Sydney replied, climbing the stairs as if she were headed to the gallows.

"Long day?"

"Long weekend. And not the good, vacationy kind."

"You eat?"

Sydney stopped on the top step and had to think about the question. "The last thing I ate was a granola bar at"—she glanced at her watch—"around one o'clock, I think."

Vivian waved an arm. "Come on in here. I made stew, and as usual, have a lot left over."

"Oh, Dr. Green, I couldn't—"

"You could. Come on. You're going to fall over if you don't get some food in that skinny body of yours."

Saying no to Vivian Green would feel an awful lot like saying no to her grandmother—something Sydney never did. She obeyed her neighbor, bypassed her own door, and went inside the next apartment.

The interior was unsurprising, in that it looked like an apartment her own grandmother might live in: neat and tidy, with small knickknacks here and there and a lot of photographs. Sydney stopped next to the table by the door and ran her gaze over the frames of varying shapes and sizes, containing photographs of people of varying shapes and sizes.

"My family," Vivian said, her smile warm. "Come on in."

Sydney left her bag near the door and kicked off her shoes, much to the blissful relief of her aching feet.

"Honestly, I don't know how you girls manage to spend an entire day in those things." Vivian tsk-tsked as she threw a glance at the discarded heels. "You were not meant to walk around on your tippy toes all day long."

"I completely agree with you," Sydney said, trying not to stop and loudly inhale the delicious aroma of beef and gravy that filled the air. "Unfortunately, my ballet flats don't go so well with this suit."

Vivian simply shook her head and indicated an empty chair with her eyes. "Sit."

Sydney did as she was told and let her attention wander around the kitchen, which she could see from the small breakfast nook where she sat. The apartment was no bigger than her own, but looked much more lived in, had tons more character. A painting of a serene-looking pond surrounded by trees graced the wall over the table. Unlike Sydney's kitchen, which was along a wall, Vivian's was galley-style with light oak cabinets, a stainless steel sink, and almond-colored appliances that all matched. The countertop was a neutral butcher block, but Vivian had used red as an accent color, her canisters, dish towels, and pot holders all adding pops of color to the expanse of beige.

"How long have you lived here?" she asked as she sat.

Vivian stopped ladling stew into a bowl to contemplate the ceiling for a moment. "Let's see, my Sidney passed…ten years ago now. So, six years? Keeping up a whole house by myself got to be too much. I didn't need all that space. I downsized."

"Your place is nice." Vivian slid a bowl in front of her and handed her a spoon. A small plate with a hunk of bread followed. "God, this smells delicious," Sydney said as she dug into the stew. Much to her surprise, a glass of red wine appeared next. She glanced up and Vivian, eyebrows raised.

"You look like you could use it," Vivian said by way of explanation.

"I certainly could. Thank you. Join me?"

Vivian paused, then gave a nod. "Don't mind if I do." She poured herself a glass and sat in the seat across from Sydney. "So. Tell me what you do."

"I'm a reporter for Channel Six," Sydney said.

Vivian slapped the table lightly. "I thought you looked familiar. You just did a story on that local beer maker, right?"

"I did."

"That was nice. I've had their beer before. It's not bad." Vivian sipped her wine as Sydney tried not to shovel stew into her mouth like a ten-year-old eating ice cream, it was that good. "You're even prettier in person."

Sydney grinned. "Thanks."

"What story has kept you working all weekend?"

Sydney took a moment to swallow, then sipped her wine. "I'm hosting the Junebug Farms telethon next weekend. So I've been working on editing and voiceovers and the schedule and all that good stuff. A lot goes into it."

"I can imagine. I watch every year. They do good work, those people."

"You watch every year?" Sydney wasn't sure why she was surprised.

"I do. It was an annual thing for my Sidney and me. Our Lucy came from Junebug. Had her for nearly fifteen years." Vivian's slightly rheumy eyes seemed to gaze at the past for a beat. "I donate every year."

"Do you have a pet?" Sydney asked, looking around the small apartment.

"Not at the moment. I think about it sometimes. It's nice to have company." She smiled at Sydney, letting her know she meant her as well. "What about you? Pets?"

Sydney shook her head. "My schedule's too crazy. I have goldfish."

Vivian chuckled. "Still counts."

"I guess." Sydney dropped her spoon into her empty bowl and let out a sigh. "That was amazing, Dr. Green. And I was hungrier than I thought. Thank you so much."

"Like I said, it's nice to have company. And I see you come and go all the time, but rarely with a grocery bag in your hand."

She gave Sydney a look of motherly concern that made her feel warm inside.

"It's a bad habit, I know. My mom will be happy I had a home-cooked meal." Sydney took a sip of her wine. "So, what kind of doctor are you?"

"Oh, I haven't worked with clients in several years, but I'm a psychologist. Had my own practice for nearly thirty-five years."

"Really? That's got to be so cool, figuring out what makes people tick, how to help them, stuff like that."

"The human mind is so complex, Sydney. You'd be amazed."

"Do you miss it? Working, I mean?"

"A little bit every day, yes. But it was also good to stop and rest. I needed it."

"Overworked?"

"Yes, very much. Like somebody else I know." Vivian raised her eyebrows poignantly, but grinned to keep it light.

Sydney chuckled, finished off her wine, then stood and took her dishes into the kitchen.

"Just leave them. I have a dishwasher."

"You're sure?"

"If I have a dishwasher? I'm not that old, honey." Vivian smiled at her own joke. "Yes, I'm sure."

"Well, thank you. I really appreciate it."

"Any time, dear." Vivian walked her to the door.

Sydney contemplated putting her shoes back on, but instead, picked them up off the floor. "It's not a long commute to my place," she said, causing Vivian to chuckle as she opened the door.

❧

The week was going by so fast, Jessica was surprised her head wasn't actually spinning. Sure felt like it should be. The Channel Six crew, along with others from various companies, was at the shelter every day, nearly all day long, and the place felt even more chaotic than usual—which said a lot. More bodies milling around. Much more noise. Adding power tools and hammer strikes to the chorus of barks and whines made for quite the symphony, and ibuprofen was circulated regularly among the shelter staff. The phone bank was nearly built, the phone company hooking up lines and getting things worked out so volunteers could answer the phones live during the telethon. There were two different "sets" that had been built in different corners of the lobby in addition to one in the barn and one near the goat house. According to Sydney, they would cut back and forth a few times to give viewers the "full scope of Junebug." Jessica had to admit, she liked the idea.

On Wednesday afternoon, Jessica hurried down the hall that housed the offices other than hers, her feet moving quickly, her head down so nobody would see her. At Catherine's closed door, she rapped twice, then opened it and entered without waiting for an answer. She closed it quickly behind her, fell with her back against it, and issued a whimper. "Quick. Hide me."

Catherine looked at her over the rim of her glasses. "Telethon preparation overload?"

"You have no idea."

"Oh, but I do. You go through this every year."

"I do?" Jessica stepped farther into the office and sat in the chair opposite the desk. Catherine's dog, Geronimo, left his dog bed in the corner where he'd been napping so he could give Jessica some love. She patted her lap and he jumped up, turned his terrier-mix of a body in two full circles, then curled up and closed his eyes, sighing in comfort.

"Traitor," Catherine muttered at him with a mock-glare. Meeting Jessica's gaze, she raised her eyebrows and made an expression that basically said, *Duh!* "Yes. Every single year. You're fine until the week before. Then prep work is in full swing and you're in full freak-out mode. It'll pass."

"I don't know. Sydney Taylor is a slave driver."

"Is that who you're hiding from?"

Jessica nodded. "She's got me doing a lot. *A lot.*"

"And that bothers you?"

"It's just…not how Janet did things."

Catherine put her elbows on the desk, clasped her hands together, and leaned slightly forward as she looked at Jessica. "Maybe it's time to let go of Janet since she's, you know, *not here anymore.*"

Jessica grimaced and stroked Mo's soft white fur as she gazed out the window at the afternoon sun.

"I think it's a good thing that Sydney's got you front and center."

"You do?"

"Totally. Especially from a promotional standpoint. You're the face of Junebug Farms, Jessica, like it or not. And call me crazy, but I would like being able to recognize the person who runs the place I give my money to, you know? It's good P.R. Ask Anna about it. She'll tell you."

"Yeah…"

Catherine squinted at her. "What's going on, Jess? You're never this stressed, even when it's warranted."

Jessica waved a dismissive hand and forced a chuckle. The last thing she wanted to do was try to analyze the confusing swirl of her recent thoughts. Mostly because she didn't want to talk about it. She'd avoided it this long; she could make it through four more days. "Oh, it's fine. I'm just being a weirdo."

Catherine studied her and Jessica had to use every ounce of energy to stay still, hold eye contact, and smile like everything was hunky-dory. It wasn't easy, but a knock on the door saved her from having to do it any longer.

Anna popped her head in. "Hey, Jess. Sydney's looking for you."

"Of course she is," Jessica mumbled. Louder, she said, "Okay. I'll be right there."

Anna hesitated for a beat before pulling the door shut again.

"If it makes you feel any better, I ran into Sydney at Happy Hour last week, and she said you're kicking major telethon ass, so…"

"She was with Anna, right?" Jessica tried not to let any opinion color her voice, but Catherine knew her too well not to hear it.

"*With her* might not be completely accurate."

"What does that mean?"

"She was with her, but I'm not sure she wanted to be. She definitely wasn't *with her* with her, if you know what I mean."

Brow furrowed, Jessica asked, "How could you tell?"

Catherine shrugged. "Just that any time Anna leaned close or tried to touch her, Sydney would reach for something or shift in her seat to prevent it. It was actually pretty entertaining to watch."

Jessica didn't know what to say to that, so she just took a beat to let it sink in.

"Anyway. Stop worrying. You got this," Catherine said with an encouraging smile.

Jessica inhaled deeply, let the breath out, gave one determined nod. "I do. I do got this." Reluctantly, she lifted Mo, who groaned his dissatisfaction, and set him back on his dog bed. "Thanks for letting me hide out."

"Any time."

Hand on the doorknob, Jessica steeled herself, then pulled it open and headed back into the fray.

By the time three more hours had passed, Jessica was both feeling better about things and also completely fried. Her eyes were scratchy, her head felt foggy, and she had the hunger shakes. But for the first time in several days, she was starting to get a feel for how the telethon was going to look...and the changes didn't seem quite so scary.

"What do you think?" Sydney asked as they stood together in the lobby and watched the crew wrapping up for the day.

"I think it's going to be good." Jessica smiled at her, a genuine smile, not the artificial one she'd been tossing Sydney's way lately, the one that didn't reach her eyes.

"Yeah?" Sydney turned to face her completely and her voice registered wonder. She hadn't dressed down today at all. Well, her suit was a pantsuit instead of a skirt, so maybe that was considered dressed down to her, but she looked incredible just the same, Jessica had to admit. And she had admitted it, to herself, several times today as she tried to take in the black pants and matching black jacket. Sydney'd had the sleeves pushed up to her elbows for half the day until she'd decided to lose the jacket all together, revealing a deep raspberry tank top that showed off her smooth-looking, toned arms.

"You sound surprised."

"I am, a little."

"Walk with me," Jessica said as she headed to her office. "Why are you surprised?"

Sydney gave her a look that, though gentle, said, *really?*

"I've been a bit...difficult, haven't I?" She was startled when Sydney stopped their progress by grabbing her arm, turning her so they were face to face.

"No," she said vehemently. "Not at all. I need you to understand that. Believe me, I have worked with difficult people and you, my friend, are not one of them." Her point made, she seemed to realize her hand was still gripping Jessica's forearm and she let go as if it had burned her. "I think…hesitant is a better word for you. Reluctant, maybe. Skeptical."

Jessica grinned and resumed the walk. Inside her office, she said simply, "You're right. And I'm sorry." She went behind her desk, moved her mouse to wake up her computer, clicked a few windows closed.

"Don't apologize. There's no need." Sydney stood in the middle of the room, looking around as if uncertain why she was there or what she should do next. Before either of them could speak further, Anna came walking in, her steps determined and quick, as they always seemed to be lately.

"There you are," she said to Sydney, barely registering Jessica.

"Here I am," Sydney said.

Anna reached out to stroke Sydney's arm. Jessica bent forward and looked at her computer screen, even though she'd already logged off. "I had really hoped we could meet up tonight, but I made these plans with my mother ages ago and she will guilt trip me for weeks if I bail."

"No problem at all. I've got plans anyway."

"Okay, good." There was a pause; Anna must have looked at her watch or something because then she said, "I'm going to scoot then. I'll call you later."

Sydney must have nodded, as she said nothing. Jessica continued looking at her blank screen until Anna was gone. Then she stood up straight. There was a beat of silence as she and Sydney made eye contact and it held. It was awkward. And kind of awesome. Jessica felt her stomach flutter.

"Want to grab some dinner?" Sydney asked softly.

"You have plans."

"I actually don't, though."

"So, you lied."

Sydney pressed her lips together, but her eyes never left Jessica's. "I did."

"I see."

"Want to grab some dinner?"

Jessica didn't so much as pause, something she'd analyze later. "Yes."

∾

Jessica and Sydney had each gone home to change clothes, and weirdly they'd shown up at the front door of Bucky's at the exact same time, approaching from opposite directions, which made them both chuckle. Bucky's wasn't terribly busy on weeknights, but there was a mellow jazz trio in one corner playing instrumental favorites and that usually brought in a nice, medium-sized crowd. Henry put Jessica and Sydney at a table in the opposite corner, a small, dimly lit, intimate table, which ended up being perfect because they could hear the music, but weren't overpowered by it. Conversation was more than possible. They ordered a bottle of Pinot Noir to share. Kim brought it to them and did the open-pour a sample-let the customer sip thing that Catherine, who moonlighted as a waitress in a nice restaurant, had taught Jessica years ago. Once approved, the wine was poured and Jessica raised her glass.

"You remembered," Sydney said, and her smile was wide, showing those perfectly straight teeth the television viewers were growing used to.

"You say that like I don't listen when you talk."

Sydney arched one eyebrow and said, "I suppose it's possible that Janet Dobson doesn't do it this way, but…"

Jessica burst out laughing. "Touché," she said, then touched her glass to Sydney's.

They sipped and Sydney nodded her own approval. "Oh, that's delicious."

"I'm glad you like it. It's a favorite of mine. People don't always think of Oregon when they think of wine, but they've got some really wonderful ones."

"I'm only just beginning to pay attention to wine, so maybe you can teach me."

"Well, I'm no pro. I've learned a lot from Henry."

"So, he's a friend of your parents?" Sydney opened the menu.

"My grandparents, yes." Jessica set her menu aside, which garnered an amused look from Sydney.

"I see you don't need a list of options." She closed her own menu. "Okay. Tell me what to order."

"Tell me what you like."

Sydney tilted her head to the side and again, they held eye contact in a way that made Jessica's entire lower body tighten. "I like meat. I like most vegetables except Brussels sprouts. I don't like fennel either. I don't love seafood, but I'll eat it if it's good."

"How are you with messy sandwiches?"

Sydney grinned. "I am exceptionally good with messy sandwiches."

"Perfect." As if on cue, Kim appeared to take their orders. "Two Reubens, please. Sweet potato fries. And an order of the pickle chips to start."

Kim nodded, topped off their wine, and was off.

"Am I drooling on myself?" Sydney asked. "Because that sounds *amazing*."

"You'll thank me."

There were a few moments of grinning and of listening to the music, which was a smooth, palatable sound Jessica loved. She watched Sydney as she watched the band. Her hair wasn't as perfect as it had been this morning—every strand in place—but this casual, slightly tousled look suited her, made her seem more relaxed and approachable. She'd replaced the black pantsuit and raspberry tank top with worn, soft-looking jeans and a simple black V-neck T-shirt. While Jessica missed the sight of Sydney's bare shoulders in the tank, she appreciated the rather low cut of the V-neck, showing a lovely collarbone and a wide expanse of skin dotted with a handful of freckles.

Sydney turned those blue-green eyes to her and smiled, and Jessica heard distinct yet gentle warning bells go off in her head, so she pulled her own gaze away and forced herself to look at the band.

"Hey, I wanted to tell you something," Sydney said, reclaiming Jessica's attention as she sipped her wine.

Jessica wet her lips and turned to face her.

"You've been doing an amazing job. I know I've thrown more at you than you're used to, but it's only because I saw your potential."

The compliment went in Jessica's ear, weaved through her body, wrapped around her heart, and settled there. "You did?"

"God, yes. You're impressive on camera. You're a terrific speaker. Not a lot of people can just ramble on about something without stuttering and stammering or using 'uh' fifty-seven times. Your speech is smooth, you know your subject matter inside and out and…" Sydney took another sip of her wine before dropping her voice slightly and saying, "And you look *fantastic* on the screen."

Jessica felt the blush creep up her neck and warm her cheeks. "Thank you for that," she said quietly. "It means a lot."

Again with the eye contact, she thought as Sydney's ocean-colored gaze held hers firmly.

This time, their shared stare was broken by Kim arriving with their pickle chips. She set the plate down and told them their sandwiches would be up soon.

Sydney looked at them. "I've never had these."

"Then you, my friend, are in for a treat." Jessica picked one up, dipped it in the tiny bowl of ranch, then took a bite, steam wafting up once the coating was broken.

Sydney followed suit. "Oh, my God. These are delicious!"

"See? Stick with me, kid. I know stuff."

"You certainly know pickles. I'll give you that."

"So, tell me how you came to be a news reporter."

Sydney chewed as she seemed to gather her thoughts. "I have always loved to interview people. Even as a little kid, I'd use a hairbrush for a microphone and just ask people questions."

"That is the cutest image." Jessica couldn't help but grin. "I see a tiny Sydney, pointing a hairbrush at her mom, asking her about bath time and why there had to be such a thing."

"Exactly!" Sydney laughed and the sound was beautiful, a thought that took Jessica by surprise. "I have watched the Barbara Walters Oscar night special ever since I can remember. I used to write down the questions she'd ask people." She popped another pickle chip into her mouth. "My best friend calls me Walters."

"No."

"Swear to God."

"That's ridiculously adorable."

"Yeah, well…" Sydney shrugged and Jessica was pretty sure she saw a little bit of pink coloring her cheeks. "What about you? How'd you end up in the shelter business? I mean, I know you inherited it from your grandmother, but why'd you stay?"

"Oh, that's a good interview question," Jessica said with a raised eyebrow and a grin. "Deep and personal, but not rudely so."

"I pride myself on those."

"The simple answer is that I wanted to carry on what my grandmother had started. The shelter meant a lot to her."

"And the long answer?"

"The long answer is that it started to mean something to me, too. I fell in love, not only with the animals, but with being the one who could help them. The one who had the space and the time and the resources to, not so much fix the problem, but to put a Band-Aid on it until a permanent solution could be found."

"So...you've got a bit of a hero complex, do you?"

Jessica laughed at that. "I suppose maybe I do. Is that a bad thing?"

"In this case? No, I don't think it is at all." Sydney winked at her and grabbed a chip.

They ate in companionable silence as they listened to the band play "The Look of Love." Jessica silently marveled at how easy it was to be with Sydney, to be quiet with her. There was no need to fill the silence. They would smile at each other and turn back to the band, completely comfortable. Kim delivered their sandwiches just as they each took a final pickle chip. She topped off their glasses with the remainder of the bottle, then left them to their meals.

Jessica watched as Sydney took a bite of her sandwich, then proceeded to make all kinds of humming noises and roll her eyes back in her head. Jessica laughed as she asked, "Have you lost the ability to speak? Use your words, Sydney."

Sydney finished chewing and swallowed. "Holy shit. This might be the best sandwich I've ever had. In my life. Is Henry a wizard? Does he use magic to cook?"

"I can tell you for certain that Henry is not a wizard." She sipped her wine. "He's also not the cook. That would be Javier. *He* might be a wizard." She popped a sweet potato fry into her mouth with a grin.

"Well, I'd like to go find Javier and kiss him right on the mouth."

They continued eating with a minimum of discussion. Once they had both finished their sandwiches and the band took a break, Jessica looked at Sydney. "I'm the kind of girl who has to have a little sugar after dinner, but I can't eat a whole dessert on my own. Share?"

"I'm going to have to spend an extra half hour on the treadmill, but…why the hell not?"

"Excellent."

"I see you have no dessert menu, so I'm going to assume you know what you want."

"Chocolate raspberry cheesecake."

"You're killing me."

Jessica smiled and within three minutes, a plate of the cheesecake was set in the middle of the table, two forks accompanying it.

Sydney blinked. "How'd you do that? You didn't even order."

"I have connections," Jessica said with a shrug.

"Apparently."

"And FYI, Javier makes this from scratch. This is not store-bought or even purchased from a bakery." She spun the plate so the point of the slice of dessert faced Sydney. "Go ahead."

Sydney dug her fork in and took a bite. More humming ensued, which made Jessica laugh. Again. Sydney seemed to have a knack for that.

"Good?"

Sydney nodded, hummed some more, nodded again. When she finally found speech, she had only one word. "Sinful."

"Agreed."

Working together, they polished off the dessert, the wine, and were close to emptying their water glasses. Sydney sat back in her chair and let out a huge breath, hand splayed across her stomach. "Holy crap, I don't need to eat for a week."

"Please," Jessica said with a snort. "I bet you hardly eat at all. Look at you."

"Hey, they're not kidding when they say the camera adds ten pounds. It's a thing, especially for the women in this business."

"How does that not make you crazy?"

"Oh, it does. But there's not a lot I can do about it, unfortunately."

"Well, that sucks."

Sydney laughed. "In a big way."

Kim stopped by with the check, and they fought good-naturedly over it until they each had a grip on it, hovering over the center of the table.

"Please," Sydney said, and Jessica watched her playful expression slip away, only to be replaced by a rather serious one. "I worked you like a dog today. No pun intended. And I'll probably do it again tomorrow. The least I can do is buy you dinner."

With a reluctant sigh, Jessica let go of the little leatherette portfolio. "Okay. This time. Next time, it's on me." *Next time?*

Sydney smiled and tucked her credit card into the little pocket. Kim collected it immediately.

With a glance at her watch, Jessica said, "Wow. I'm not used to being out of work so early. I can't believe it's not even nine."

"Really?" Sydney glanced at her own watch. "Huh. I'm usually still at the station."

"I'm usually still in my office."

"Well," Sydney said and sat back in her chair. "I don't know about you, but I'm having a great time. I kind of don't want the evening to end." As soon as the words were out, she looked as if she hadn't meant to say them. Wanting nothing more than to make her feel better, Jessica spoke quickly. And honestly.

"Me neither." That got not only a smile, but an easing of the tightness around Sydney's mouth.

"What should we do?"

"My place isn't far from here." *What? Who said that? What am I doing?*

"Neither is mine. Though yours is probably much less…sparse."

"My place has wine."

"Your place it is then."

Sydney signed the check and they gathered up their things. Jessica waved to Henry as they passed the bar on their way to the door, could feel his weighted gaze. He'd have questions next time she saw him—of that, she was sure.

The night was beautiful. Warm for early spring, which you could tell by the number of people wandering the streets on a Wednesday. A few shops had stayed open late, restaurants and bars were bustling, the overall atmosphere was bright, friendly, and jovial. Light spilled from different establishments as Jessica and Sydney strolled slowly along the street, Sydney stopping to peek in a window every so often.

"I didn't realize all this was here. That one night I saw you at Bucky's was my first night out and I was just following the sound of jazz."

"You should pay more attention to your surroundings," Jessica teased, but meant it, as she was paying *a lot* of attention to her current ones. Specifically, the wildly attractive woman walking next to her, how differently they interacted when not working, the fact that she wore slight heels even with her jeans, the way she smelled like honey, how the trio of men they passed looked for an extra beat. Oh, yes, Jessica was very, *very* aware of her surroundings.

In less than ten minutes, they were on the front steps of Jessica's building and she was sliding her key home.

"This is nice," Sydney said, her head tilted up as she took in the outside of the large house. "Is it all yours?"

"It is. I have the top two floors and my tenant lives on the first floor."

"Not sure I could be a landlord," Sydney said, a touch of hesitation in her voice.

"Not sure I can either," Jessica said with a smile as she led Sydney up a flight of stairs. "I inherited this house from my grandparents, along with the current tenant, who is a dream. If he ever leaves, I'm not sure what I'd do."

Sydney chuckled as they stopped at the top. "My thing is, I don't like to share my stuff. I'm an only child, so never really had to. I guess that stuck in a not-so-great way. If I owned a house, I don't think I'd do well with a stranger in there, putting holes in my walls and spilling sticky stuff in my cupboards."

Jessica turned to look at her. "Those are pretty specific," she said, raising one eyebrow. "Do you have issues I don't know about?"

Sydney scoffed. "Tons, I'm sure."

Jessica pushed the door open and stepped inside. "Welcome." The cats showed up from three different directions to greet their mom and inspect the visitor. Sydney immediately squatted and reached out to pet each of them.

"Hi, guys," she said quietly. "It's nice to meet you." She looked up at Jessica and told her, "You have a few cats."

Jessica nodded and pointed. "Fred. Shaggy. Scooby."

"Awesome names."

"Thanks. I watched a lot of cartoons as a kid and I much prefer the older ones. *Scooby-Doo. Tom and Jerry.* Et cetera."

"I completely get that." Sydney stood, Shaggy in her arms. "This guy likes me."

Jessica smiled and refrained from mentioning that Shaggy liked everybody. "Wine?"

"Yes, please."

They moved into the kitchen where Jessica pulled a bottle from a small countertop rack and held it up for Sydney's approval. "Or I have beer."

"That's perfect." Sydney gestured to the wine with her chin. The apartment had been modernized before Jessica moved in, so it was basically open concept. As Jessica pulled a corkscrew from a drawer, she watched Sydney wander her living room, taking in the art on the walls (mostly from Target), the framed photo of her grandparents on the mantel of the gas fireplace, the wicker basket filled with cat toys. "You don't have a dog?"

Jessica poured the wine as she answered. "No. Not currently. I think about it, but my hours are so long and unpredictable."

Sydney gave her a look. "You run an animal shelter. I don't think the boss would mind if you brought your dog to work."

Jessica laughed as she walked into the living room and handed Sydney her wine. Shaggy abandoned her arms as she grabbed the glass. "Catherine says the same thing. I could do that."

"How come you haven't?" Sydney looked at her with those eyes, intent and expectant and, more than that, genuinely interested.

"Are you wearing your news reporter hat now?" Jessica touched her glass to Sydney's, then sipped, watching as Sydney grinned knowingly. Over the rim of her glass, Jessica said quietly, "I will definitely have a dog in the future. I just...haven't met the right one yet."

"That, I can understand," Sydney said quietly as their gazes held.

This?

This right here?

Not at all where Jessica expected to be tonight.

Not having dinner with Sydney Taylor. Not genuinely enjoying the time and conversation with her. And certainly not in her own apartment, standing a few inches away from her, about to lean in and kiss those gorgeously full lips. None of this was what she'd expected when she woke up that morning. Not even close. And yet here she was, about to lean in, about to take a taste. About to—

"I should go," Sydney whispered, and took a step back. Jessica opened her eyes before realizing they'd been closed, and if she'd been paying any less attention, she'd have fallen over forward—she was that far into her move.

"Oh," she said, for lack of anything more in-depth, and stood up straight. "Um, okay."

"I'm sorry," Sydney said, and sounded like she meant it, but suddenly all that delicious eye contact was withheld. Her eyes darted as she looked around the room, her gaze landing on the well-lit kitchen, and she quickly moved in that direction. Jessica blinked once. Twice. Finally followed. "It's been a long day and it'll be another one tomorrow. You know? I should get some sleep. You should, too."

"Oh, sure. Absolutely." *It's fine. Everything's fine. That wasn't embarrassing at all.* The thoughts ran fast and furious through Jessica's brain, but she kept a gentle smile plastered on her face because she'd be damned if she was going to let her disappointment—or worse, her embarrassment—show. No, she wasn't going to give Sydney Taylor another ounce of power over her. She'd given her too much already.

In the kitchen, Sydney set her nearly full wine glass on the counter and grabbed her purse from the spot where she'd left it. "I had a great time tonight," she said, her eyes still not quite meeting Jessica's.

"Me, too." Jessica opened the door for her.

"See you tomorrow. Bright and early."

"You certainly will." With a nod, Jessica watched her descend the stairs. With a half-hearted wave over her shoulder, Sydney pushed through the front door and was gone. Her head against the edge of the door, Jessica stood there for long moments, eyes on the empty front foyer one floor down as she tried to figure out two things.

First, what had just happened?

Second, how the hell was she supposed to handle tomorrow?

CHAPTER THIRTEEN

THURSDAY DAWNED GRAY AND rainy. Foggy. A little chilly. Very much like Sydney's mood.

She'd woken up with a pounding headache, probably from lack of sleep, since she'd done nothing more than lie there in her bed, eyes open, thoughts swirling. At 3 a.m., she'd hopped onto her computer, having given up completely on even dozing, and checked on some of the reels she'd sent out. There was a reply in her inbox from a channel in Austin that asked her a few questions. She'd typed up a response, but left it in her draft folder, figuring she'd better proof it when she wasn't bleary-eyed and when her brain wasn't taken up with something altogether not about work.

Last night had been so good. And then so bad. How she'd let it go from one to the other so quickly was beyond her. She replayed and analyzed and dissected and came up empty. All she could think was that she needed to be much more careful because she had been *this close* to making out with Jessica Barstow last night and that would have been bad on so many levels.

Mostly one, she thought as they pulled into a parking spot at Junebug Farms. Mixing her work and her personal life was just bad judgment. Unprofessional, not to mention unethical. A reporter had to stay neutral. And yes, it was just a telethon, not a damning or exonerating interview, but still. Someday it would be hard-hitting journalism, and she didn't want her behavior on some fluff piece from her past to come back to haunt her. Neutral was key. She'd let it go further than she should have last night, but the bottom line was that she'd stopped it. Right? That was the important part. Not how much she'd wanted that kiss—God, had she wanted that kiss—but that she'd stopped it before things went way beyond complicated. Determined that she'd made the right decision, she slid out of the Channel Six van and saw Anna St. John entering the front door of Junebug Farms. Luckily, Anna didn't see her, and that was a good thing because Sydney wasn't quite ready to deal with her yet. Not on top of everything else.

"How do I get myself into these situations?" she asked softly.

"What situations?" Connor asked, his eyes never leaving his tablet. "Telethons? News vans? Having a near-debilitating crush on your producer?" He looked up then and winked at her, the lenses of his glasses showing a subtle mist.

"Ha ha. Not quite." Sydney shouldered her bag and turned to walk with Connor toward the shelter, the crew to follow behind.

"Okay, today we'll rehearse the live stuff, give Jessica a few chances to wing it, see how she feels. Yeah?"

Sydney nodded her agreement and let out a small sigh.

"Everything all right?" Connor asked and Sydney genuinely appreciated his concern. She did her best to give him a small smile.

"Yes. Everything's fine." *Business. This is business.* Three more days and she would be done with this. But the real question remained: could she get Jessica out of her head? Last night had surprised her. They seemed like a different pair of women when they weren't talking about work or dealing with work or stuck in their work roles. Here at the shelter, Jessica was authoritative, in charge, formidable. Nobody with half a brain would mess with her when it came to the good of her shelter. But last night she'd been charming. And funny. And super sexy.

And no matter what other complications factored in, she'd wanted to kiss Sydney last night. Sydney was sure of it.

"Hey there, gorgeous."

Anna St. John seemingly appeared out of nowhere with her cheerful voice and bouncy ponytail, interrupting Sydney's train of thought—which was probably a good thing. "Hi, Anna. How are you this morning?"

"I'm great. I see it's still misting out there." She reached a hand toward Sydney and fussed with her hair before Sydney had a chance to duck out of the way. "I hope you brought Bridget with you," she said with a wink. "The mist made your hair a little frizzy."

"It's okay," Sydney said, stepping back—she hoped—subtly. "We're just rehearsing today." She saw a tiny dimming of Anna's smile before the wattage kicked back up again.

"Oh, well that's good. Less formal." Anna's eyes raked over her. "Not that you'd know it by this"—she lowered her voice— "really sexy outfit."

Sydney looked down at her navy slacks and navy-and-white striped short sleeved-sweater and sexy was not a word that came to mind. Professional, yes. Neat, yes. Classy, yeah. Sexy? No. "That's not exactly what I was going for, but thank you," she said politely, looking over Anna's shoulder to see where Connor had walked off to, if somebody needed her. Hell, she'd even take Jessica at this point, knowing how awkward they might be, over trying to walk this very, very thin line Anna had her on.

"You're very welcome," Anna said, her eyes twinkling like she and Sydney shared a secret. She laid a warm hand on Sydney's upper arm, just below her sleeve, but before more could be said, Connor approached them.

"Okay, here's the list of things I'd like to run through today with Jessica." He showed them a list of timed segments on his screen. "I sent this to you both last night. Anna, I'd like to showcase this one company a little bit." He pointed to an organization that gave the shelter sizable amounts of money each year. "Can you clear that for me? Get me somebody to talk to? I figure as public relations head, you probably have contacts with most of the donors."

"I do." Anna nodded, but her expression had hardened just a bit. "You'll want to talk to Emily Breckenridge." She said nothing more, even as Sydney and Connor waited expectantly.

"All right, well I'll let you lead me on that one. Sydney, let's go over this stuff with Jessica." He made a show of looking around the lobby. "Anybody seen her?"

This was her chance and she snagged it. "I'll get her," Sydney said, heading off in the direction of Jessica's office before anybody could offer an alternative. This was good. This would give them a few moments to maybe clear the air about last night, touch on a few issues, fix things so the entire day wasn't awkward. She wasn't sure what to expect. After all, she didn't know Jessica very well at all, so she had no idea how she handled uncomfortable things. At the closed office door, she knocked three times.

"Jessica? It's Sydney. You in there?"

"Come in." Jessica's voice was cheerful. Sydney pushed the door open. Inside, Jessica was nowhere to be seen, but her voice issued from the corner where Sydney believed the bathroom was. "Just fixing my hair. Be right there."

"No problem," Sydney said. She stood in the middle of the office, hands clasped in front of her, then on her hips, then behind her back. She hated that feeling of not knowing what to do with them. She settled on clasping them in front when Jessica came out of the bathroom, looking nothing short of amazing.

Sydney's brain started sifting through its own internal thesaurus. Jessica looked stunning. Astonishing. Beautiful. Striking. *How does she manage to do that in jeans?* Granted, the jeans were apparently tailored to her body, but they were neat, almost refined. On top, she wore a simple, royal blue T-shirt with a deep V-neck, white tank visible underneath. Also visible was a healthy glimpse of cleavage and a nice length of collarbone and what the hell was it about Jessica's skin that Sydney couldn't take her eyes off it? Any of it? Her long arms looked so smooth, a white plastic watch buckled around her left wrist, face turned in. Silver ballet flats finished off the outfit, giving it a hint of sophistication. Jessica's rich auburn hair was pulled back in a ponytail, which hung in a corkscrew from the rubber band. Her makeup was perfect and Sydney was envious to see no telltale signs of a lack of sleep. No dark circles. No puffy face. No red-rimmed eyes.

I hate her a little bit right now. It's true. Can't help it.

"Good morning," Jessica said with a wide smile. "How are you?"

"Good." Sydney furrowed her brow a bit. "I'm good. You?"

"I'm great. Ready to do this thing." She laughed, then picked up a sheet of paper. "Connor e-mailed me the segments you guys want to rehearse today."

"Oh. Good. That's good."

Jessica seemed to study her. "You okay?"

Sydney looked at her for a beat before saying, "Yeah. I'm fine. I just…I wanted to say something about last night is all."

"Last night? I had a great time. I hope you did, too." Jessica glanced down at the paper in her hand, seemingly done with the subject.

"Oh, I did. I did. A great time. I…when I left, though…it was a little…" Sydney had no idea what to say or what she wanted to say or even what she was trying to say, so she let her voice just trail off.

Jessica waved a dismissive hand and made a sound like steam coming out of a pipe. "Please. No big deal. We had a nice time. Let's leave it at that."

"Oh. Okay." Well, that went better than she'd expected. It made sense, really, Jessica's immediate dismissal of the whole thing. "Okay," she said again. "Let's get to work then, shall we?" She watched as Jessica smiled—a smile that Sydney understood because it seemed slightly...brittle?—walked past her without a second glance, and headed out to the lobby. When she approached the crew, she greeted Connor loudly and actually hugged the man. Over her shoulder, Connor looked at Sydney with raised eyebrows, his face clearly radiating, *WTF?*

Sydney shrugged and shook her head at him, wanting to say, *Sorry, dude, totally my bad,* but staying quiet instead. Okay. If this was the way it had to be, with the two of them pretending nothing had happened, then this was the way it had to be. Sydney worked to reprogram her mind, to wipe last night, the almost-kiss, and anything related to Jessica Barstow that was not work-related right out of her brain. *It's better this way.* She had to tell herself that more than once. Believing it proved to be a challenge.

❧

Jessica had spent the night with her brain doing its best impression of a tornado, whipping her thoughts around in circles, blowing her feelings all over the place. When she woke up this morning, she decided the best course of action would be to ignore everything that had happened—or almost happened— last night. Sydney had obviously wanted to address it, but Jessica had been more than humiliated enough, so she decided to play the game of Don't Be Silly, That Was Nothing. And it had worked for hours now.

Had her face cracked yet?

That was the main question in Jessica's head for the majority of the day because having to display this fake smile the whole time, pretending everything was magical as a Disney movie, was very nearly killing her.

Why?

That was the other big question. Why had this affected her so and why was she having such a hard time shaking it? So, she'd been embarrassed last night. It wasn't the first time and she was reasonably sure it wouldn't be the last. Why did she allow Sydney Taylor to hold so much power over her? Jessica was no pushover. She wouldn't be where she was today if she were. No, she was tough. She was no-nonsense. She was a bit of a control freak. So who the hell was Sydney Taylor and why did she make Jessica feel like such a discombobulated mess? This was unfamiliar and Jessica didn't like it. At all.

Maybe she'd simply had a much better time than Sydney had. That was possible, right? They'd had interesting, stimulating conversation, but maybe it was one-sided. Maybe Sydney had been bored. Though…she hadn't hesitated to come back to Jessica's place…

God, this was going to drive her insane.

Forcing herself to focus, she did her best to shove everything else aside and work.

The segments they rehearsed went off without a hitch, and Connor and Sydney made sure to constantly tell her what a pro she was in front of the camera. It really wasn't hard when you knew what you were talking about, and if there was one subject Jessica was literally an expert on, it was this shelter. She knew everything about it, how it ran, why it worked, what had to be done each day to keep it successful, and how to get money. This was her baby and nobody knew it like she did. Luckily, she was a decent enough speaker that those facts came shining through as clear as a sunrise on a July morning.

It was after six again by the time they finished up for the day. Both Connor and Sydney seemed very happy with the direction things were going.

"This is going to be a piece of cake," Sydney said, her television smile firmly in place. Jessica could recognize it now; she'd been around Sydney long enough to notice. It was slightly different than her actual smile, and the fact that Jessica was getting the fake one made all the insecurities she'd shelved early come tumbling down around her.

"I hope so," Jessica replied as she glanced around the lobby, watching the crew tweaking the set, wondering if she could help them. She'd much rather swing a hammer than stand here next to Sydney feeling uncomfortable.

"I have no doubts."

"Good. Well." Jessica looked around to make sure her volunteers had things under control. She saw Lisa and Catherine talking near the dog wing doors. The phones had quieted and only Regina was left working behind the front desk, but she'd be heading home soon. They'd closed to visitors at six, so there was nobody milling around other than employees of the shelter or the television station. Glancing back toward Sydney, but not able to keep her gaze there, Jessica said, "I've got a ton of work to catch up on, so I'm going to get to it." Without waiting for a response, she turned and took the path to her office, so relieved to be away from Sydney, she almost cried.

She hadn't been kidding about the work. Two full days of rehearsal had put her very far behind on paperwork, e-mails, and phone calls, and she spent the next three hours doing her best to catch up. Or at least get close. She'd seen the Channel Six crew leave when she'd glanced out the window, but Sydney hadn't stopped in to say goodbye and for that, Jessica had been grateful.

Now, eyes scratchy and head beginning to ache from fatigue, Jessica finally dropped her pen and mentally called it quits. There was no way she could read one more word. Her eyes couldn't see them. Her brain couldn't comprehend them. She was done.

With a defeated sigh, she pushed away from her desk and crossed to the corner mini fridge where she found a Diet Coke. With a pop, she opened it and took several swallows, then headed out into the lobby of the shelter.

Even Bill was gone, the nighttime lighting casting a soft glow along the faux marble flooring and glass windows of Paws & Whiskers. Farther in, the cat wall reflected her in its clear squares, several of the cats awake and watching her. She smiled at them, then pulled open the door to the dog wing.

This was as quiet as the dog wing ever got, which was not to say it was quiet. There was always a dog or two whining or whimpering or barking, even in the dim lighting of the night. Most were curled up in balls on their beds, doing their best to get some sleep, but many sprang into action any time the doors opened. Jessica honestly wasn't sure how Lisa managed to sit at her desk with all the chaotic noise every single day and not go completely out of her mind. Junebug was lucky to have her—that was for sure.

Jessica didn't do this often...only when she was feeling particularly vulnerable or if she ached emotionally, or a dog did. And it had been a while now, so she was due. She wandered slowly down the aisle until she found the right one for tonight and opened the door to the kennel.

The dog was a mix but had that super distinctive look of a pit bull. With her big square head, her wide-set eyes, and her barrel of a chest, Millie looked like she could tear the arm off just about anybody with a minimum of effort. She was strong and intimidating and she scared a lot of people.

"If they'd just take a minute to look," Jessica said quietly as she closed the kennel door behind her and moved toward Millie, whose stump of a tail was wagging with glee. "They'd see that all you need is a comfy couch and lots of snuggles. Isn't that right?" She sat down next to the worn dog bed and Millie did that thing that all excited dogs did: her body literally vibrated with joy. She stayed quiet—Lisa had noted on her chart that she rarely barked—but she sidled as close to Jessica as she could get before depositing herself halfway into her lap. With a contented sigh, she settled her head against Jessica's stomach, happy as can be.

For the first time that day, Jessica felt herself relax a bit as she kicked off her shoes. Her muscles finally unclenched; she hadn't even realized she'd been tensed up. Her stomach stopped its incessant sour churning, though she really did need to eat. Her heart rate slowed a bit and her lungs seemed to calm their frantic in-and-out pace, instead pulling air in slowly, letting it out just as slowly. Her hand stroked Millie's short, white fur, traced the black spot on her side and another on her rump. The dog was warm and soft and Jessica, like Millie, let out a contented sigh. Though she wasn't a woman who felt the need to hunt for peace very often, she knew that this was it. When she sat with an abandoned dog late at night, in the dark quiet of the shelter, that was when she felt true peace. Her grandmother had told her the same thing, but Jessica hadn't experienced for herself until she'd run the place alone for the better part of a year. Since that moment, "going to the dogs" had taken on a whole new meaning for her. She came to the dogs whenever she felt the need for solace. They never failed her.

Continuing to stroke Millie's velvety fur, Jessica leaned her head back and closed her eyes, wishing to leave the day behind her.

The next thing she knew, Millie was lavishing warm kisses on her face and the red of the early morning sun was streaking through a window. Jessica blinked rapidly, then winced as her muscles and spine cried out in anguish from having spent so many hours on a concrete floor. A quick glance at her watch told her it was not quite 6 a.m.

"Shit," she muttered, and as soon as she moved to stand, the cacophony of barking and howling began. Lisa and at least one volunteer were usually there by seven to take care of breakfast, so that meant Jessica had time to get to her office and use the personal bathroom her grandfather had installed for her grandmother, complete with a shower. Thank God she kept a change of clothes handy.

Grabbing up her shoes, she stooped to give Millie a kiss on the head. "Thanks for keeping me company," she said, then let herself out of the kennel and hurried down the hall to the double doors. She had her hand out to push one open when it opened on its own. Both Jessica and Lisa jumped at the sight of one another.

"Oh, my God," Lisa said, pressing a hand to her chest. "You scared the shit out of me."

"Yeah, well, right back at you." Jessica, too, had a hand over her heart as she worked to catch her breath. "You're here early."

"And you never left."

"It's not the first time," Jessica said, with a shrug.

"True. Let me guess. Millie?"

With a smile, Jessica nodded. "She's such a sweetheart."

"For God's sake, take that little girl home already. You want to. I mean, I made the decision for Catherine. I can make it for you, too, you know." Jessica chuckled as she recalled how Catherine had fallen in love with the little stray escape artist. Any time he managed to slip away from his handler—and it was often—he found his way to Catherine. Nobody knew how or why he'd become so attached to her, but he had, and he'd made his way to her over and over again until she'd finally given in and adopted him as her own. She named him Geronimo because he leaped before he looked, and he adored her more than life itself. Jessica was pretty sure the feeling was mutual.

"I'll let you know if and when I'm ready."

Lisa shook her head. "Fine." They sidled past each other. "More telethon rehearsal today?"

Jessica tried unsuccessfully to stifle a groan. "Yes, but not as much as we've done in the past few days. Tomorrow is the big dress rehearsal. Today should be bearable."

"Good. 'Cuz it's Friday and we're doing Happy Hour and you're coming."

"Oh, I don't know. I've got so much to do. I'm way behind."

"I don't care. You're coming."

"God, does Ashley put up with this much bossiness?"

"Yes, because she likes it," Lisa said with a wink.

"Ew, okay. Enough." Jessica held up a hand to forestall any more comments, and laughed as she headed toward her office.

A very hot, very long shower helped immensely with the aching muscles, but it didn't completely restore them. "I am too old to sleep on the floor," she muttered to her reflection as she unzipped the little toiletry bag she kept under the sink and took out a tube of mascara. The circles under her eyes weren't super dark, but they were definitely there. Terrific. She found some cover-up she hardly ever used and did her best to make herself look normal. "I'll be damned if I let Sydney Taylor, she who never looks less than fresh as a daisy, see me looking old and tired."

Fresh, clean clothes always went a long way in making Jessica feel better and she almost moaned with delight as she slipped her leg into a pair of worn jeans that smelled like fabric softener. The purple T-shirt had the same scent, and once she was fully dressed and had dried her hair with the tiny blow dryer that she cursed every time she used it, vowing to get a better one—though she never did—she felt much better and ready to face her work day.

And that meant facing Sydney Taylor.

Jessica recalled the feeling of the almost-kiss, but didn't allow herself to dwell. "Shakin' it off," she said as she literally shook out her limbs and rolled her shoulders. "Just shakin' it off."

CHAPTER FOURTEEN

SYDNEY HAD SUCCESSFULLY SHAKEN it off. She was sure of it. The few things she'd wanted to go over with Jessica Barstow had run super smoothly. Jessica was a pro—there was no denying that. She instinctively knew where the camera was going to be the whole time, never missing a beat or looking in the wrong direction. She smiled perpetually, and it actually seemed genuine, not forced, which would go a long way in getting people to call and part with their money. Nobody wanted to donate their hard-earned cash to someone who seemed fake. Jessica was far from it. She was warm, charming, and approachable.

"Okay, next we'll do a piece with another dog," Sydney explained. "But I'd like to have the camera follow you right into the dog wing and stay with you while you get one to talk about. Is that okay?"

"Sure." Jessica pushed a lock of hair behind her ear. She'd left it all down today and the waves of auburn seemed to catch any source of light they could find to reflect back.

Sydney clenched her fingers into a light fist.

"It's going to be loud, though."

"Right. Maybe we'll follow you, but keep the dialogue to a minimum until you bring the dog out. Yes?"

Jessica gave an agreeable shrug. "Let's try it."

They went through the motions a couple of times, and Jessica wasn't kidding. Any time anybody pushed through those double doors, the barking and howling kicked up several hundred decibels until Sydney had to consciously *not* clamp her hands over her ears.

"Hmm," she said as they went back out into the lobby, which now looked more like a telethon set than an animal shelter. The phone bank was complete. The two separate sets at opposite ends of the lobby had been painted in cheerful colors. "Maybe that's too much. We don't want to deter people from coming by showing them how deafening it can be."

"Good point," Jessica said as she nodded. "In their defense, though, a lot of people have been milling around. Way more than usual. The dogs sense the change and it's got them more excitable. They're not always this spazzy."

"Well, we've got Lisa. Maybe we just have her bring the dogs out. While I'd like to show the size of the dog wing, I'd like to avoid the noise. Maybe we shoot from the door?" Sydney looked to Jeff for his opinion. He gave a nod. "Let's try that."

The afternoon went on like this, trying different methods, focusing on things that were or might become issues. All recorded interviews with volunteers and adopters had been completed and edited. She had a list of times and where everything fit. Brad had said just this morning how impressed he was with the way she'd managed the whole thing. She tried not to puff up with pride at the time, but that's how she'd felt. Live guests were lined up and scheduled and would be at the dress rehearsal tomorrow. Everything went smoothly and there was no residual discomfort from Jessica. In fact, it was as if the other night had never happened. Sydney couldn't decide if she was relieved or disappointed by that.

Despite Anna's constant, very close proximity, Sydney was impressed with the way she'd handled the social media end of things. Between her and David, word was out and anybody who couldn't actively watch television but wanted to follow the telethon could do so on Twitter, Instagram, Facebook, and

Tumblr. The shelter's website would show videos of adoptable animals for the next week.

All the bases were covered.

Back at the station that evening, she went over the schedule again, watched video, tweaked a few things, and generally made sure that every single thing that would happen on Sunday was planned and executed by her. She was in control. This was her baby and she was going to knock it out of the park. She'd told Laura exactly that when she'd answered her call while sitting in the editing bay.

"I'd love to say I'm surprised, Walters, but I'm not." Her voice held a smile that Sydney could almost feel. "You were resistant, but I knew once you relented and put your mind to it, you'd own this project."

"I'm hoping to bring in the most money of any of the telethons they've had in the past. That's my goal. You should hear some of the stories. They're amazing. This shelter has touched a lot of lives."

There was a beat before Laura said, "Who is this and what have you done with my very professional college roommate who doesn't let herself become emotionally involved?"

The comment was meant to be light—and it was—but Sydney bristled a bit. "I'm not emotionally involved."

"Okay, okay." This time, she could feel Laura take a step back. "All I'm saying is it sounds like you like this place."

Sydney closed her eyes and pinched the bridge of her nose, and it was as if the past three days of late nights and hard work simply fell on her. "I'm so tired, Laura."

"I was just going to ask if you're getting enough sleep."

"I'm not. And when I have the time, I don't sleep well."

"New surroundings?"

Yeah, let's go with that. "Uh-huh."

"Hang in there, kid. It'll pass. Just takes time." She paused for a beat. "What else is new? Make any new friends?"

"I got an e-mail from a station in Austin. They want to see more of my work, so I was thinking I'd wait until Sunday is over, then send them some clips from the telethon."

"That's great, but that's not what I asked you." Again, she could feel the gentle smile in Laura's voice. It helped to soften the rebuke.

"A couple. I haven't been here that long." Sydney tried to keep the defensiveness out of her voice, but was pretty sure she failed.

"I'm just checking on you. It's my job to remind you not to pour every minute of your time into your job. That's all."

"I know. I know. I promise I'm not doing that."

"Good. That's all I ask."

They talked about a few more mundane things, Sydney sent her love to Zack, then ended the call and focused on the monitors in front of her. She had just glanced at the clock, noticed it was going on eight, when her phone rang. She snapped it up without looking at it.

"Sydney Taylor."

"I love when you get all newsy and professional," Anna said. "It's very sexy."

Crap. "Hey, Anna. What's up?"

"I'm cashing in on your promise. You're late, but I'm going to allow it."

"My promise?" Sydney searched her brain, but came up empty.

"Yes. From this afternoon? I told you we were going to Happy Hour and you should come, and you said it sounded great."

Sydney didn't want to tell Anna she had zero recollection of that conversation, but she had zero recollection of that conversation.

"You were talking camera angles with Connor and Jeff?" Anna phrased it as a question, obviously realizing that Sydney was drawing a blank. "And I mentioned Happy Hour at Sling and you said, 'yeah, that sounds great, let's do it.' Remember?"

Feeling worse by the second, Sydney caved. "Oh! Yes. Yes, I remember now." She just needed to keep everything copasetic until Sunday evening. Then she could feel free to ignore Anna's calls if she wished.

"Well, get your cute butt down here," Anna said, clearly relieved. "I'll save a seat for you."

"Great." Sydney ended the call, then rubbed her face with both hands. She was really not up for more of Anna. And truthfully, she'd much rather walk to Bucky's, sit at the bar, and enjoy the jazz while she scanned the place for... She shook the thought away and began packing up her things.

The bar was barely ten minutes from the station, so she was there in no time. It was also hopping, if the overflowing parking lot was any indication. She showed her ID to the very large, frighteningly strong-looking, female bouncer, nodded when she smiled at her, and headed inside. It took a few moments for her eyes to adjust to the ultra-dim lighting, and once her ears were able to distinguish voices from the pulsing house music, she heard her name being called before she managed to see Anna clearly.

"You made it." Anna had changed her clothes, from her usual jeans and polo to nicer jeans and a snug navy blue shirt with capped sleeves. Her signature ponytail was gone, her blonde hair just skimming the tops of her shoulders. She looked very cute and was so clearly happy to see her that Sydney allowed herself a genuine smile.

"I said I would."

"I wasn't sure." Anna's expression of doubt made Sydney feel the tiniest bit like crap, so she turned up the wattage on the smile. "What can I get you?"

They sauntered over to the bar together and Sydney let Anna order her a beer. The bartender made tons of eye contact with Sydney, which she tried to deter for Anna's sake, and soon they headed to a corner table where three other women sat. Sydney knew Catherine and Emily, but not the other woman.

"So, you know these two," Anna said, waving a hand at the two without looking at them.

Sydney shook their hands. "Good to see you both."

Emily smiled, her brown eyes sparkling, and pushed a hunk of dark hair out of her face, as she said, "Nice to see you again."

"And this is Ashley," Anna moved on, indicating a pretty blonde. They also shook hands as Anna said, "She's with Lisa."

"From the shelter?" Sydney asked, failing to mask her surprise.

Emily chuckled. "Yeah, there's something in the water over there. Obviously."

"I'm just enjoying the fact that I'm here and *Lisa* is the one who's late." Ashley sipped from her clear drink.

"Ashley is notorious for her inability to be anywhere on time," Catherine said to Sydney. "In fact, we've taken to telling her that things are scheduled to start a full half hour before they actually are. That way, she's only a little bit late."

"Hey!" Ashley playfully swatted at Catherine and Sydney decided she immediately liked these people. They seemed genuine, down-to-earth. Not qualities she found a lot of in the business of television.

172

"So, Sydney." Catherine again. "Tell us how it's going with the telethon. Is it going to be okay or quietly disintegrate like a sand castle at high tide?"

"Oh, my projects don't disintegrate," Sydney said, holding eye contact with Catherine. A beat passed and she grinned. "Wow, that was obnoxious, wasn't it?" With a laugh, she sipped her beer. "Sorry about that. I'm a little punchy. Not enough sleep."

Instead of being irritated, Catherine laughed. "I like you, Sydney. You tell it like it is."

"I have to in this business. If I sugar coated things, I'd be run over before I even realized what was happening." She looked around the table. "The telethon will go off without a hitch. You guys have a great organization, a terrific cause, people love animals, and Jessica is amazing, both in her business and in front of the camera. I am nothing but confident."

"Speak of the devil," Emily said, then raised her arm and waved.

"There's my girl," Ashley said.

Sydney had her back to the door, so she turned around to look. Walking toward the table was Lisa, followed closely by Jessica. Jessica met Sydney's eyes, did a barely noticeable stutter-step, then approached the table with a smile that only looked slightly pasted on.

"Finally," Ashley said, as she stood and gave Lisa a kiss.

Lisa jerked a thumb in Jessica's direction. "This one tried to bail. I wasn't about to let that happen." Meeting Sydney's eyes, she smiled. "Hey, Sydney. I didn't expect to see you here."

"I dragged her," Anna said with a grin and a slight tone of possessiveness that set Sydney's teeth on edge.

Soon drinks were ordered and everybody settled in, talking loudly to be heard above the dance tracks that had a good-sized crowd on the dance floor. Sydney found herself sitting with Anna on her right and Jessica on her left and she forced herself not to make the face she really wanted to. The one that said, *Really, Universe? Really?*

Trying to ignore both the body heat radiating from Anna, who had inched her chair so close their thighs touched, and the intoxicatingly musky scent of what had to be Jessica's perfume or lotion, it took several beats for Sydney to register Emily's comment.

"Sydney was telling us what a television star you are, Jess."

Jessica's smile this time was genuine, if not a little bit self-deprecating. "Yeah, well, Sydney has to say that. She doesn't want me storming off the set in a huff."

Sydney chuckled as she shook her head. "Don't want that."

"She's been really amazing in front of the camera," Anna chimed in, and Sydney had to consciously not roll her eyes. Anna obviously had a thing about being in the middle of things, seeming important, and while Sydney could sympathize a little, she mostly found it grating.

"Yeah, yeah," Jessica said, literally waving a hand to wipe the words away. "Emily. How's the new job?"

"It's great," Emily said, and the glance she tossed Catherine's way was so clearly meant for only her that Sydney felt a tiny pang of envy.

"What do you do?" Sydney asked. She knew who Emily was in relation to the shelter, but not on a personal level.

"I run the marketing division of my company," Emily said, her smile friendly. Next to her, Jessica rolled her eyes.

"Please. What she's not telling you is that she runs the marketing division of Breckenridge and Associates, and her 'little company'"—Jessica made air quotes around the word—"is one of

174

the most successful companies in the city. They give a ton of money to Junebug Farms every year. You did know that part."

"Blah, blah, blah," Emily said with a wink. "My mother is a sucker for animals. I say let 'em rot!"

Catherine gave a mock gasp next to her. "I am telling both Mo and Dave that you said that."

"Dave?" Sydney asked, her eyes darting from Catherine to Emily to Jessica and back. "I've met Mo. Who's Dave?"

"Dave is Emily's sweetheart of a mutt," Jessica told her, leaning closer. Not that Sydney noticed or anything. Nope. "That she rescued from Junebug Farms."

"My mother rescued him, thank you very much," Emily corrected. "I don't really care about the beast one way or the other."

"Right. And that's why he sleeps in the bed between us," replied Catherine before sipping from her glass of wine.

Laughter rang out around the table and Sydney grinned. Yeah, she liked these people. She spent the next ninety minutes listening to stories about the shelter, updates on various relatives, and discussions about television shows. She didn't contribute a whole lot, but she had a great time listening and did a lot of laughing. She paced herself with the drinks, alternated with water, knowing she had to drive home soon.

"So, Sydney, what do you think of our fair city?" The question came from Ashley.

"It's nice," Sydney said. "I haven't seen much yet, but it's okay so far."

"Oh, but Sydney isn't staying," Jessica said, and Sydney turned to look at her.

"Well," Sydney said, feeling Anna's eyes on her as well as every set at the table.

"That's what you said, isn't it? You want bigger." Jessica finished the vodka tonic she was drinking. Sydney didn't know her well enough to know how alcohol affected her, but if she had to guess from this moment, she'd say it probably made her say things she normally wouldn't, and with a slight edge.

"I get that," Anna said, surprising Sydney. And everybody else at the table, judging from their expressions. "I mean, this is a nice city, but it's certainly not the big time. If you want more, you have to strive for more, right?" She looked at Sydney, her expression plainly broadcasting her need for Sydney's approval.

"Right," Sydney said with a nod. She felt movement next to her and when she turned back to Jessica, she was muttering, "excuse me," and heading to the doorway in the back with the *Restrooms* sign hanging over it.

There was a beat of silence at the table, and then Ashley said something about a movie she and Lisa had seen and conversation started up again.

"I'll be right back," Sydney said quietly and went off in search of Jessica, almost as if her body moved of its own volition. She didn't want to go find Jessica, didn't want to know what exactly was bothering her, didn't want to talk it through with her. Did she? But regardless of the dialogue happening in her head, her feet continued to take her to the restroom until she pushed through the door and found Jessica standing at the sink, hands braced on the counter, head hanging down between her shoulders. She looked up at the sound of the door, had brief eye contact with Sydney, then made a sound like that of a child who got a tuna fish sandwich in her lunch instead of the anticipated PB&J.

"You okay?" Sydney asked quietly, not really sure where to start. Or why she was even in this tiny room with two stalls that smelled much too strongly of the floral air freshener in the wall outlet.

Jessica didn't look at her. "Yep."

"Convincing." They were clearly alone and Sydney leaned her back against the closed door, flipped the lock so they wouldn't be disturbed.

"Look." Jessica finally made steady eye contact. Her jaw jutted forward slightly, telling Sydney she was angry. "I've had a rough, very busy week, and I had one too many cocktails, and I'm a little cranky. That's all."

"That's all?"

"Yes. That's all."

"Because it seems to me you're really bothered by the fact that I don't plan to stay here." *God, what are you doing? Just leave it alone.* Her brain screamed at her, but Sydney couldn't seem to keep the words in.

"I'm not."

"No?"

"No." Jessica's blue eyes were flashing now, flinty with anger and…something else. "I don't care what you do."

"Right. Because you don't even like me."

"I don't. You're right. I don't like you."

"Why not?" Sydney's tone was as hard as Jessica's and they sparred like tennis players, batting words back and forth. Folding her arms across her chest, Sydney refused to see the gesture as any kind of shield. Which she knew it was. The only reason she'd need a shield was if these words from Jessica stung. Which they did.

"You changed my entire telethon."

"I did. For its own good, yes."

Jessica seemed to abruptly run out of steam.

Sydney waited a beat before saying, "That's it? That's the reason you don't like me?"

Jessica looked down at her feet, took in a slow breath and puffed it out in frustration. "You could at least *see* the city, get to know it before you decide to leave." Her voice was very quiet, louder than a whisper, but not by much.

Sydney cocked her head to one side and raised her eyebrows. "What in the world could there possibly be in this city to make me stay?" she asked honestly.

She didn't even see Jessica move, didn't realize she'd closed the three steps that separated them, until Jessica grabbed Sydney's head with both hands and crushed their mouths together. And then she couldn't see. She couldn't think. She could do nothing but feel. And taste. And melt. Jessica's mouth was soft and yielding, yet aggressive and demanding. A dichotomy made of flesh and heat. She kissed like a goddess and Sydney's knees went weak as she thanked God she was backed against a door, something solid and sure to keep her from collapsing to the floor in a heap of desire, of want.

This was exactly what she'd tried to avoid the other night. *This* was exactly why she'd avoided that earlier almost-kiss. Because *this* was heaven. It was bliss. It was euphoria. It was also opening a can of complicated, unprofessional worms, but Sydney did her best to ignore that part.

And then she didn't care because Jessica's tongue was in her mouth and Jessica's body was pushing against hers and it felt indescribably *amazing*. Sydney cupped the side of Jessica's face with one hand and used the other to grasp her waist, pull her roughly, impossibly closer, and kiss her with abandon, driving all the cautions from her head and away like a lion tamer with a whip and a chair. Their tongues battled as Sydney gave as good as she got, the only thought rushing through her head now being *Oh, my God, we kiss* fantastically *well together.*

She had no idea how long this went on, but the rattling of the doorknob followed by the insistent knocking that sent vibrations through Sydney's back were enough to yank the two women back to reality. They returned reluctantly, as the frustrated and annoyed expression on Jessica's face probably mirrored Sydney's, she was pretty sure Jessica hadn't wanted to resurface either. They stood for a beat, silent, before Sydney finally spoke.

"Well. That was a hell of a sales pitch."

Jessica smiled and her already flushed face turned a deeper red. "You don't think I oversold it?"

"Oh, no. No, not at all," Sydney said quickly with a light chuckle. "This city should give you a raise." She paused for a beat, then continued. "It was…surprising. To say the least."

"Yeah…"

More banging on the door. "Come on!" a voice said from the other side. "Get a room and let people who have to pee in!"

"Okay! Just a second." Sydney's eyes never left Jessica's as she spoke. She didn't let go of her; they were still close enough to start another volcanic-level-hotness make out session, and Sydney had to admit she was tempted to do just that. "What do we do now?" she whispered.

"I have no idea," Jessica whispered back.

"At least we're in agreement." Sydney's grin was tender, as was the one Jessica gave back to her. "Okay. You go out. I'll hit a stall and wait a couple minutes."

Jessica nodded, but didn't move, and they held each other for another long—but not long enough—moment before more banging ensued. "We were talking about tomorrow's rehearsal. Got it?"

"Got it." Sydney couldn't help it: she kissed Jessica once more, gently, softly, then pulled away and headed to a stall without looking back. She closed the door to it just as she heard a voice say, "Jesus Christ, it's about damn time," followed by Jessica's mumbled apology. Sydney sat down on the lid of the toilet, dropped her head into her hands, and sighed.

What the hell had just happened?

She could hear the two women who'd come in talking animatedly about the DJ and the music. One was at the sink, the other closed in the stall next to Sydney. Apparently, Stall Girl had requested a song and was irritated by how long it was taking it to be played. Sink Girl tried to tell her to be patient. Sydney silently wished she had that simple a problem right now, because, as awesome as that kiss just was, there were consequences. Effects. So many. So, so many. There was the telethon and the fact that she and Jessica had to work together, all day long, for the entire upcoming weekend. There were complications. Like Anna. Like the Austin television station. Like the Raleigh television station. And the three others reviewing her reel. Like she wasn't really a relationship kind of girl, but she was almost certain Jessica was. And yes, she was jumping way ahead here. So incredibly far ahead, but she couldn't seem to help it. At all. Because in order to see herself with Jessica, she could only manage to see a full-fledged relationship. There was no casual sex. It wasn't scratching an occasional itch. It was an honest-to-goodness relationship. That was all she could see, and she wasn't equipped for that.

She shook her head.

"What the hell do I do now?" she asked quietly as she heard the two women leave.

Not surprisingly, nobody gave her an answer. She returned to the table with the question bouncing around her head nonstop.

What the hell do I do now?

It was weird how their little group seemed to disperse immediately after that. Before Sydney even had time to understand that it was just the two of them left at the table, Anna whirled on her.

"What the hell, Sydney?" Her voice was the perfect combination of hurt and anger, as was the expression on her face.

"What do you mean?" A lame response, for sure.

"Do you think I'm stupid?"

"Of course not. No. I don't think you're stupid." Sydney felt awful. She could feel nervous sweat break out under her arms, and she tried to swallow down the sourness that was creeping up from her stomach.

"I don't do that," Anna said then, downing the remainder of her drink. "I don't share. If you're with me, you're with me. You don't get to have your cake and eat it, too."

Okay, hang on a minute. Sydney didn't say those words out loud, but instead squinted at Anna, forced herself to mentally count to five before busting out with what she was really thinking. *Just two more days. Keep the peace for two more days.* "To be absolutely clear, I never said I was with you, Anna." She paused to let those words hopefully sink in. "But you're right. I was rude tonight, and I apologize if I embarrassed you." That was good, right? Clearing up the assumption of possession, but still being a good human.

"You did embarrass me."

"I know. I'm sorry."

"Fine."

In the parking lot, it was clear Anna was still hurt and—shockingly—didn't seem to want to talk. Using that to her advantage, Sydney apologized once more, squeezed Anna's upper arm, and got the hell out of there, swearing out loud her entire drive home.

Later that night, her phone buzzed indicating a text, but when she saw Anna's name, Sydney simply set the phone back down and ignored it. She didn't have it in her. She didn't want to fight with Anna and she didn't want to think about the softness, the heat, the responsiveness of Jessica's mouth on hers.

God, she wasn't sure how much longer she could do this.

And now she'd tossed Jessica directly into the fire...

CHAPTER FIFTEEN

BY 6:30 ON SATURDAY morning, Jessica had already been lying awake in bed for nearly three hours. The cats surrounded her as if they were keeping her from tipping over, one warmly tucked into her stomach, one leaning against the small of her back, the third in the crook of her knees. She'd watched the clock, hoping sometime around 3:45 that their gentle purring would lull her to sleep, but she wasn't that lucky. She watched the red numbers as they changed, stared at the sky outside her bedroom window as it went from black to deep indigo to dusky purple to crimson red. Rubbing an eye, she pictured the dark half-moons that would probably underscore them and thought with amusement that Bridget would finally have her work cut out for her.

What have I done?

She should be up, showered, and well on her way to the shelter by now. Instead, this question pinballed around her brain in the wee hours. On the one hand, it had felt good—*God, could Sydney kiss*—felt good to release the frustration she'd been bottling up for a while now. She was attracted to Sydney Taylor. Ridiculously so. That was fact, and acting upon that fact hadn't been entirely crazy. It felt right and Sydney had kissed her back in a big way, so there was definitely something there for both of them. Which was an enormous relief, because throwing caution to the wind and kissing somebody who didn't really feel what you did would be horrendous and awful. It made her ill to even entertain what might have happened if Sydney had pushed her away.

But she hadn't.

The rest of the night at the bar had been blissfully short, which was good because, though she'd said nothing, Anna had glared at her for the remainder of their time together. The others had given her quick looks, but nobody said anything about what they *must have* suspected had gone on in the ladies' room. Lisa and Ashley wanted to get home, and as Lisa was her ride, Jessica was able to bid the table farewell and get out of there before too many questions were asked. Though she got a very poignant look from Catherine and knew she'd have some explaining to do. She'd also have to deal with Anna today.

Today.

It was rehearsal day and then tomorrow was the actual, very live telethon. Jessica wasn't normally that nervous about it at this point. She was a little; that was to be expected. But she'd done this for five years now, and by this time in the proceedings, her nerves had calmed. She was almost a seasoned pro. Granted, Sydney had her participating in way more on-air segments than she was used to, but she could do it.

Sydney.

Scooby shifted and Jessica was able to roll onto her back (finally) and stretch her legs out (*finally!*) even as the beautiful face of Sydney Taylor drifted through her mind's eye. She'd be with Sydney for a large percentage of the next two days. With her, next to her, seeing her, smiling at her, smelling her. *That's* what had her so nervous. At least she could admit it.

"Okay. Enough of this uselessness," she said aloud, gently nudging each feline. "Move your furry bodies and let's get some coffee."

In less than two hours, she strolled into the shelter, feeling guilty that she was later than usual. It was still a bit of a surprise to walk in and see all the sets in the lobby, the lighting equipment and phone cords running under industrial mats that had been brought in just for the purpose of covering them. They didn't need anybody deciding a trip-and-fall lawsuit would be fun.

It didn't look like any of the public had arrived yet, though they would, as Saturdays were notoriously busy. But Junebug Farms had just opened, so the only people shuffling around were volunteers. Nobody from Channel Six had even arrived yet.

Thank God. Now Jessica had time to prepare herself for facing Sydney. They'd had no interaction other than a wave goodbye last night once they'd exited the ladies' room, so there'd been no discussion of what had happened. Jessica wasn't sure there should be. But she also didn't know what Sydney was thinking, how she was feeling, if any of this kept her up or if she'd slept like a baby.

"I guess I'll find out," she said aloud as she headed into her office.

"Find out what?" Catherine was right behind her, and Jessica gave a little yelp.

"God," she said, hand pressed to her chest. "You scared the crap out of me."

"Sorry," Catherine said as they entered the office.

Jessica set her stuff down on the desk. When she looked up, Catherine had made herself comfortable in one of the chairs, crossed her legs, folded her hands on her lap, and looked expectant.

"What?" Jessica asked.

"You know what."

Damn it. Jessica sat down and looked out the window. The day had dawned brightly and now the grounds were sunny, inviting, the grass lush, the petunias in full bloom. She chewed on her bottom lip for several moments before turning in her chair to face Catherine.

"We sort of…made out. Last night. In the bathroom."

"You *sort of* made out?"

"Okay. Fine. We made out. We were making out in the bathroom." Jessica held Catherine's gaze for a beat before covering her face with both hands and groaning loudly.

"Yeah, no kidding." Catherine said. "Now what?"

Jessica looked at her, tried to read the very neutral expression on her face, and threw her hands up. "I have no idea. I have no idea what." She shook her head. "I have never been this out of sorts before, Cat. Over a woman, for God's sake. It was a kiss. One kiss." She wet her lips. "One super long, super awesome kiss, but still. One kiss. And now it's like my brain has short-circuited. It's all wonky. I can't think straight."

"Here's a crazy idea," Catherine said as she sat forward in her chair. "Have you talked to Sydney about it?"

"What? No! No, of course not. I'm sure it was nothing for her. I was kind of drunk. I made the move. We know she made out with Anna there as well. She's on television. It's probably no big deal to her. I can't have her thinking I've got some sort of crush or something. I'd be humiliated."

Catherine seemed to think about her next words, sort through them in her head before finally saying them out loud. "Do you think that's how it would go? That Sydney thinks you have a crush on her and that you're…what? Silly?"

"Probably." Jessica sounded like a pouting three-year-old and she knew it.

Catherine cocked her head and arched one eyebrow.

"Okay, fine. Fine. Probably not." Jessica wrinkled her nose. "I hate you, you know."

"Oh, I know." Catherine sat back, elbows on the arms of her chair, laced her fingers together and tapped both forefingers against her lips. "So…what do you think you should do next?"

"I don't know."

Another arched brow. "Okay. Let's look at your options, shall we?"

"I hear sarcasm."

"You have good ears."

"Ha ha."

"Option one: you say nothing. You coexist. It's probably awkward and uncomfortable today and tomorrow. But then tomorrow is over and you probably don't see each other again if you don't want to. Yes?"

"Yeah." Jessica grudgingly listened. Catherine was good at listing pros and cons, and while it made Jessica grind her teeth at times, she was almost always able to see clearly afterward.

"Option two: you talk to the woman. You can be light about it. Joke about the bathroom make out session. You can be serious about it. Ask how she felt and how she feels now. You can get heavy, pour out your heart, tell her you were up all night worrying about it." At Jessica's raised eyebrows, Catherine gave a gentle scoff. "You look like you're playing outfield with those dark circles."

"Terrific. Thanks."

"No worries. That's why God created makeup." Catherine looked at her for a long beat. "So? What's it gonna be?"

Jessica sighed in defeat. "Fine. I'll talk to her."

"I thought you might."

"I hate you."

"So you've said." Catherine stood with a grin and turned to go. Looking back at Jessica, her smile softened as she said, "Jess. It'll be okay. Stop worrying."

Jessica nodded and gave a smile back, watched as Catherine left her alone in the office with her thoughts. She replayed all the conversation from last night and a glance out the window showed the big, white Channel Six van pulling into a parking spot. She watched as a sedan pulled in next to it and Sydney exited the passenger side. She was looking down at her tablet, but the sun glinted off her dark hair like it was bouncing off spun silk. Unsurprisingly, she wore business attire. Tan dress slacks and a black short-sleeved top. A black-and-tan lightweight scarf was draped around her neck and the gold watch on her arm slid loosely up and down as she gestured to Jeff near the van, then moved toward the door of the shelter.

Jessica took a deep breath and let it out slowly.

"I guess it's now or never."

≪

How ridiculous is it that I don't get butterflies before going on live television, but I have them now when I'm about to see the woman I made out with last night?

Sydney shook her head at herself. This is how her train of thought had been going since the wee hours of the morning. Sleep had laughed at her and left her bedroom to find more deserving people to visit while Sydney had lain awake trying not to replay every moment of the bathroom incident, but doing exactly that.

Which was infinitely better than replaying that scene with Anna after everybody had left.

She did her best to box up the subject and put it on a high shelf in her brain for now as she pushed through the front doors of Junebug Farms. It was blissfully quiet for the moment—or as quiet as an animal shelter can conceivably be—and Sydney walked into the lobby in full-on TV personality mode. It was the best way to keep control. She directed Jeff to where she wanted his camera. She accepted a steaming cup of mediocre coffee from

Regina – Volunteer. She went over the rehearsal schedule with Connor.

I got this. I'm running things. I'm the boss here.

Well, Connor was really the boss, but Sydney didn't care. This was working. The mantra ran in her head, loud and strong, for the better part of twenty minutes. She was in her zone. In the groove. She snapped her fingers and people did what she said. The wheels were turning on her well-oiled machine. This was going to be great.

Then she looked to her left and saw Jessica walking toward her from the hallway to her office. And the wheels came right off that well-oiled machine. Just...popped off. Spun away in different directions, never to be seen again.

"Hi," Jessica said, and her smile was pretty, but seemed a bit forced.

"Hey," Sydney said back, and felt immediately that her own smile was much too wide.

"How are you?" Jessica asked.

"I'm good. You?"

"I'm good."

They stood facing each other, eyes darting, hands fidgeting, voices silent. Sydney swallowed. Jessica looked off into the distance as the sound of barking seemed to increase for no reason.

"God, good thing I brought my cover-up," Bridget said from behind Sydney, startling both her and Jessica. "What the hell happened to you guys last night? Neither of you look like you slept a wink." She shook her head and walked over to the pile of equipment where her makeup case was stacked.

Sydney turned to Jessica, who had flushed a deep red. Their gazes held for a beat before they both burst into nervous laughter. Which actually helped, Sydney realized, as it seemed to break a bit of the tension.

Connor approached them then and began talking about the schedule and that also helped keep any awkwardness at bay. Sydney had to work at it, but she was able to shift her focus to the job at hand. And from the way Jessica seemed to relax over the next hour or so, she seemed to have the same success.

Thank God.

Jessica's part in the rehearsal went off without a hitch, which did not surprise Sydney at all. The woman was a natural. That lasted about three hours, as there was time built in to the six-hour telethon for video clips, interviews, commercials and other things that didn't involve either Sydney or Jessica. After the three hours, she set Jessica free and focused on the phone bank volunteers who'd be answering calls, the regular shelter volunteers who would be on camera here and there, and guests who'd be appearing live to bring in their donations. One of those was Emily Breckenridge.

"My mom usually does this," she told Sydney as they went over her part, where she'd stand, where to look, all that good stuff. "But she's away on vacation, so she asked me, given my...ties to the shelter."

"Yeah, I'd say you're pretty attached here." Sydney had really grown to like Emily, and today that opinion was solidified. She seemed genuine and fun. "How long have you and Catherine been together?" she asked, keeping her voice low in case it wasn't public knowledge.

Emily's volume stayed the same, so Sydney had to believe it was known, at least here at the shelter. "Not that long, really. A few months." She glanced over Sydney's shoulder, then went on. "We met at the beginning of last winter, but it took me a while to win her over. Lots of expensive wine and fancy gifts. She's all about my money."

"She could stand to learn a few things about wine, though," came a voice behind Sydney, and she turned to meet the smiling face of Catherine Gardner. Catherine looked at her girlfriend and muttered, "Smart ass."

"You wouldn't have me any other way," Emily said.

"This is true," was Catherine's reply, and while they didn't kiss or even touch, their feelings for each other were so obvious and solid that Sydney was sure she could smell them in the air. Taste them. Hold them in her hands if she wanted to.

Not one to have ever been envious of somebody's relationship, Sydney found herself in unfamiliar territory and it made her feel weirdly unsteady to watch these two. She shook the thoughts from her head and focused on the task at hand, going over things with Emily a second time, then did a quick rehearsal. Concentrating on the work and purposely not looking at Emily while she stood anywhere near Catherine seemed to help a tiny bit.

"You got this," Sydney said when they finished. "I'm not worried." And she wasn't. While Emily wasn't as naturally relaxed in front of the camera as Jessica, she was good enough. A little nervous, a little jumpy, but mostly fine. And she would only be on for a minute or two. "Be here tomorrow by…" Sydney ran her finger down the schedule on her tablet. "Two. You go on at 2:45. Sound good?"

"Yes, ma'am." Emily tossed her a salute, then she and Catherine left the set and walked toward the hall where all offices except Jessica's were.

Jessica…

They hadn't really had much of a chance to talk about last night, it had been so chaotic all day. And while she'd initially

191

thought that was a good thing, the not talking about last night, now she had the weird desire to. At least a little. Like, just address it, so it didn't sit there like an enormous pink triangle in the middle of the telethon tomorrow. Today had been chaotic, yes, but tomorrow would be worse, so maybe she should just get it out of the way.

"I guess it's now or never," she muttered as she watched the cleanup process around her for a beat before heading toward Jessica's office.

Sydney stopped in the doorway and just stood there, watching, as Jessica leaned a hip against her desk and gazed out the window, her back to Sydney.

The royal blue top she'd worn today couldn't have been more perfect for showcasing the sensual beauty of her coloring. It was short-sleeved and had a V-neck, perfect for highlighting her creamy skin and the blue set off her eyes to the point of nearly making you gasp in surprise at the depth of their color. Sydney had almost said something, almost told her how amazing she looked, but didn't want to embarrass her in front of all the people present. Plus, Anna was nearby and Sydney figured complimenting Jessica might not go over so well with her.

Two more days.

She actually stood there, just watching Jessica, just taking her in, for a long moment before gently clearing her throat.

Jessica turned to look at her, and the blue of her eyes struck from all the way across the room. "Hey," she said with a hesitant smile.

"Hey back," Sydney said, then shut the door behind her and walked slowly into the office. "You did great today. Tomorrow will be a cakewalk."

"Don't jinx me," Jessica said, chuckling quietly as she pulled out her chair and sat.

"No worries. You'll be fine." Sydney sat in one of the chairs in front of the desk and there were several beats of silence. "So," she said, finally. "About last night…"

"About last night…"

"Yeah."

"What about last night?" Jessica propped her elbows on her desk and set her chin in her palms as she watched Sydney struggle to find words.

"I thought…we should probably talk about it."

"Probably."

"You want to go first?"

Jessica's laugh punched the air. "Um, no."

Sydney grinned. She couldn't help it. "You know what? I was really nervous to come in here, but now I'm not. Now? Now I feel happy. And I'm really glad to be sitting right here with you." *Wait, what?*

"You should see the look on your face right now," Jessica said, pointing at her.

"Yeah, well, this is the face I make when I open my mouth to speak and something I hadn't planned on comes out."

"Must be hard in your line of work then."

Sydney kept grinning.

"So…you're *not* happy to be sitting here with me right now? That was a lie?"

"No," Sydney said with a firm shake of her head. "That was the absolute truth. I'm happy now. And I was happy last night in the bathroom of the bar. I also learned something then."

"Yeah? Care to share?" Jessica had shifted so her chin rested against just one fist as she gazed at Sydney with such intensity Sydney was sure she could feel the heat from it.

"Yes. I learned that you kiss just as amazingly as I imagined you did."

"You imagined kissing me?" Jessica asked, and her cheeks flushed a bit.

"I did. And you blush a lot."

"Shut up, I do not."

"Yeah, you do."

"You like to tease me," Jessica said, and her voice had gone husky. And sexy.

Sydney swallowed hard and said, "I didn't come in here to tease you. Honestly, I was just going to leave it alone, not mention anything. Like last time. But…" She stopped, worried she'd already gone too far. It was as if her mouth had a mind of its own, just saying random things that she'd had every intention of keeping to herself. What was it about this woman?

"I was, too. And then Catherine said—"

"Wait. Catherine knows?" Sydney sat up a little straighter.

Jessica gave her a look. "Yes. And I'm surprised I didn't burst into flames and turn to a pile of ash given the eye daggers Anna was throwing my way. I just have to ask…are you two…officially a thing?" She didn't like asking the question, that was obvious.

"No." Sydney put every ounce of certainty into her voice that she could. "We're not. Officially or unofficially. She's become a little…inexplicably possessive, considering I've never indicated, intimated, or even pretended we were together. We're not. And we never were."

Jessica still didn't look completely convinced

"Look." Sydney released a huff of frustration and regret. "I didn't know she worked here. We met in a bar once, before I was even assigned to the telethon, and—"

"Uh, yeah, I know about that. You don't have to…"

Sydney really wanted to explain, but she let it slide for the moment. "How did Catherine know?" Sydney asked.

Jessica arched an eyebrow. "Really? 'Cuz I'm pretty sure everybody knew. We were in the bathroom together for a long time. With the door locked. I imagine my face was red when I came out. Your lips were swollen…" Jessica's eyes dropped to Sydney's mouth.

"They were?" Sydney asked very softly and raised a hand to her lips.

Jessica nodded, her eyes going a little bit dark, and Sydney watched, entranced, as Jessica stood up, rounded the desk, her gaze never leaving Sydney's. Once in front of her, she took Sydney's hands, pulled her to her feet, gently cupped her face with both hands, and pressed their mouths together.

Sydney's breath hitched. Her heart rate kicked up dramatically. Her eyes closed. Her hands landed softly on Jessica's waist, held tight as the kiss started tentatively, but quickly went from sweetly harmless to something a bit deeper, and then a bit deeper still. With Sydney in her heels, they were about the same height, so when she pulled Jessica closer, their thighs pressed together, their breasts melded.

God, this woman.

Sydney couldn't understand it, but she couldn't get enough. She pushed her tongue into Jessica's mouth, wanting to get closer somehow, knowing it was impossible, but trying anyway. Jessica's tongue pressed back, and Sydney heard herself release a breathy moan as she cupped Jessica's chin in her hand, seriously contemplating the idea of making out with her all day long.

And she might have…if the stunned voice hadn't interrupted them.

"Wow."

Both of them jumped, the sudden sound startling them apart, and Sydney turned to meet the pained eyes of Anna St. John standing in the doorway.

Jessica made a sound of anguish. "Anna…"

"What the hell, Jessica?" Anna stared, her eyes full of hurt and accusation. "Has every woman in this place decided to make sure I can't be happy? Is there a rule I don't know about?"

"Oh, Anna, no." Jessica took one step toward her, but Anna held up a hand and the expression on her face must have warned Jessica back, as she stopped. It would have kept Sydney rooted to her spot, too.

"And you," Anna said, and in an instant, the anguish turned to rage. "What's your deal? Are you trying to make out with every woman here? Do you have a bet with somebody? Who's next on the list? Catherine? Lisa?"

Sydney swallowed hard, couldn't manage words. Instead, she lamely shook her head, feeling so many things all at once: embarrassment, anger, indignation, sympathy. Also, horrible. She felt horrible.

"Sure seems that way." Anna turned flashing eyes back to Jessica. "Do you think I'm stupid, Jess? Do you think I didn't know what was going on in that bathroom last night? While I sat at that table feeling like a fool? You apologized, so I thought I'd give you the benefit of the doubt that you actually meant it, but then I walk in on…" She moved her hand in an all-encompassing gesture. "*This.*"

"Anna," Jessica tried again, and it was as if Sydney could see her shift into Placation Mode, something she must have to do with donors at times. Or people who surrendered animals maybe. It was damage control and, despite the gracelessness of the situation, it was soothing. "Nobody planned this. We didn't plan this." She tried again to take a step toward Anna, but stopped after one. Her voice was gentle. "I'm so sorry we hurt you. It wasn't our intention."

"*We* didn't plan this? It wasn't *our* intention? There's a 'we' now? You guys are a thing?" Anna turned her angry gaze on Sydney again. "You work fast."

Sydney shook her head again, annoyed that it seemed to be the only response she could come up with. "There's no we," she said quietly, feeling like a scolded ten-year-old, thinking things couldn't get any more awkward until they did, as Connor showed up, peering over Anna's shoulder from the hallway.

"What's going on?" he asked, his confused eyes darting between the three women, his face obviously registering the tension.

"Oh, no big deal," Anna spat. "I just came in here to ask Jessica something and found her with Sydney's tongue down her throat. You know, nothing unusual. Just another day at Junebug Farms." She turned and pushed her way past Connor, disappearing down the hall.

Several moments passed while Connor looked from one of them to the other, Jessica brought her fingers to her lips and closed her eyes, and Sydney stood still, shaking her head slowly from side to side.

"Well," Connor said. "That wasn't awkward at all." He waited another beat before saying to Sydney, "I've got a few things to go over with you when you get a minute. I'll be"—he jerked a thumb over his shoulder—"out there."

Sydney, grateful for a reason to stop shaking her head, nodded instead. "I'll be right out."

Connor held her gaze for a moment—she couldn't quite read his expression—and then he turned to go.

The room was quiet as Sydney looked after Connor for a beat. When she finally turned her gaze back, Jessica was looking at her shoes. Several beats went by.

"I can honestly say," Jessica began. "I have never had something go from so good to so bad quite so fast."

"I'd have to agree with you," Sydney said. "And I work in television, so that says a lot."

Their smiles were faint, but they were there.

"I feel awful," Jessica said with a grimace.

"Me, too."

"Can I ask you something?"

"Of course."

"Did you…lead her on?"

Sydney pressed her lips together and turned her gaze out the window. She could lie. She could feign indignation, throw Anna under the bus. But this was Jessica asking, and for some reason, Sydney wanted to be honest. She blew out a breath. "I think, in her mind, maybe I did. It wasn't my intention, I swear. But…yeah, if you asked Anna, she'd probably say I did."

"Why?" There wasn't any accusation in Jessica's voice, which surprised Sydney. She seemed more curious than angry.

"I didn't want to rock the boat." At Jessica's raised eyebrows, she said, "I know. I know. It's ridiculous, now that I look at it. I just…Anna and I had that…encounter a few months ago. A one-time, meaningless little…thing. We kissed, really. That's all. We didn't even know…each other." She released a sigh of frustration. "You know all that, it's just embarrassing to admit. I knew I had this project, and I wanted to do a good job. I didn't know I'd run into her here. I never expected to run into her again, to be honest. But, there she was, and I just didn't want there to be any weirdness. I thought if I could play along, not upset her or make her feel bad, just keep things in a good, friendly space until after the telethon, it would make life easier. Turns out that was a really bad call." She gave a half-grin/half-grimace.

"Did you two…you know…?" The idea of it didn't sit well with Jessica, if the look on her face was any indication.

"No," Sydney said adamantly. "I swear to you. No. I haven't even kissed her since…"

"Since that first time in the bar?"

"Since *only* that time in the bar, before I knew she had anything whatsoever to do with Junebug Farms. Yes." Being honest felt good and Sydney took a step toward Jessica. "I am really sorry about this," she said quietly, reaching out to toy with the ends of Jessica's hair. "I knew she had a thing for me and I should've been really clear that I didn't feel the same way."

"Yeah, well, now *I* have a thing for you. Have for a while now."

"Yeah? Good, because I've got a thing for you, too."

"Thank God. You're a little slow, you know."

Sydney laughed outright. "Really? Because it's not like your signals are glaringly obvious. You don't *like* me. Remember? For one totally lame reason."

"Oh, I remember. That hasn't changed much."

Sydney stepped in closer. "No?"

Jessica shook her head. "No."

Sydney grasped her waist, tugged her closer, so their lips were scant inches apart. "How about now?"

"It may have changed slightly. May have. *Slightly*."

"Yeah? How about now?" There was no hesitant schoolgirl kissing this time. No chaste pecking. This was serious *making out*. Lips, tongues, teeth. When hands started to wander, though, Jessica pulled back. Just enough to be able to speak, but not enough to step out of Sydney's grasp.

"We need to stop," she said, and she was breathless, which made Sydney grin.

"I know." She was right. Connor was waiting. Anna may have been all over the Internet by now voicing her betrayal. And there was a telethon to run. "Can we...do you have some time later?" Sydney's voice was small and hopeful and she hated that.

"Absolutely," Jessica said. "Meet me at Bucky's?" Sydney tamped down her disappointment but Jessica must have seen it first. "I think we need some neutral territory to talk. You know?"

Sydney nodded. Jessica was right. Again. "Okay. I'll meet you there at...when?"

"I'll be here until at least seven. Meet me at eight?"

"You got it." There was a moment when they simply looked at each other, held eye contact, and the connection between them was like a power line, warm and charged and sexy, and Sydney groaned, which made Jessica grin. "What is happening here?" Sydney asked, bewildered. "I don't understand it."

"I don't know," Jessica said, but the grin remained. "We'll talk about it tonight, okay?"

Sydney nodded, blew out a breath.

Jessica gave her a quick peck on the lips. "Now go."

Sydney did as she was told, but at the doorway, couldn't stop herself from glancing back over her shoulder. The fact that Jessica was still looking at her with darkened, hooded eyes made everything south of her waist constrict deliciously. It was hard to keep going, but she managed.

Out in the lobby, Connor was all business. As soon as he saw Sydney, he punched up the schedule on his tablet and went over it with her. "I think this, this, and this are tight," he said, pointing to three different segments. "Edits are just about done on these two pieces," he informed her about a couple video interviews. Then he looked up and pointed at the phone bank. "Lines are good to go. Volunteers are all lined up and know what shifts they have. Everything seems to be running smoothly."

There was an edge to his voice. Sydney simply looked at him and waited. He sighed, kept his eyes riveted to a far corner of the lobby and said quietly through clenched teeth, "Except my host is apparently banging my shelter CEO."

Sydney waited a beat, let the angry wave rush through her and out before she spoke. She kept her voice even and low, despite how insulted and embarrassed she felt. "First of all, who I'm banging is none of your business. Second, I'm not banging her. And really? Banging? Are you fourteen? How about a little respect, for God's sake?"

Connor inhaled, let it go very slowly. "You're right. I'm sorry. It's just…a snag I wasn't planning on."

Sydney snorted. "That makes two of us, dude."

They stood next to each other, gazing at the sets, at the people milling around—both visitors of the shelter and employees of Channel Six—and were quiet for a beat. Anna was nowhere to be seen, and for that, Sydney was grateful. She'd really stepped in it there and was going to have to fix it, but right now, her mind was so full, so overwhelmed, she didn't think she'd be able to form actual words for Anna, let alone have them make sense. She'd wait until she had time to think.

"Back to the station?" Connor asked. "We can go over some final details, make sure we've got all our bases covered?"

Sydney glanced at her watch. It was 2:46 in the afternoon. She had a good three and a half hours before she needed to think about getting ready for tonight. And just the thought of it made her heart skip in her chest, her stomach flutter.

She had a date.

CHAPTER SIXTEEN

I THINK I HAVE A DATE.

That simple thought brought such a huge smile to Jessica's face she actually looked around to make sure nobody saw her, lest they wonder what was making her look like a giant weirdo, walking around with a massive grin. It was close to seven and there was no way Jessica was staying past then. No way.

She glanced out the window at the parking lot for what seemed like the fiftieth time since Anna's blowup at her, but still didn't see her car. Apparently, she'd left right after that, and nobody had seen her since. Not that Jessica could blame her.

A rap on her door had her glancing up while praying it was something simple. Catherine stood there.

"Hey, have you seen Anna? I need to run something by her for tomorrow."

Jessica bit her bottom lip. "I haven't."

Catherine squinted at her and there was a beat of silence from her while Jessica tried not to squirm in her chair. "Okay. What's going on?"

"Damn you. How do you do that?" Jessica sat back in her chair, indicated for Catherine to sit across from her. When she was settled, Jessica told her the story. All of it, from she and Sydney addressing last night to her bold assertiveness to Anna walking in on them.

"Oh, shit," Catherine said, summing it all up nicely.

"Yeah."

"And she left when?"

"Like, three hours ago. She's not answering her cell?"

"Straight to voice-mail," Catherine said with a shake of her head.

"Son of a bitch." Jessica felt irritated and awful at the same time. Awful because she'd caused this. Irritated because Anna had a job to do, damn it, and she needed to do it regardless of how pissed off she was or at whom.

"What happens now?" Catherine asked.

"I don't know," Jessica said honestly. "I guess I wait her out. I mean, if she doesn't want to answer, she's not going to answer. There's not much I can do about that."

"I meant with Sydney," Catherine said, one eyebrow arched in amusement.

"Oh."

"Yeah."

Jessica was annoyed to feel her face heat up. Apparently, Sydney was right about the blushing. "I'm not totally sure, but...we have a date tonight."

"You do?" Catherine sat forward in her chair with renewed interest. "Jess, that's great."

"I mean...I think it's a date."

Catherine gave her a look. "Explain."

Jessica took a deep breath and then did, ending with, "So, she asked if I had some time later and I suggested Bucky's."

"That certainly sounds like a date."

"Right?"

"Picking a public place was a good idea. There's no pressure that way. What will you talk about?"

"I have no idea what I'll say." Jessica blew out a breath. "This is all so weird, Cat. I mean, it started in such a different place from where it is now."

"I know. I totally get it. Same thing happened with me and Emily."

Jessica remembered the beginning of Catherine and Emily. How they hadn't really gotten along. How Catherine had judged Emily for her money. How Emily had worked like an obsessed person to win Catherine over. How others had nearly ripped them apart, herself included. How happy they were together now. "So. I guess we'll just see what happens."

"Can I offer a piece of advice?" Catherine asked, and her expression was so full of friendship that Jessica's eyes welled a bit.

"I'd love it if you did."

"Be honest."

"I can do that. I really have no idea what's happening." Jessica chuckled. "I'm attracted to her. Have been since the beginning. But I have no idea if it's anything beyond that."

"So find out."

Jessica gave a nod.

"In the meantime, what do we do about Anna?"

With a frustrated sigh, Jessica said, "I guess we figure out what she's taking care of tomorrow, just in case, and make sure somebody else can cover if necessary."

Catherine's eyes widened in surprise. "You think she won't show?"

"You know her better than I do. Do you?"

Catherine thought about it. "I don't know. I honestly don't."

"I don't either," Jessica said, and suddenly felt so weary, she was pretty sure if she put her head down on her desk, she'd fall immediately asleep. "I do know she was hurt and angry. I'd also like to think she's responsible enough not to completely shirk her duties, but…" She looked out the window as if Anna's car may have magically appeared since the last time. "I feel terrible."

"Yeah, I know, and not to sound callous, but you have a telethon to worry about. Not to mention a date in…when?"

Jessica glanced at her watch. "Oh, my God, in forty-five minutes! I have to change!" She sprang out of her chair like somebody had pushed the ejector button, gathered up her things, Catherine watching her the whole time.

"Well, this is going to be fun."

"Stop it," Jessica said, but grinned.

"No way," Catherine said with a chuckle, as she stood to get out of the way of the Got a Date whirlwind. "You made things tough for me with Emily at first. I'm going to enjoy watching you figure this out." Her wink took away any sting the words may have carried.

"This is not a you and Emily thing. Sydney's not even planning to stay here," Jessica said as she shook her head, gathering her things. Instantly, her stomach soured. Right. What was she doing? Sydney didn't even plan to *stay*— No. She wasn't going to dwell on the future, damn it, except so far as making it to Bucky's on time. "It'll work itself out," she mumbled.

"Hey," Catherine said.

Jessica glanced at her.

"You said it yourself," Catherine said softly. "It'll work itself out." She laid her palm on Jessica's forearm and gave it a gentle squeeze. "Let it."

Jessica nodded, then they hurried out to the parking lot together. When they parted ways to go to their respective cars, Catherine's voice stopped her one more time.

"Jessica Barstow."

When Jessica looked up from her keys, Catherine smiled at her.

"Just. Breathe."

"Okay." Jessica gave a wave and dropped into the driver's seat of her car. Just breathe. How could such a simple directive seem so impossibly hard right now? She concentrated on her lungs, on taking in a slow, full breath, on letting it out very slowly.

Why was she so nervous? *It's just Sydney.*

≈

It's just Jessica.

Sydney kept saying those three words in her head over and over again as she sat at the bar in Bucky's and sipped one of the best Cosmopolitans she'd ever had in her life. *It's just Jessica. And Jessica is a client of the station. She's a cohost. She's a subject. Nothing more.*

Then she laughed. Out loud. Causing Henry to give her the side-eye. Not for the first time.

She'd arrived early, as was her habit. You were never, ever late for an interview because somebody else could scoop up your subject, just like that. You arrive early, you have things ready to go, you make them feel important. The icy martini next to her, extra dirty, was proof of this philosophy. She'd told Henry it was for Jessica…that's when the first side-eye had come. He'd made no comment. Just gave her a look and made the drink to perfection. So much so that Sydney had a hard time not picking up the glass to take a sip, it looked that good. Saving a stool on a Saturday night was no easy feat, but she'd managed, and at exactly 8:02, Jessica came through the door. And Sydney's heart stopped for a beat.

She'd gone home to change. Gone was the casual, denim-based shelter uniform she usually sported. Instead, she wore a casual, lightweight black dress with capped sleeves and tiny flowers printed all over it. Sydney had to pretend not to notice the neckline, which plunged more than she trusted her eyes to observe, leaving so much skin visible she had to take a large gulp of her Cosmo to swallow down a surge of desire. On her feet were wedges, and Sydney thought about how much taller than her Jessica would most likely be. Also a massive turn-on. From the shoes, Sydney's eyes wandered back up—too much bare leg to think about—until they locked with Jessica's. Her smile was smoldering and Sydney was suddenly at such a complete loss, she had no idea where things would go from here. That was disconcerting. Sydney always had a schedule. A plan. But not now. Not tonight. It was as if, over the past twenty-four hours, Jessica Barstow had walked in, taken Sydney's precious schedule in her hand, crumpled it into a ball, and tossed it over her shoulder with a laugh.

I am so out of my league...

"Jessie!" Henry's voice boomed across the bar, yanking Sydney from her trance-like state. She blinked rapidly and watched Jessica's gaze move away from her and to the bartender as she crossed to Sydney and took the stool next to her.

"Look at that," she said, picking up the martini. "You remembered my drink and had it all ready for me. Impressive."

"Well, I did remember your drink, but the truth is, Henry beat me to it."

"And honesty as well." Jessica held her glass toward Sydney, who picked up her own. They clinked. "Hi there."

"Hey," Sydney said. They sipped, each watching the other over the rims. After a moment, she added, "You got out when you said you would."

Jessica grinned. "Yeah, consider yourself lucky. I'm actually very bad at that."

"I believe it. And I do consider myself lucky."

Jessica made herself comfortable, hanging her purse on the hook under the bar and resting her forearms on the mahogany top. "So. How was the rest of your day? Is my telethon going to run smoothly tomorrow?"

"Smoothly? *Smoothly?* Oh, no. Your telethon is going to rock."

Jessica lowered her chin, but raised her eyebrows. "Those are big words, Ms. Taylor. Big promises."

"I never make promises I can't keep, Ms. Barstow."

"I see." Jessica's gaze moved so she was looking over Sydney's shoulder just before a voice registered behind her.

"Aren't you on the news?"

Sydney turned to face the young man. He had sandy hair cut in a fade and a very neatly trimmed beard to match. His blue eyes held intelligence. His hand held a frosty mug of beer. "I am. Sydney Taylor. Hi."

"I thought you looked familiar. Channel Six, right?"

"You are correct." She held out her hand, which he shook. His hand was warm, his grip firm but not crushing.

"Mitchell Crane."

"It's nice to meet you, Mitchell." Without missing a beat, she turned so Jessica was included in the discussion. "And this is my date, Jessica Barstow."

Jessica covered her surprise nicely and shook Mitchell's hand. "Nice to meet you."

"You, too." He turned back to Sydney. "Your date?"

Sydney nodded. "Mm hmm." She sipped her drink.

"As in date-date?"

"As in date-date, yes."

"So…" He cocked his head to the side. "I don't really stand a chance here, then, do I?" His grin was hangdog and Sydney found him kind of adorable.

"I'm afraid not, big guy. Sorry."

208

"Ah, well. Can't blame a guy for trying," he said, lifting one shoulder in a half-shrug. Then he gestured to Henry. "I'd like to buy these lovely ladies a drink, please." Henry gave a nod and placed two shot glasses upside down near each of them.

"You're a good guy, Mitchell Crane," Sydney said as Jessica held up her glass in thanks.

He blushed, the pink weaving its way under his beard to his high cheekbones. "Take care," he said, and left them alone.

"That happen often?" Jessica asked after a moment.

"More often than you'd think," Sydney said with a sheepish grin.

"Well, I would think it happens all the time."

"Okay, maybe a bit less often than you'd think."

Jessica laughed and Sydney couldn't help but smile. It was that kind of laugh, full of joy and warmth. "I'm your date, am I?"

"As far as I'm concerned, you are. That a problem?" Sydney surprised herself with the bold confidence coloring her voice.

"Not for me, no." Jessica held her gaze and Sydney suddenly understood what it meant to have an electric charge run between two people. She felt it in the pit of her stomach—and someplace much lower. "So," Jessica said, cleanly changing the subject, thank God. "Tell me about you. Siblings? No, wait—you said you were an only child."

"Correct. My parents got it right the first time."

"Same here."

"I know. You told me." Sydney lifted her glass. "To only children who never learned how to share their toys."

"I'll drink to that."

"Close to your parents?" Sydney asked.

"Unfortunately, no," Jessica said. "Mine were killed in a car accident when I was nine. I lived with my grandparents until I went to college."

Realization dawned on Sydney then. "So that's part of why you were so close to your grandmother. She raised you."

Jessica nodded once. "Pretty much. And Henry here"—she jerked her chin in the bar owner's direction—"was my grandfather's best friend from the service. So he had a hand in it all as well."

Pieces were falling into place now and Sydney found Jessica growing even more interesting as they talked. "You were brought up by people a generation older than your parents."

"I was. I'm kind of an old soul because of it." Jessica finished her drink, gave Henry the signal for refills.

"Where'd you go to school?"

"I got a business degree from Syracuse University, then came back here. I wasn't going to stay. I had big plans to work in New York City. But I went back to working at the shelter, like I had pretty much my entire life, and I just...really got into it. And once I had my degree, Grandma started to step back, gave me more and more responsibility, started leaving decisions up to me. She was a terrible businesswoman." Jessica laughed. "She loved the animals and knew everything about them, but the books and the numbers and the donations used to make her eyes glaze over, so I started to take that part over. I learned the ins and outs of the shelter and the animals from my grandmother. I came to Henry for questions about running a business."

"And your big plans for New York City?"

Jessica shrugged as Henry placed two fresh drinks in front of them and took the markers away with a wink. "Plans change. That's the thing about life."

"The thing about life is that plans change?" Sydney furrowed her brow.

Jessica chuckled. "No, the thing about life is that you don't always know. Yeah, plans change. Sometimes. Sometimes, they don't, but…sometimes when they do, it's the right thing."

"Deep." Sydney teased, winking at Jessica.

Jessica bumped her with a shoulder. "Don't mock me. I am wise beyond my years. An old soul, remember?"

"I believe that."

"I'm just saying." Jessica's gaze met hers, held, and her voice took on a more serious tone. "Plans change."

Sydney blinked at her and it was as if the rest of the bar just faded away. All the sound, all the people, everything. Gone. It was Jessica and Sydney and the space between them. That was it. *What is happening here?* Sydney's mind posed the question, but she had no answers. Or she did, but refused to examine them. "I want to be alone with you," she heard herself say. Quietly. Pleadingly. Full of promise. And desire.

Jessica made no verbal response, but her head bobbed up and down in an enthusiastic nod. She signaled to Henry for the check.

Henry took his sweet time sauntering over to them and Sydney clenched her teeth tightly in frustration. "You want something to eat?" he asked, his eyes on Jessica.

"No, thanks. Just the check," Jessica told him.

"You sure? Javier made an amazing gazpacho today."

"I think we're good." Jessica did a much more admirable job of being patient than Sydney ever would have.

"It's *really* good," Henry said, and Sydney noticed his eyes never met hers. "Cool and delicious. Got a little kick to it, just the way you like it."

If Sydney hadn't known to look for it, she'd have missed the zap of warning that flashed across Jessica's eyes. Henry saw it as well, and Sydney chuckled internally, making a note never to mess with Jessica when she was not up for being messed with. "Just the check, Henry. Please."

His jaw set, Henry gave one nod and his eyes brushed Sydney's as he turned to the cash register. When Sydney looked at Jessica, she rolled her eyes good-naturedly.

Out on the sidewalk, Sydney blew out a loud breath. "Wow. He did *not* want you to leave with me."

"He's the closest thing I have to a father figure," Jessica said, and her voice was light, but Sydney could sense the tiny sheen of defensiveness for Henry. "He's just looking out for me. He promised my grandma."

"I can accept that," Sydney said, and she meant it. "I wish I had somebody looking out for me with that kind of loyalty."

Jessica turned to look at her, her blue eyes subdued in the dim light of the street. "Your dad?"

Sydney waved a dismissive hand. "He and my mom are busy. They have a lot going on. They don't pay a lot of attention to my life." She could feel Jessica's eyes on her, even as she looked off down the street. She stretched her neck, rolled her shoulders, felt uncomfortable. And then Jessica's mouth was right next to her ear, her breath causing a ripple of arousal as it brushed her ear.

"Come to my place and I'll pay a *lot* of attention to you."

What woman in her right mind would say no to that?

◈

Every fiber of her being was screaming at her that this was a bad idea, that Sydney wasn't going to hang around for long, that she'd just end up hurting her, but Jessica didn't listen. She didn't care. All she cared about was getting her hands on Sydney Taylor. Like, now. They climbed the flight of stairs in silence and she slid her key into the lock, alarmingly aware of the heat of

Sydney's body behind her, painfully aware of how close she was, disturbingly aware of every little thing she wanted to do to her. Absently, she wondered if they'd even make it to the bedroom.

The door barely closed behind them when Sydney was on her, grabbing her with those beautiful hands, turning her around, coming at her with those full, sensuous lips. Jessica's back hit the door and she let out a small "oof" as Sydney's mouth crushed against hers. This kiss. *Oh, my God, this kiss.* Jessica admitted to herself then that she'd been thinking about, hoping for, waiting to experience this kiss all damn day. She'd ignored the thought, pretended not to notice it. But it had been there. All day. Any time Sydney had come near her, pointed out a direction or offered a suggestion, Jessica's heart rate kicked up and her stomach had tightened. She'd ignored it, but... Now, Sydney's hands were everywhere. Her mouth was everything. Jessica was quite certain she could kiss Sydney Taylor for the rest of her life and be perfectly happy.

How had this happened?

A war went on inside Jessica's mind. An epic battle. Logic versus pleasure. Business versus pleasure. Using her head versus pleasure. And pleasure was winning. In every fight and in a big, big way, pleasure was winning, because her body responded to Sydney like it hadn't in a very long time. Her blood rushed through her veins, all of it heading south. Her head was light, forcing any serious thought to the outskirts to be dealt with later. Her hands moved like they had minds of their own, skimming along Sydney's curves, burrowing under fabric to find hot, bare skin, scratching against it, squeezing it. Any time she was able to wring a moan or a gasp from Sydney, she gave herself a mental point and searched for another way to do so. And they hadn't even made it out of the foyer yet.

As if reading her thoughts, Sydney managed to ask, "Couch? Bed? Anything?"

Their foreheads touching as they breathed raggedly, Jessica chuckled. "I have both."

"Thank God. Take me to one of them. Now."

The demanding tone sent an erotic chill dancing along Jessica's spine as she slid her hand down Sydney's arm, grasped her hand, and whispered, "Come with me." Thanking the Universe she'd come home first and fed the cats so they weren't making nuisances of themselves now, she tugged Sydney to the stairs. This was not going to happen on a couch. No way.

Jessica rarely made her bed in the morning, but she'd made it today. Another stroke of luck from the Universe, as she led Sydney into a neat and tidy bedroom, wondering in a split second what she thought of the colors, the décor, the art on the walls. But it was made clear pretty quickly that Sydney was noticing none of those things. Her hands were on Jessica again, cupping her face and kissing her so deeply, Jessica whimpered. When the backs of her knees hit the edge of her bed, she sat abruptly, looking up at the most beautiful woman she'd ever seen.

They hadn't turned on the lamp. There was only moonlight, streaming through the open blinds and tinting the ivory room a sensuous blue. Sydney was gorgeous, still in her work clothes, her white button-down top open at the throat, open far enough to pull Jessica's eyes, even as she tried to resist. Jessica reached up from her sitting position, grasped the placket, began to unbutton.

"I've wanted to do this all day," she said, working the buttons.

"You have not," Sydney said, not stopping her.

"Oh, yes. I have."

214

Sydney looked down, watched Jessica's hands, and that alone was such a turn-on Jessica thought she might explode. One by one, as slowly as she could force herself to go, Jessica worked, and when she reached the last button, opened Sydney's blouse, pushed the sides apart, exposing the light pink bra lined with lace. *Pink. Good God. Pink.*

Before she could form any more coherent thought, Sydney took her face in both hands and kissed her again. With gusto. Jessica slid her hands up Sydney's torso, skimmed over her breasts, and pushed the fabric off her shoulders. Sydney let go of Jessica's face, wrenched their mouths apart, and shook her arms out of the sleeves. She stood there in front of Jessica in her dress pants and bra and Jessica was positive she'd never seen a sexier sight in her entire life.

"You're so beautiful," she whispered, her eyes never leaving Sydney's.

Sydney smiled and knelt down in front of her. Warm hands caressed Jessica's bare legs, up and down in a slow, lazy motion and while Sydney's gaze held hers, she lifted Jessica's right leg and removed her shoe. The other leg followed, and then Sydney straightened up on her knees so she and Jessica were nearly face to face. Jessica could feel Sydney's fingertips trail up the backs of her legs to her knees, stroke the backs for what wasn't nearly long enough, then Sydney's hands capped each knee and slowly pushed them apart. Jessica could feel every move Sydney's hands made, but she couldn't take her eyes from that sensuous mouth until Sydney leaned forward and kissed her again. And then everything moved into sensation. Jessica's eyes were closed, but she could feel everything. Sydney's soft lips against her own, Sydney's tongue pressing into her mouth, Sydney's hands sliding up the sides of her thighs, taking the fabric of her dress with them. Jessica dug her fingers into Sydney's dark hair, feeling the thick softness, smelling the scent of peaches or mangoes maybe. She made a small gasping sound as Sydney's hands found her center, one fingertip stroking her through her bikinis.

"Oh, my God," Sydney whispered, their lips mere millimeters apart. "You're so wet."

Jessica felt her face flush. "Your fault. It's what you do to me."

Sydney's finger continued to move, very slowly, up and down along Jessica's center, the only movement the two of them made aside from the hitch in Jessica's breath, which was growing more ragged by the second. The searing eye contact between them only made it that much more intense, and Jessica was surprised to hear herself whimper—a sound that tugged one corner of Sydney's mouth up and caused her to arch an eyebrow. Without taking her eyes from Jessica's, she slid her hands around to Jessica's hips, curled her fingers around the waistband of the bikinis, and gave them a tug.

"Give me these," she commanded in a nearly inaudible whisper.

Her hands flat on the mattress, Jessica pushed her body up, lifting her hips and allowing Sydney to slid the fabric down her legs and off. Their gazes never wavered from each other the whole time, and Jessica marveled at the intensity of it. She didn't have time to marvel long, though, as Sydney captured her mouth once again, this time pushing into her until she lay back on the bed. Somewhere in the back of her mind, Jessica wondered how she'd gone from holding all the cards on this date to having every ounce of control stripped gently from her without her even realizing it. *How had that happened?* She wondered for a moment, but then all thought was chased from her mind as Sydney's alarmingly adept fingers were again stroking through the wet, hot folds of flesh between her legs and unrecognizable sounds were being pulled from her throat.

When Sydney pulled back from her face, Jessica was shocked to see how very dark with arousal those gorgeous blue-green eyes had become. At that moment, she realized she might be having a similar effect on Sydney as the one Sydney was having on her. Taking that thought and running with it, she grabbed Sydney's face with both hands and kissed her like her life depended on it. When Sydney wrenched their mouths apart moments later, she was breathing as raggedly as Jessica had been.

"Wait," she huffed out. "Just…wait. My God."

Jessica grinned. "Just trying to give as good as I was getting." It was not lost on either of them that Jessica's lungs were working overtime as well.

Sydney looked at her and her face grew serious again. Jessica couldn't remember ever having looked at a woman and known—without the tiniest sliver of doubt—that the woman wanted her more than anything else in the world in that moment. That's exactly how Sydney Taylor was looking at her right now. And without another word, Sydney flipped the skirt of Jessica's dress up and buried her face between Jessica's legs. No warning. No preamble. Just a relentlessly determined mouth on the very core of her being.

Jessica cried out a strangled sound she'd never heard herself make before as it felt like every nerve ending in her body stood at attention, waiting for Sydney's command. Suddenly, they were back to sensation. Jessica couldn't pinpoint anything, but she could feel it all. She had no idea what was Sydney's tongue, her lips, her fingers. She only knew that her body was being owned—touched, tasted, stroked, higher and higher until she was sure her limbs would simply melt, that she'd spin off into oblivion, never to be seen again. And despite expecting it, the orgasm somehow took her by complete surprise, ripping through her body like a tsunami, wiping out every part of her until she was left wasted, a quivering mass of flesh on the bed, still nearly fully dressed, unable to remember her own name.

"Oh, my God," she managed, her arm thrown over her eyes. "Oh, my God."

Sydney moved, but Jessica didn't have the energy to lift her arm and look. And then Sydney's voice was closer, and she whispered, "Again," and Jessica's arousal cranked up a dozen notches unexpectedly just from the commanding tone of that one word.

Sydney didn't give her much time to warm to the idea, as her fingers were suddenly pushing inside and finding a rhythm, and it was like Jessica's body had completely disconnected from her brain, taking charge, moving with Sydney's hand, no thought or bargaining required. Just lust. Stretching her neck up, she caught Sydney's mouth with her own, kissed her for all she was worth, and before she had time to think, a second orgasm grabbed her with both hands, lifted her off the bed, and wrung her like a dishrag, squeezing every last bit of pleasure from her before dropping her back to the mattress in a heap of utter, wiped out exhaustion.

Jessica had no idea how much time had passed while she tried her best to recover, but when she opened her eyes, Sydney was kneeling above her, the smile on her face so smug it was almost comical. Jessica grinned for a moment, touched her fingers to Sydney's swollen lips before the grin slid away to be replaced by a much more sensual expression, if her train of thought was any indicator. She pushed herself to a sitting position, forcing Sydney to stand, and without a word, she reached up, unsnapped the front clasp of Sydney's bra, and took a nipple into her mouth.

Firmly.

Sydney gasped and Jessica could feel the fingers of both hands digging into her hair, holding her head in place. "God," Sydney said softly, and Jessica felt her back arch slightly, pushing her breast into Jessica's mouth farther. Jessica moved from one breast to the other, loving the surprising size of them. When her mouth was on one, her fingers toyed with the nipple of the other, back and forth, until Sydney could barely keep still…exactly the reaction Jessica had hoped for.

As wonderfully explosive and surprising as her double orgasm had been, Jessica was determined to draw this out. She wasn't going to push Sydney, wasn't going to force her over the edge. She was going to savor her, pull her along gently so that she didn't see the edge, wasn't even aware she was close to it, until she'd slipped over.

At least, that was the plan.

And she stuck to it as she lavished attention on each ample breast. Stuck to it as her palms ran over the smooth plane of Sydney's back, her nails lightly scratching, causing Sydney to drop her head back and hiss in a breath. Stuck to it as she moved around to the front and unfastened the fly on Sydney's pants, dropping them to the floor around her ankles. She stuck to the plan right up until the moment she slipped her fingers into Sydney's bikinis and felt just how drenched she actually was.

The plan dissolved like a sugar cube in a cup of hot coffee.

With a moan of desire and a growl of want, Jessica reversed their positions, spinning Sydney around so she landed on her back on the bed, and a small squeak of surprise popped out of her mouth. Before she could say anything else, though, Jessica silenced her with a crushing kiss as she pushed her fingers through the hot slickness waiting between Sydney's thighs.

Jessica quickly found a rhythm with her fingers even as she ran her tongue along the side of Sydney's gorgeous neck, licked a shoulder, lightly bit down on a nipple. Sydney was vocal, and Jessica found it to be such a turn-on, she thought she might erupt in flames right there on the bed. Every demanding "more," every satisfied "yes," and every whimpered "please," just pushed Jessica's own arousal higher, made her work harder, concentrate more, drove her to be closer, deeper, until Sydney finally crested with a stunned, high-pitched whisper of, "Oh, God, Jessica..." that devolved into a ragged cry of release. Hips came up off the bed, her neck strained as she arched her head back, squeezed her eyes shut, and Jessica winced as Sydney clenched a handful of her hair, but it was an exquisite pain and worth it for a view that Jessica was certain was the most beautifully erotic sight she'd ever witnessed.

The only sound now was the gently steady breathing coming from each of them as Jessica rolled off Sydney's body to lie on her back beside her. Sydney reached blindly for her, patting different parts of her body until she found Jessica's hand, brought it to her lips, and kissed the knuckles.

"You are a goddess," she said softly, eyes still closed.

Jessica's shoulders moved as she chuckled. "I'll take that. Slight exaggeration, but I'll take it."

"No," Sydney said, shaking her head, still with her eyes shut. "No exaggeration. I'm positive. Goddess." She pointed in Jessica's general direction and sighed. "Goddess."

"Well, if you're positive, I guess I can't argue."

"You can't."

The most interesting thing to strike Jessica in that moment was the ease. The overall, general relaxation. She turned to look at Sydney, to study her profile, the straight nose, the smooth skin, the sexily tousled hair, and the after-sex flush of her cheeks.

And she wasn't nervous with Sydney any longer. Not even a little. It was like any worry or trepidation had been expelled from her body with her orgasm (okay, two orgasms). She was perfectly content to just lie there next to Sydney, stare at her face, feel the heat from her body, the warmth of her hand.

She wasn't sure what to do with that.

Trying not to overthink, she turned onto her side to face Sydney. "I'm going to get some water. Want some?"

"I do." As Jessica moved, Sydney added, "And wine?"

"Demanding," Jessica said, one eyebrow raised.

"I'll make it worth your while."

"In that case, one water and one glass of wine coming right up."

She padded to the kitchen still in her dress, sans underwear, and her cats followed, twining around her feet as she got glasses, opened a bottle of Cabernet, and grabbed a bottle of water. When she returned to the bedroom she was surprised to see that Sydney was dressed. Jessica stopped in the doorway.

"You're leaving?" She hadn't meant to sound like a petulant child, didn't want to, but was afraid that's exactly how it came out.

Sydney smiled as she buttoned her shirt, but her eyes darted away. "I didn't realize how late it is. Big day tomorrow."

"But…the wine." She held up the glasses lamely.

"Yeah, I'm sorry. I didn't realize the time…"

She didn't really have a leg to stand on. Sydney was right. She'd just been hoping…what had she been hoping? Refusing to delve any deeper for an answer, she shrugged. "Yeah, you're right. This was fun, but…big day tomorrow." Annoyed that she couldn't even come up with her own line, Jessica set the wine and glasses down on a dresser. Picking up the water bottle, she handed it to Sydney. "Don't want you getting dehydrated."

"Thanks." Sydney stepped toward her to take the bottle, kissed her softly on the mouth. "I'll see you tomorrow."

"Okay."

And she was gone. Just like that.

Jessica stood alone in the empty room, hurt, confused, and angry.

ॐ

"What the hell just happened?"

Sydney said it aloud, but quietly, once she was out onto the street and walking in the direction of her own apartment. It was barely 10:30. Too early even to be doing a walk of shame. And yet she'd left. Just left. Actually, ran away was much more accurate. She ran away.

Why?

She'd been looking around the bedroom, taking in Jessica's personal items, the décor. The room was warm, inviting. There was art on the walls. There was a lush, thriving plant on a stand by the window. There were photos on the dresser of her and an older couple that had to be her grandparents. Another of her and Henry standing in front of the shelter. A third of Jessica, Catherine, and Lisa, smiling and happy, holding up champagne flutes in celebration of…something. Jessica's life was here. All of it. She had roots.

The thought made Sydney both envious and terrified.

She could still see Jessica's face, a mix of shocked surprise and disappointment tinted with a hint of confusion. "Big day tomorrow," Sydney said in an unkind mimic of her own voice, then shook her head. What was the matter with her? Seriously.

Her apartment building was fairly quiet, though the same couldn't be said for those around her. Several college-age and twenty-something partiers mingled on the sidewalk, red Solo cups in hand, obviously overflow from a nearby party. She breathed a sigh of relief when she slid her key into the lock and shut the apartment door behind her, muffling the music and conversation wafting up from the street.

The only light in the room came from the gently humming fish tank. Sydney tossed her keys on the counter, plopped herself onto the end of the couch nearest the tank, put her chin down on the arm, and watched Marge and Homer swim around aimlessly. There was something calming, relaxing, about staring at the fish as they swam, not a care in the world.

I can't get attached.

The thought came out of nowhere and snapped at Sydney like a wet towel in a locker room. But attachment hadn't ever been a problem. She wasn't a girl who got attached, so that shouldn't be an issue. Somehow, though, it had become an issue with Jessica.

Because Sydney could totally see herself becoming attached. In a big way.

Sydney closed her eyes, tried to push the thought from her head. Instead, her brain painted her a vividly erotic image of the view she had earlier. The view she had when she looked up from Jessica's center where she'd buried her face, her mouth. The view of the long, lean body clad in black fabric, auburn hair tousled and spread over the ivory comforter, chest heaving. God, she hadn't even gotten her hands on Jessica's breasts. Hadn't even undressed her completely, she'd been so blinded by arousal, so driven to touch Jessica's most intimate place, to hear her ragged breathing, to cause the sounds she made.

"If I'm honest, Marge," she said quietly to the fish. "I have to admit that my plan had been to end it there." Despite admitting it to a mere fish, Sydney still felt shame at the statement. "I just wanted to *touch* her." This time, she whispered it. "That's all. I just wanted to touch her. I didn't count on her turning the tables so quickly." *God, had she turned the tables.* And then the image in her mind's eye shifted until Jessica was above her, those blue eyes boring into hers, those long fingers working some kind of magic between Sydney's legs. "I had to get out of there. It was that simple. I had to." Sydney turned so she lay with her head back against the couch. "She went to get water. And wine. And I lay there thinking about cuddling with her and does she like that or is she not a cuddler and which side of the bed does she like to sleep on and would she be warm enough under just the sheet or would we need the comforter, too, and…I just panicked. It was too much. I just couldn't. I panicked. I panicked and I ran."

Even though it was the truth, Sydney was ashamed. Even Marge must've been disgusted, as she turned fin and swam in the opposite direction.

And tomorrow was the telethon. Not only would she and Jessica be together all day long, they'd be together all day long in front of a bunch of people and on live television.

My timing could not possibly suck more.

Trying not to dwell on that turned out not to be an option, because she tossed and turned for the rest of the night, pinballing between checking her phone every ten minutes, being disappointed that Jessica hadn't texted her, and hating herself for not having the balls to text Jessica first.

Sleep stayed well out of her grasp.

CHAPTER SEVENTEEN

DID SHE HAVE TO look so good?

Jessica had made up her mind about the role she'd play today. Aloof. Unconcerned. Maybe a little flighty even. So Sydney'd had sex with her—ridiculously hot, mind-blowing sex, but whatever—and then hightailed it out of there like the place was on fire, but that didn't mean Jessica had to dwell on it. Right? So they'd had a one-night stand. It certainly wasn't Jessica's first. Probably wouldn't be her last. She could play this part. No problem.

But did Sydney really have to look so damn good?

She was casual but not. Jeans, which were so not her professional attire, but fit like they should be and hugged her ass like a possessive lover. She—or the station, more likely—had had a camp shirt made for her with the Junebug Farms logo on one side and the Channel Six logo on the other, and the deep teal color of it made her eyes look even more intense than they usually did, and that said a lot. Her dark hair was shiny, the ends curling just a bit, and it looked so soft Jessica balled her hands into fists to keep from giving in and walking across the lobby to dig her fingers into it. Again.

Bridget had worked some magic and Sydney now sported her on-air makeup, which made her look prettier—something Jessica didn't think was possible. When Sydney had walked into the shelter, Jessica had literally felt all the air leave her lungs and had actually muttered, "Damn her," then looked around, hoping nobody had heard.

Completely contrary to Sydney Taylor, Jessica looked like a corpse that had been run over by a truck. Twice. Her pallor was gray. Her hair was limp. She had those damn dark circles under her eyes, announcing to everybody that she'd gotten little sleep. She blamed it on nerves, and that was only a partial lie, but it was mostly because she couldn't shut her brain off after Sydney had left last night. She warred with herself about whether or not to text. Sydney had been right: today was a big day. And if she'd stayed, they'd have most likely gotten even less sleep than Jessica had alone. So, she couldn't really hold it against Sydney, and she'd decided not to text. It was just…the idea of waking up with her had painted a really nice picture. So then she would sigh, feeling a bit of disappointed anger seep in. Then she'd flash back to their lovemaking and her view would soften just a little bit. All told, she figured she'd gotten maybe two hours of sleep. Maybe. And that had been somewhere just before her six o'clock alarm.

Bridget spent fifteen minutes doing damage control on Jessica's face, her silence enough to tell Jessica that she wasn't wrong about the state of her appearance. But one glance in the mirror had her smiling. "You're a miracle worker," she said.

"It's not hard when I have a good basic canvas," Bridget replied with a wink.

"Today, I will take that," Jessica said and squeezed her shoulder in thanks.

It was now or never. Time to face the music. Pay the piper. And any other cliché that meant it was time to be within the same three feet as the woman who'd turned her into a quivering mass of sexual pleasure last night.

She could do this.

Before she had a chance to cross the lobby, though, David approached her. He looked amazing, as usual, in his jeans and

226

black, tight-fitting T-shirt that showcased his hard-earned musculature, but his face was worried.

"Have you seen Anna?" he asked quietly.

Damn it.

"No," she responded. "I tried calling her this morning, but it went straight to voice-mail."

"Me, too." He gazed across the lobby, looking for everybody like they were having an everyday, normal conversation.

"David." Jessica looked at her shoes, not wanting to expose her private life, but feeling like she had to in this instance. "This is my fault."

David furrowed his brow, silently asking what she meant.

Without going into the nitty-gritty details of her sex life, she told him that Anna had liked Sydney, and Jessica had ended up spending a lot of time with her, which Anna discovered.

David was not happy about it; she could tell by the look on his face. She immediately flashed back to when she'd discovered Catherine and Emily were seeing each other, her concern for appearances, the disapproval she'd conveyed. "Listen, I'm not thrilled about any of this either. It wasn't intentional," she said to David, immediately recalling that Catherine had said almost the same thing to her.

"It never is," David retorted, but immediately seemed to regret his tone. "I'm sorry. It's just…bad timing."

"I know. I've talked to the TV people and we'll figure it out. I'm sorry."

He gave a curt nod and walked away, leaving Jessica to feel guilty, inadequate, and immature. And goddamn Anna and her unprofessionalism. Yes, she'd been hurt. By a friend and unexpectedly, if Jessica was going to be honest. But she had a job. And grown-ups did their jobs even when they were angry.

227

"Shit," she muttered, looking around the lobby at all the volunteers, TV people, and visitors readying for the telethon.

"Hey." Sydney's voice hit her before she was ready, before she was able to take a moment and prepare. *Damn her.*

"You know, you could at least pretend you were affected by last night." She'd snapped out the words before she could stop herself and now she was embarrassed, color flooding her cheeks.

Sydney didn't look at her, just stared at the schedule in her hand and said quietly, "I am affected. I am very affected. Give me some credit, for God's sake."

"I'd give you all the credit in the world if you hadn't fled like a rat from a sinking ship."

"Ouch."

Connor came up to them at that moment, began discussing the schedule, the timing, which cameras they'd be looking at, and that was a good thing because Jessica needed to pull herself together. She couldn't be this edgy, this snippy. Today's focus was on the shelter and raising money for it. She needed to concentrate on that, not on her wreck of a sex life. Not on the ridiculously attractive woman at her side that made her want to clench her thighs together just from being next to her.

She also, however, needed to deal with her missing public relations manager.

"I'm sorry," she said to Sydney as Connor went off to speak with the volunteers who'd be answering the phones. "I'm just nervous. I didn't get much sleep and…I'm nervous."

Sydney smiled tenderly at her. "You have no reason to be nervous. You're going to be great."

She was all business and Jessica guessed that was probably a good thing for the moment. She offered a crooked grin and said, "Hey, while we're on the subject of awkward moments, have you heard from Anna?"

"If you don't count the giant scratch on my car that I suspect was made by her key, then no." Sydney didn't look at her when she spoke, her eyes still focused on the schedule in her hand, but her voice was clipped, tense.

"What?" Jessica's eyebrows raised in surprise.

"Yeah. I came outside this morning to a giant scratch running from my front passenger side tire all the way to the rear bumper." Sydney didn't seem angry about it, though. She seemed…sad. Resigned. Guilty. Finally, she looked up at Jessica. "Why?"

"Because nobody has been able to get ahold of her since last night. And frankly, she has responsibilities today."

"I know. But…" Sydney looked off into the distance with those gorgeous eyes of hers. "Don't you feel a little bit guilty? I mean, we did this."

Jessica sighed. "Yeah. I know."

What else could be said?

Sydney looked at her. Really looked at her. Almost studied her. Then a smile broke across that beautiful face and she said, "You look amazing. You know that?"

Jessica felt the heat rush up from her chest, cover her neck, rest in her cheeks, and she looked down, the epitome of the shy girl. "Thanks," she said quietly.

"Let's just get through today. Okay?"

"Yeah."

They split up then, Sydney heading off to the control area to talk to the director and Jessica heading back to her office to try Anna one more time. On the way, she hit up both Catherine and Lisa, neither of whom had heard from her. In her office, she dialed the number and went unsurprisingly into voice-mail.

"Anna, it's Jessica. Listen. I know you're upset with me and I'm sorry about that. I honestly don't know what to say. You've known me for a long time and you have to know that I'd never do anything to intentionally hurt you. I just…people here are worried about you. I'm worried about you. Can you just call? Please?"

While Jessica did subscribe to some of what Sydney mentioned—the guilt, the shame for betraying a friend, however unintentionally—she was also the boss. And as the boss, she found Anna's irresponsibility grating.

Do your job. And if you can't do your job, at least call in sick so someone else can do your job. That's what her grandmother would've said.

She set the handset in the cradle. She'd done all she could. She'd be damned if she was going to let this ruin the day for the shelter. The telethon brought in more money than any other fundraiser during the year. It was huge and important and Jessica knew that Anna's disappearing act had been carefully timed for maximum damage. With a sigh, she headed for the door. The only course of action to take was to assume Anna wasn't going to show. It was time to delegate her jobs.

৵

The first three hours of the telethon had flown by. And even more smoothly than Sydney had hoped. She and Connor exchanged many a glance, as Jessica continually knocked it out of the park with her approachable professionalism and incomparable knowledge. She never stuttered, never stumbled over words, and gave off an air of knowing exactly what she was talking about without making you feel dumb because you didn't. The volunteers sitting at the phone bank were enamored of her when they weren't busy answering phones, their gazes glued to her every move, whether she was on the air or not.

At the commercial break, Sydney could hold it in no longer. "You're amazing at this, Jessica," she said as she sidled up next to her.

Jessica's expression was dubious. "You sort of have to say that so I don't have a crisis of confidence on the air." She gave a half-grin.

"True, though I don't think it's possible for you to have one of those. But I'm not saying it because I have to. I'm saying it because it's true. I can't believe your last crew didn't have you in front of the camera more. You're a natural."

And there came the blush. Sydney had to admit that she'd waited for it, loved seeing it, loved being the cause of it even more. They stood in silence and Sydney absorbed the company. After a moment, she glanced at her watch and said, "Halfway done."

"Thank God," Jessica replied. "It's so nerve-wracking. Every year, I look forward to the telethon because it's so good for the shelter. But I'm always thrilled when it's over because it's not good for my stress levels."

"Only three hours to go. Then you can subdue those stress levels with a glass of wine. Sound good?"

"Is this wine you're actually going to drink? Or will you be leaving me with it again?" Jessica's direct tone held a hint of teasing, but she looked at her then, right in the eye, and Sydney had a flash of the previous night. The muscles in her abdomen tensed up in that delicious way and she swallowed hard as a rush of heat shot through her body.

"Oh, no, I'll be drinking it," she said, her voice throaty.

Jessica said nothing, simply nodded in response and moved to her mark as the count was given until they went live again.

Over the next hour, Sydney watched and worked and the amount of donated money climbed higher and higher. David, who sat in a corner of the control area with the production assistant who was running the social media tickers threw her a thumbs-up and a big smile every time she glanced his way, which made her laugh after the fifth or sixth time. They were trending on Twitter and had snagged over 100 new followers on Instagram in the last forty-five minutes. *Not bad. Not bad at all.* The video featuring Maddie and Rex played next and there was yet another noticeable uptick in phone calls, just as Sydney had expected.

"You weren't kidding. That's a great interview," Connor said quietly in her earpiece. She nodded and gave him an I-told-you-so look just before the camera cut back to her and they moved directly from the video about an adoption success story into the next dog available for adoption. Lisa brought out an obvious mixed breed of some sort with a huge, broad chest, sweet brown eyes and a wagging stump of a tail.

"Here's Lisa Drakemore again, the head of adoption here at Junebug," Sydney said, shifting her gaze from the camera to Lisa. "Hi again, Lisa."

"Hey, Sydney." Though a bit stiffer and obviously more nervous than Jessica, Lisa wasn't bad in front of the camera. Sydney was used to walking inexperienced people through interviews and such, so this was no big deal.

"And who do we have here?"

"This is Millie," Lisa said, resting her hand on the huge square head. "She's been here for a while, so we've gotten to know her pretty well. She's a big sweetheart."

"She looks a little…intimidating," Sydney said, following the "script" she and Lisa had come up with to put people's fears around mixed breeds—especially those thought of as pit bulls— at ease.

"She does," Lisa said and ran with it. "But what we need to keep in mind is that there are really no bad dogs, only bad owners. A lot of the dogs here at Junebug are brought to us because they've been seized from less than ideal conditions and they're simply in need of love and an owner with the patience to teach them kindness."

The whole time she spoke, Sydney stroked Millie's broad back, rubbed her velvety ears between her fingers. "She's so sweet," she said.

"She really is. Kind. Smart. Lovable. Good with other dogs. Cats, too, from what we've seen."

"And up for adoption today?"

"Absolutely. Though I'll tell you guys a little secret." She leaned toward the camera in a perfect display of mock collusion and stage whispered, "Jessica, our fearless leader, and Millie have a little bit of a thing going, so if you want Millie, you may have a fight on your hands."

"Really?" Sydney said, grinning.

"Scout's honor," Lisa promised, crossing her heart.

"Hey!" came Jessica's voice from off stage and the phone bank volunteers laughed. It couldn't have happened more perfectly.

❧

By hour five, people were starting to get a little punchy, Jessica noticed. Herself included. Who knew doing a live, six-hour telecast could be so draining? Well, she did, but hadn't been this involved with the actual telethon...ever. She was on the air nearly as much as Sydney was and by the fourth hour, didn't even care anymore. She felt like an old pro, knowing which camera to turn to even before the red light went on. More than once, she'd caught Sydney smiling with something that certainly looked like pride, though Jessica was tired and might have been imagining it.

They'd gone through a quick-and-dirty history of the shelter early on in the first hour of programming, but it only scratched the surface. Now that it was going on 5 p.m. and they had the older demographic, Sydney wanted to delve into that a bit more. At least, that's what she'd told Jessica when asked. Now she watched as Sydney talked to the camera, giving the viewers a bare-bones overview of Jessica's grandmother's vision of Junebug Farms.

"I can stand here and talk at you," she said to the camera. "But I thought it might make more of an impact if you heard it from Junebug herself."

What? Jessica's brow furrowed as she turned her gaze to the monitors so she could see what was being broadcast live and there was her grandmother. Smiling and jubilant and talking right to the camera. Jessica recognized it as an interview she had done about ten or twelve years ago. Then the voiceover came on. Sydney.

For the next five or six minutes, Jessica was lost in memory, in love for her grandmother, in delight at being able to see her and hear her again. She watched in awe, as there were four more interview clips of her grandmother talking about how important animal rescue efforts were, how vital the participation of the public was. She was adamant and strong and well-spoken, just like Jessica remembered her. No-nonsense, but soft-hearted. There was video of the barn being built, segments from previous telethons, even a couple shots of a much younger Jessica when she was still learning the ropes. She hadn't noticed how her eyes had welled with tears until one slipped over the edge and slowly coursed down her cheek, a salty droplet of joy and love. When the video ended and they cut to commercial, she turned her gaze to Sydney, who stood across the set looking at her, and whose smile was so wide and gorgeous that it momentarily stole the breath from Jessica's lungs. She mouthed *thank you* and Sydney gave her a nod.

The money board continued to jangle and ring, as did the phones in the phone bank, and the next hour went by so swiftly that when Sydney started to do her wrap-up, Jessica was startled.

"That's it?" she asked aloud, on the air, before she could stop herself.

Sydney laughed. "What, six hours on live television isn't enough for you? You want more?"

Jessica chuckled, too, and hoped she wasn't blushing too badly as she felt the heat in her face. "It just seems like it went so fast."

"I feel the same way," Sydney said. "Let's take one last look at the donations."

They turned to the big board with the large red numbers that shuffled like a Vegas slot machine. When it stopped, the final number left Jessica completely speechless, her jaw dropped open like it had disconnected from her skull. She whipped her head around and caught David's eyes across the set. He wore the same expression.

Sydney announced the final number, thanked the sponsors, the volunteers, and everybody who'd helped make the telethon the huge success it had been. She mentioned the animals, invited viewers to drop by and visit, or better yet, volunteer. Then she laid a gentle hand on Jessica's shoulder.

"And this woman," she said to the camera, then turned to look at Jessica. "This woman is one of the most amazing people I've ever met. She works tirelessly for these animals, carrying on the tradition of love and support that her grandmother started.

She is here seven days a week, sometimes fifteen, sixteen hours a day. Sometimes more. She has seen more cruelty and heart-wrenching sadness than any of us should have to, and yet she continues on because of her love for the animals and the rewards they give. This city and these animals owe her more than we could ever possibly repay." Turning back to the camera, she went on, even as Jessica's eyes welled up yet again and she felt her cheeks warm. "You can donate to Junebug Farms all year long, so if you missed out today, no biggie. Like us on Facebook. Follow us on Twitter, Instagram, SnapChat, and Tumblr. Visit our website shown at the bottom of your screen. Not every city is lucky enough to have a Junebug Farms, because not every city is as lucky as our city. Thanks so much for spending time with us."

A beat went by, then a voice shouted, "We're clear!" And suddenly, everybody who had remained quiet burst into noise and movement. Applause rang out. Hands were shaken. High fives were slapped. Whoops went up. A pile of papers was tossed into the air and floated to the ground like too-large confetti. Jessica watched it all happen, a huge smile on her face, her eyes overly wide. She managed to keep from openly crying, but it wasn't easy. She just kept smiling instead.

"You know, you look just this side of creepy with that enormous grin." Sydney's voice was close. And teasing.

"Shut up," Jessica replied with a laugh. "I can't help it. This was an amazing day. I'm just...I'm speechless. All I can do is smile this creepy smile right now. Deal with it."

"Yes, ma'am."

"Hey, Sydney?" Jessica lowered her voice so that in the din, only Sydney could hear her.

"Hmm?"

"That piece? On my grandmother?" A lump closed Jessica's throat for a moment and she had to stop, swallow, collect herself.

"Did you like it?" Sydney's face, her tone of voice, the way she caught her bottom lip between her teeth, all told Jessica that she was honestly worried Jessica would say no. Seriously? How could she think that?

"It was beautiful. You captured so much of who she was. Smart, compassionate, obstinate but a sweetheart. I don't know how to thank you."

Sydney's expression was one of obvious relief. "You don't need to thank me."

"Where on earth did you find all that stuff?"

"I researched. I questioned. I dug." At Jessica's raised eyebrows, Sydney cocked her head. "I'm a reporter. It's what I do."

"Well, you're damn good at your job."

"I know." Her wink took away any hint of conceit.

By seven, the important equipment and paraphernalia was packed up and headed back to Channel Six. Most people had headed home and Bill Tracey locked up the front doors behind the last straggling visitors. Jessica was in her office, sitting in her chair and letting her brain decompress from the constant activity of the day. Outside, she watched Jeff loading the last of his stuff into a van, Connor talking to him as Bridget climbed into the passenger seat. A couple spots over, Lisa was getting into her car, and she waved to Connor. Jessica blew out a long, slow breath, closed her eyes, and leaned her head back against the chair.

"Tiring day, huh?" Sydney's voice was soft, gentle, so it didn't startle Jessica so much as stroke her back to attention.

"Exhausting." She opened her eyes and turned her head to smile in Sydney's direction. "Hi."

"Hey, you." Sydney came into the room.

"How do you do this all the time?" For the first time that evening, Jessica noticed the slow pace of Sydney's step, the increased blinking of what were probably scratchy eyes, the way she sunk into the chair slowly as her breath left her lungs. Sydney was beat, too.

With a quiet chuckle, Sydney said, "Six hours of live television? I *don't* do this all the time. This is definitely not a normal work day for me."

"Me neither."

They sat in silence. Comfortable silence, for the most part. "Wow," Sydney said. "Even the dogs must be tired. They're hardly making any noise."

"That happens after a big day of constant people. They're as overstimulated as we are." They were quiet again for a beat before Jessica leaned her head back and closed her eyes again. "So here's my problem."

"Tell me."

"I'm starving, but I can barely get out of this chair, let alone decide on a restaurant and drag myself there."

"That *is* a dilemma."

"Right?"

"Might I offer a solution?"

"Sure."

Sydney sat up, forearms on knees. "What if we ordered a pizza, have it delivered to my place, and just hang out for a while? Decompress a bit?"

Warning bells went off all over the place.

"Oh, I don't know. I really have some things to take care of here."

"You've been here all day. What could you possibly need to do?" Sydney's voice was calm. Reasonable.

"Yes, I've been here all day, but I've been on TV, not doing my work." Sort of lame. Okay. But not a lie.

Sydney cocked her head. "You worked your ass off today. You deserve a break." Jessica hesitated. Sydney obviously saw her opening. "Come on. Just this one night, leave before you think you should. What's it going to hurt?"

The warning bells continued to clang, but Jessica fought to ignore them, instead nodding and saying, "That sounds perfect," before she could talk herself out of it. Meanwhile, the other voice in her head screamed, *What are you doing? She's dangerous. You like her too much already and you saw where that got you last night. Spending more time with her will only make things worse!*

Wondering when she'd become so adept at ignoring her conscience, she took a deep breath, pushed herself up from her chair, and began to gather her things together. "I'll meet you at your place in…an hour?"

Sydney grinned widely and looked almost surprised, which made Jessica wonder if she thought she'd put up more of a fight and ultimately end up with the answer being no. *As it should have been!* the voice shrieked.

"I'll text you my address," Sydney said, pulling out her phone.

CHAPTER EIGHTEEN

SYDNEY'S BUILDING WAS NICE, a neatly kept large house—as many of the apartments in the downtown area were—that had been broken up into a handful of individual dwellings. The siding was a deep slate blue, the trim a clean white, the fixtures brass. Jessica climbed the front steps, inhaled, and blew out the breath slowly. With a swallow, she reached for the bank of doorbells and pushed the one that said, "Taylor."

The door buzzed less than two seconds later, and Jessica smiled at the possibility of Sydney waiting for her. Then she furrowed her brow and tried to shake off any delight as she reached for the knob. No, she'd thought about this on the drive home. Sydney had some explaining to do. If last night had been nothing more than a one-night stand, so be it, but Jessica needed to know, needed to hear it from Sydney. Of course, she didn't really *want* to hear it, but...

Her thoughts were interrupted by Sydney's voice from above her. "You found it." She stood one flight up, forearms braced on the railing. She'd changed her clothes and now wore cute gray workout pants and a white, feminine T-shirt with a logo so faded, Jessica couldn't make it out.

"Wasn't that hard." Jessica smiled and headed up the stairs. "This is a nice place."

"Thanks. I like it." Before either of them could say more, the door to Sydney's left opened and an elegant looking elderly woman came out from the apartment next door with a trash bag. "Hi, Dr. Green," Sydney said and reached for the bag. "Can I take that down for you?"

"You're in your pajamas," the woman said, but still handed over the bag.

"I won't let anybody see me," Sydney replied with a wink, then turned to Jessica. "Jessica Barstow, this is my neighbor, Vivian Green."

Vivian stuck out her hand as she said, "I know you. You run that animal shelter. I saw you on TV today. Gave you some money, too."

Jessica shook her hand. The skin was soft and papery, but the grip much firmer than she'd expected. "Well, I and the animals thank you for that. It's nice to meet you."

Sydney pushed the door to her apartment open. "Go on in. I'll be right back." She headed down the stairs. Vivian smiled at Jessica and retreated into her apartment and Jessica entered Sydney's.

"This is nice," Jessica said as Sydney returned. She looked around. "A bit on the sparse side, but nice."

"Thanks."

It *was* a nice place. Jessica could tell that despite the lack of color or almost anything personal. The walls were white, the furniture was basic. There was nothing on the walls and only two photos she could see. One that had to be Sydney and her parents—she looked just like her mother—and one with Sydney and a blonde woman, both in graduation attire. She picked it up. Studied it. Sydney looked happy and the blonde was beautiful. A friend? Roommate? Ex-girlfriend? It bothered her that it bothered her that she didn't know who it was.

"That's Laura," Sydney said and pointed at the pizza box on the counter. "Hungry?"

"Famished. Who's Laura?"

"College roommate. Best friend. Voice of reason."

"Ah. It's good to have one of those."

241

"She's talked me off a ledge more than once." Sydney got plates out of the cupboard and set them on the small counter that separated the living room from the kitchen. "She helps me with career stuff and life stuff and gives great advice. I'm waiting for her to call me back. I got an interesting e-mail from a station in Austin. I want to know her take, if she thinks I should counter. She's really smart about life and always helps me see things from a perspective that never occurred to me."

"Austin…Texas?" Jessica tamped down her uneasiness and put the photo back. She moved to the counter across from Sydney, watched her dish out the pizza, which looked so delicious her mouth watered, despite the sudden sourness of her stomach.

"Is there another Austin?" Sydney asked with a laugh. "You want beer or wine?"

"I think a cold beer sounds terrific." Jessica forced herself to shake off whatever weirdness had enveloped her and focus on the moment. They'd had a great day. Things couldn't have gone better. *Stop looking for things to stress about.*

"You got it." Sydney turned to the fridge, pulled out two bottles, and popped off the caps. She handed one to Jessica, then held up the other. "I'd like to propose a toast."

"Irish," Jessica said in a mock-scoff.

Sydney chuckled, but then her expression became serious. She looked Jessica in the eye. "To an amazing job today. You were…so impressive. You did great."

"Right back atcha," Jessica said. "Did you see the final number?"

"I did."

"It's never been that high."

"No?"

"No. It's never even been *close* to that high."

"Well, then, here's to a job well done." They touched the tops of their bottles together and Sydney continued to hold her gaze as they sipped.

"I owe you an apology," Jessica said, surprised when the words slipped out before she had a chance to screen them.

"You do?" Sydney took a bite of her pizza.

"Yes. I'm really sorry I was difficult."

Sydney watched her, squinted at her a bit. "Difficult? You?"

Jessica grinned. "Ha ha. Yes, I was. You know it and I know it. I just wanted to say I'm sorry. All the changes you made, the alterations, they worked. You were right. I'm sorry I didn't believe in you from the beginning."

"That's not how Janet did it," Sydney said in a high-pitched tone, causing Jessica to burst out laughing.

"I know. I know. That's what I mean." She chewed her bite of pizza, swallowed, and studied Sydney for a beat. Her silky hair. Her creamy skin. Those ocean-colored blue-green eyes. "I'm sorry."

"You're forgiven."

They ate in silence, Jessica looking around the apartment from where she stood. Her eyes landed on the humming tank at the end of the couch, its blue light casting an eerie glow on the bare wall. "Oh, hello there, fishies."

Sydney chuckled. "That's Marge and Homer."

"Ah, a *Simpsons* fan, are you?"

"Used to be. Watched it all the time in college. Laura and I still quote it sometimes."

Without taking her eyes from the tank, Jessica asked, "Is she your ex?"

Sydney choked on the swig of beer she'd taken. "Laura? No! God, no. And she would find that absolutely hysterical."

"Why?"

"Because she could never be in a relationship with me. She'd kill me. We both know it and we've laughed about it more than once." She popped the last bite of crust into her mouth and said around it, "Also, she's straight."

"Ah, well, that does pose a problem. Though not always." Jessica winked.

Sydney feigned a gasp. "Why, Ms. Barstow. Are you telling me you've bedded a straight girl?"

"They're all straight until they're not," Jessica said with a lewd wag of her eyebrows. Then she shook her head. "I'm just kidding. And no. I never have. I'm pretty certain both my girlfriends were gay. Well, one was gay. One was bi."

"Just two?" Sydney tried to hide her surprise, but was unsuccessful because Jessica saw it immediately.

"Just two. One at college and one a couple years ago. Neither lasted terribly long."

"How come?"

"Well, let's see." Jessica sipped her beer and squinted at the ceiling. "The first one, we were in college. That's always dicey anyway. Close quarters. Pressure. We were both dealing with our newfound sexuality and neither of us was doing it well. By the end of our junior year, we did nothing but fight, so we called it quits. It was mutual. We're still friends. We chat on Facebook every so often. I keep track of her life through that."

Sydney didn't comment, just watched her intently.

"The second one…" Jessica grimaced, took a sip of beer, and studied the label while wondering how truthful she should be. But when she looked up at Sydney, she saw nothing but openness and safety in those eyes and decided to tell the truth. "She wanted me to choose."

"Between?"

"The shelter and her."

244

"No." Sydney looked shocked, and for that, Jessica was grateful.

"I'm afraid so. Now, in her defense, I was there all the time. Not unlike I am now." She gave a self-deprecating laugh. "She said I worked too much, that I didn't have enough time for her. That was her argument."

"So she threw down an ultimatum?"

"She did."

"Wow. That's cold."

"Well…" Jessica held out her flat hand, tilted it one way, then the other. "Yes and no. I *did* work too much. I *didn't* make time for her. The ultimatum was harsh, but it was the only way she could figure to find out where my priorities were."

"And the shelter came first."

"Yeah." She swallowed the last of her beer. "I wasn't happy about it. Don't get me wrong. But my grandmother had just died and I was buried in learning the ins and outs of being in charge, not to mention drowning in my own grief that I kept tamped down so I could continue working and not miss a beat. She went home to Boston and I went into therapy. In hindsight, the best moves for both of us."

Sydney got two more beers out of the fridge, popped the caps, then came around the counter to stand next to Jessica rather than across from her. She held her bottle up. "To therapy."

"You've been?" Jessica asked as they touched glass.

"Oh, God, yes. Hasn't everybody?"

"In a perfect world maybe. I went for a couple years, until I started to feel not insane anymore." She sipped. "I still go back every few months for a 'mental health tune-up.'" She made air quotes.

"I think that's smart." Sydney was quiet for a moment before saying, "You know, I realized something today during the telethon and it was even more obvious when you met Dr. Green next door."

"What's that?"

"You're kind of a local celebrity. A lot of people know who you are when they see you."

Jessica gave a nod. "That's true. Anna has been trying for years to get me to be 'the face of Junebug' and I initially resisted. But she's slowly made it happen."

"Was that hard for you and your last girlfriend?"

Jessica thought about it, took a bite of pizza and pondered as she chewed, as it wasn't something she'd ever really considered before. "Well, I don't know that it was hard for her, but I can tell you it was hard for me for a while."

"Yeah? How come?"

"Because I didn't want to stay here. I was going to New York, remember?"

"Oh, that's right. I'd forgotten about that."

"But the more known I became, the more people associated me with the shelter, the less comfortable I became with leaving. And then after a while, I didn't *want* to leave."

"Why not?"

"Because I belong here." Jessica smiled widely, remembering the day she came to that realization. "It was a day just like any other day. A Wednesday, I think. And it had been crazy. Abuse cases were brought in. Three dogs from a dogfighting ring, two of which had to be put down. There weren't enough volunteers working. It was a disaster of a day all around. I was exhausted. And it was, like, nine at night and I collapsed in my chair in my office and just sobbed. Cried like a baby. I was so beat up and felt like I'd been running in place all day, running as fast as I could and getting absolutely nowhere. I was so sure I was failing everybody around me, every animal, and the memory of my grandma. So I moved to put my elbows on my desk so I could hold my head and cry some more and there was a pile of mail that Regina had opened and stacked there for me. And on top was a letter from Maddie, that little girl you interviewed. There was a picture of her and Rex and her letter just gushed about how happy she was and how she and Rex were helping each other learn to get along with their disabilities and she must have said thank you six or seven times throughout and…" Jessica looked up at the ceiling, felt her eyes well up a bit at the memory. "That was it. I knew I was exactly where I was supposed to be. The tears dried up. The doubt just…left. I…I *knew*."

When she looked over, Sydney seemed to be awed, enamored. "That is an amazing story," she said quietly.

"It was a big moment for me. I'll never forget it. And I flash back to it on bad days. So, being known for the shelter wasn't as hard on me as it was on my then-girlfriend, because she lost." A beat passed while they sat with that. Then Jessica shifted to lean on the counter. "What about you?"

"What about me?"

"Past relationships? Besides Anna, I mean."

"You're hilarious. Yeah, the only reason I'm not doing anything about the scratch on my car is because I kind of deserved it." Sydney took a bite of pizza. Chewed. "And also, I can't prove it was her."

"Oh, it was her."

"You think?"

Jessica nodded. "It's exactly the kind of thing she'd do. I'm surprised she hasn't keyed mine."

"Yet."

247

Jessica snorted.

"Not surprisingly, I have had very few long-term relationships."

"You *are* only thirty, so no, it's not surprising."

"The longest was Claire. We met at my first job out of college, not far from my hometown in Pennsylvania. She was still in college and working as a production assistant part-time at the same station where I'd been hired to write news."

"And how long did that last?"

"Until she graduated and got a job offer in Florida." Jessica watched Sydney's face and was sure she detected a quick flash of pain zip across. "She wanted me to go with her, but I had my own plans. A reporting position in a bigger city. It was only a matter of time. So she went without me. And that was the end of that." It was obvious she was trying to keep it light with her half-shrug and unaffected tone, but Jessica wasn't buying it.

"So...she kind of gave you an ultimatum as well." At Sydney's furrowed brow, she elaborated. "My career or yours. She said come with me or wait here until you get what you want. That's essentially my career or yours, isn't it?"

Sydney seemed to ponder that for a moment before responding. "You know what? You're right."

"It happens."

"I bet it happens a lot."

"Well..." Jessica shrugged and feigned modesty.

Sydney laughed and when their eyes met this time, their gazes didn't waver and Jessica held her breath. She'd vowed on the way over that she wasn't making any moves this time, that the ball was firmly in Sydney's court. So she waited, and the wait paid off as Sydney leaned forward and kissed her. Softly and tenderly, like they hadn't a care in the world.

When Sydney pulled back, Jessica stayed still for a beat, licked her lips, then opened her eyes. So many questions careened through her brain, so many words, so many thoughts. *What are we going to do about this? Are we just a fling? Are we just having fun? Is there something more here? Does it mean anything to you? Does it mean anything to me?* She just needed to give voice to one and the rest would come pouring out. She knew this about herself. If she could just ask one question, put one of them out there, she'd be able to stop this feeling of...of what? What the hell was it that Sydney made her feel? Crazy? Uncertain? Confused? Beautiful? Sexy? Ridiculously turned on?

Yes! Yes, all of those things! Every one of them. Yes!

And before she realized she was going to do it, she grabbed Sydney's face with both hands and kissed her for all she was worth.

It was the only way to stop the questions.

Because if Jessica were going to be honest—with herself or with anybody else—she'd have to admit that she really didn't want any of the answers. Not today. Not now. Right now, she wanted to lose herself. In Sydney's kiss, in Sydney's body, in Sydney.

Any surprise Sydney might have had by Jessica's move seemed to disappear quickly because in a matter of seconds, she was kissing Jessica back. Enthusiastically. And even as Jessica's inner voice kept shouting warnings at her, she continued to push herself as close to Sydney as she could get, to pull Sydney against her. Nothing existed but Sydney's mouth, the warmth of her body, her arms that had moved around Jessica, her hands splayed across Jessica's back. She could feel every single part of Sydney that touched her as if she left a shadow of heat in each spot.

They were moving now. They'd gotten halfway across the living room before Jessica had even realized it, and soon they were in Sydney's bedroom. And everything seemed to speed up. Clothes were suddenly gone, and they were under the covers before Jessica knew it, hands roaming, mouths searching. She'd never become so completely lost in somebody physically before. But being with Sydney…it was bliss. Heaven. Perfect.

They battled for the upper hand and it was playful, then serious, then playful again. *It's one of the things that makes us so good together in bed.* That thought zipped through Jessica's head just before Sydney's mouth caused her first orgasm to obliterate all conscious thought. As she lay there in the aftermath, getting her breathing under control, trying to relax her tensed muscles, the rest of the thought appeared in her head: *But what about places other than bed? Are we good together then?*

Jessica waited only long enough to let the words sink in before she growled and spun a surprised Sydney onto her back, preferring to lose herself in the glorious body underneath her rather than deal with the simple question her subconscious was asking.

She knew exactly what she was doing as she took a nipple into her mouth and sucked hard enough to make Sydney hiss. She'd never considered herself a person of avoidance, but yeah, avoiding was totally what she was doing. And in the moment, she didn't give a crap. She knew the questions wouldn't go away, but pushing her fingers into Sydney's body certainly did take her focus from them. She gave her head one hard shake and concentrated on the sensual, sexy form underneath her, on the sounds she could pull from Sydney's throat, on the way Sydney's fingers ran up and down her back, then dug in when she arched her back and came, Jessica's name floating into the air on a moan.

But Jessica didn't stop there. She couldn't. She moved lower, took Sydney into her mouth, started off with gentle movements that gradually became firmer, more demanding, until Sydney's fingers dug into Jessica's hair, tugged it as a second orgasm hit, and Jessica basked in the sounds Sydney made, basked in the knowledge that only a few people on earth ever got to hear them.

Then the only sound in the room was the two of them breathing raggedly. Jessica's forehead rested against Sydney's stomach, her fingers still inside, Sydney's warmth holding them there for a few beats longer as the contractions subsided and Jessica gently slid them out. Letting herself shift up, Jessica tucked her head under Sydney's chin, kept one leg draped over Sydney's thigh, and settled against her. She drew lazy circles along her collarbone with a finger.

"Wow," Sydney whispered after some time had passed and she was no longer gasping for breath. "You were…assertive."

Jessica could hear the smile in her voice. "Yeah, that happens sometimes."

"It was awesome."

"I'm glad." She felt Sydney move her head in an attempt to see Jessica's face, but the angle was impossible.

"Hey. You okay?"

"Mm hmm."

"Well, that was convincing." Sydney was trying to keep it light. Jessica could hear it in her voice, feel it in the gently movement of her fingertips against her shoulder.

She doesn't want to deal with things any more than I do. And something about that understanding made Jessica suddenly sad. "Oh, no. It's fine. I'm fine. Everything's good." She waited, counting exactly five seconds before she shifted herself to a sitting position and then got out of the bed. "I'm going to head home."

"What?" Sydney's surprise was clear and Jessica heard her sit up, even though she didn't allow herself to look as she searched for her clothes and got herself dressed. "Why?"

"Because that's how this works, isn't it?"

Sydney flinched slightly, but she got it, understood completely what was being said; Jessica could see it on her face.

"This." Jessica made an all-encompassing gesture between the two of them. "Us. This is what we do. We talk. We have great sex. One of us goes home." She could almost hear the wheels turning in Sydney's head as she tried to come up with the right reply. Jessica wanted to stop, to take a breath, but once she'd started, she couldn't seem to find the brakes. "Besides, you've got to talk to Austin, right? Get things set up down there? You don't need me distracting you from what you really want."

"I have no idea. I haven't really..." Sydney's voice trailed off, as if she'd just forgotten how to speak. Jessica could feel her eyes on her as she pulled on her shirt, her jeans, grabbed her shoes.

Jessica knew she was being cold. She couldn't care, though, because she had to get out of there. If she didn't, she was going to fall for Sydney and fall hard—it wasn't lost on her that she may have already done so—and Sydney was only going to leave. She'd made that clear. How many times had she expressly said she wasn't staying? And Jessica didn't think she could take it if they started something serious and *then* Sydney left. It would hurt way too much.

"I'll see you around, okay?" With the lamest wave known to man, she fled Sydney's bedroom, her apartment, her building. She was able to hold the tears in until she reached the street and then she silently cried her way home.

CHAPTER NINETEEN

BY 6:30 MONDAY MORNING, Sydney had scoured her bathroom, mopped her boot-tray-sized kitchen floor, and returned from the gym where she'd run four miles that had nearly killed her.

I should've gone after her.

That thought tortured her all night, poked at her any time she dozed off, slapped her when her brain drifted toward another subject.

She was stumbling back into her apartment on legs that felt like wet noodles when her iPhone chirped. She dug it out of her bag and saw it was a FaceTime call from Laura. The mixed emotions hit immediately. She needed to talk to Laura. She didn't want to talk to Laura. But she needed to. But she really didn't want to because...Laura never let her get away with anything.

Damn it.

It was barely dawn and she already felt like she was losing her mind.

"Hey, you," she said as she answered the call and held the phone up so she could be seen, doing her best to look totally normal.

"Holy shit, what happened to you? Bus? Mugger? Vicious raccoon?"

"Nice. You're funny."

Laura laughed. "Seriously. Your face is all flushed. Your hair's a mess." She gasped. "Wait! I didn't interrupt you and"—

she dropped her voice to an obnoxious stage whisper—"one of the animal shelter chicks, did I?"

"If you had, I wouldn't have answered the phone," Sydney said, but her voice was low-key and she didn't feel like joking around, even with Laura, who picked up on it instantly.

"What's the matter?" Laura asked, growing serious, her brow furrowed. "I don't have to be to school for another hour. Talk to me."

"Oh, Laura. I don't even know where to start." It was the truth. Sydney felt…stuck. Like she was wading through oatmeal. It was why she hadn't been able to reconcile what had happened last night. Or even think about it clearly.

"Start at the beginning."

So she did. With a deep, fortifying breath, Sydney dove in and told Laura everything. Not that she didn't already know most of it, but she told her anyway. Everything. She reiterated the Anna situation, but then added in Jessica and the crazy chemistry they'd had from the beginning. "I tried to avoid it," she said, feeling she was being truthful.

"Why?" Laura stared at her, in her eyes, through the iPhone's screen. Sydney loved and hated FaceTime for exactly this reason. She couldn't fib, couldn't gloss over, couldn't pull a fast one on Laura if her face was visible. Laura knew her too well.

"Because I didn't want to get too close to her."

"Why?"

"Because I knew we'd end up in bed."

"And did you?"

"Twice."

"And?"

Sydney sighed. How did she describe what it was like to be with Jessica that way? Where did she begin? How honest should she be?

"I'm going to get it out of you sooner or later," Laura said, but with a gentle smile. "You might as well just tell me."

"I know." Sydney's cheeks puffed as she blew out a breath, ran a hand through her still-sweaty hair, and pursed her lips in thought as she tried to find the right words. "When we were together the first time…it was…surreal. Just…surreal. In a good way. An amazing way. But…" She gazed off in the distance as she remembered how different being with Jessica had been from anybody else she'd slept with. That wild, unfamiliar connection and how much it had scared her.

"You ran afterward, didn't you?" Laura's voice pulled her back.

"What do you mean?"

"You know exactly what I mean. You left. You didn't spend the night." Laura gave her a look of disapproval and even through the tiny screen, it shamed her.

"I left. Yeah." Lying to Laura was of no use.

"Jesus, Sydney."

"I know. I know." Sydney rubbed her forehead with one hand.

"What am I gonna do with you? Huh?" Laura shook her head from side to side and finally broke eye contact, looking off into her kitchen as if she couldn't bear to look at Sydney's face any longer.

"I don't know. I don't know what my problem is." A tiny crumb of self-pity snuck into her voice.

"I do." Laura's voice was stern now.

"What's that tone? Are you *mad* at me?" Sydney was taken aback.

"I'm not mad at you." Laura grimaced. "But you frustrate the crap out of me. I just wish you'd pay more attention."

"To what?"

"*To yourself,*" Laura said, her irritation so obvious it was almost tangible. "To your patterns. If I can see them, why can't you?"

"What patterns?" What the hell was she talking about? Sydney felt a tiny spark of indignation ignite deep down in the pit of her stomach.

"You can't stay still, Syd. You always have to move, move, move. You leave school and get a job as a PA, but you're waiting for the next thing. And in the meantime, you have a really nice girl who loves you and wants you to follow her to her new job. But you don't. Because that'd make sense. So you get another good job and you like it and you do well, but then a new job comes along and you drop everything and take *that*. And you do well there. You're doing well there, right? And you like this girl. I know you and I know when you like a girl. But then an e-mail from Austin comes in and *bam!* You're looking to go *there*. As soon as something seems good—too good, maybe?—you're on to the next thing. You don't know how to sit still and breathe, not in all the years I've known you. *That* is your pattern. I wish you could see it as clearly as I do."

"Wow." It was about all Sydney could come up with.

"Yeah, well." Laura was actually a little out of breath. "As somebody who loves you, it's kind of hard to watch."

Sydney gave a snort.

"So, you said that was the first time you were together. What happened the second?"

Again, Sydney gazed away from the screen, watched Homer swim in adorable circles, chewed the inside of her cheek.

Laura, of course, waited her out.

"She left this time." Sydney's voice was quiet when she finally said it.

"She left…you mean Jessica left? I need details, please."

Sydney sighed in annoyed defeat for about the sixth time during this conversation, hating to have to spill the truth to Laura, but having no other recourse. She told Laura the rest, how the telethon had rocked, how it had brought in way more money than expected, how amazing it had been to be side-by-side with Jessica all day, to see the awe in her eyes when the final total was revealed.

"And then came the adrenaline crash." Sydney grinned. "We were so tired, but…it was like we weren't ready to be apart quite yet. So we ordered a pizza and came back here."

"And ended up in the sack."

"Not right away, no. We talked. We talked a lot."

Laura's right eyebrow arched, but she made no comment.

"We got to know each other a bit better. It was nice." Sydney realized in that moment that she was telling the truth. It *was* nice talking with Jessica. She enjoyed conversation with her.

"And *then* you ended up in the sack."

"And *then* we ended up in the sack. Yes."

"And?"

"She left."

Laura blinked at her and was silent for a beat. "Wait. What?"

"She left."

"You made it known that you wanted her to?"

Sydney gave a humorless laugh. "No. That's the ridiculous part. I actually kind of wanted her to stay."

More silence. More blinking.

"I don't understand what's happening here," Laura said finally.

257

"She was just doing what she thought I would've done." Sydney went over the conversation with Laura, telling her what had been said and how. "It was self-preservation. It sucked, but I got it."

"You didn't go after her?"

"I was naked." Laura gave her a look through the phone. "Okay, fine. No, I didn't go after her, and I should've."

"You most definitely should have. Man, you may have really screwed this up, Sydney. What the hell am I going to do with you?" It was the second time she'd said it and it didn't sting any less.

But Laura was right. Sydney knew it. Jessica had pretty much been saying her goodbyes last night and Sydney had pretty much let her, even though—she understood now—that wasn't what she wanted. "Love me forever?" she asked in a small voice.

"Well, that's a given, you dumbass."

They chatted for a bit longer, but didn't come to any conclusions—aside from Sydney being a dumbass—or hammer out any solutions. Still, it was good to talk it through.

After hanging up with Laura, Sydney gathered her garbage from last night's pizza and took it out into the hall where Vivian Green was coming up the stairs.

"Hey, Doc," Sydney said by way of greeting.

"Your friend left rather abruptly last night," the elderly woman said, stopped halfway up the staircase.

Sydney was so surprised by the observation, she wasn't sure what to say.

"She didn't look happy about it."

"You saw her?"

"I was having trouble getting to sleep, so I decided to take a walk." Dr. Green's rheumy eyes bored into Sydney's with an unexpected intensity that made Sydney shift her weight from one foot to the other. "She wasn't happy."

Sydney swallowed, hung her head. "I know."

"Things we need don't come along in this life very often, Sydney. When they do, we should grab onto them with both hands. You know what I'm saying?"

"Yes, ma'am."

"Good." Dr. Green continued on her way up, leaving Sydney to stay rooted to the steps while she stared at her in dumbfounded disbelief until she went into her apartment and shut the door.

"What the hell?" Sydney whispered aloud, feeling like she'd just unwittingly taken part in a romantic comedy from the eighties. Collecting herself, she blew out a breath and took her garbage out. She knew she had some serious thinking to do, some major self-analysis. And she needed to do it alone.

She wondered if she'd ever see Jessica again.

و

For the past two weeks, Jessica did what she'd always done to combat something that was bothering her: she threw herself into her work. The shelter had been bustling steadily since the telethon, and that was a good thing. They were set to have a record number of adoptees this month, which was always cause for celebration.

Jessica had done something else as well, something slightly out of character for her. Something that she hadn't thought twice about. Something that, shockingly, had given her nothing but joy. As if on cue, Millie snuffled in her sleep from the round dog bed in the corner of Jessica's office. Despite her intimidating appearance, Jessica had never known a gentler animal—and that said a lot given her job. When Jessica had shown up at Millie's kennel the day after she'd run from Sydney's, leash in hand and a smile on her face, Millie had jumped up and spun in circles on the concrete, making happy dog sounds and—Jessica would swear to it—smiling. Once leashed up, she pranced along next to Jessica as if she'd known all along she was coming, had simply been waiting for her to arrive and put her in her rightful place beside her. At Jessica's house, Millie had lain on the kitchen floor and let each cat come to her, sniff her, paw at her, crawl on her (in Shaggy's case), waiting patiently for them to give their approval. Which they had, in less than two days.

Not surprisingly, Millie also seemed to get the sadness inside Jessica, the ache in her heart. Jessica found the dog "checking in" with her often. Jessica would look up and Millie would be looking at her. Millie would come to her and nuzzle her for no reason, as if she was making sure Jessica was okay, as if she was simply saying, "I love you. I'm here for you. It's going to be okay." Jessica had never been so grateful for anything in her life.

Though it tended to be muffled when in her office, Jessica could still hear the sound of the shelter today. The barking, howling, meowing, conversation, all of it making up the soundtrack of her life. It brought her comfort, even now as she sat in her desk chair, her new dog napping nearby, and gazed out the window at the sparsely populated parking lot, the dusk fading rapidly into darkness, and tried hard not to think about Sydney.

The story of her life lately.

There'd been no contact since the Sunday of the telethon, so Jessica had no choice but to believe this was how Sydney wanted it, how she'd meant it to be from the start. If Jessica was going to be honest, she had to admit that was okay. It was allowed. Casual sex was not uncommon—hell, she'd had it herself more than once. And if that's what Sydney'd wanted, who was Jessica to judge? It was her own fault she hadn't asked for specifics before jumping in and finding herself liking Sydney a lot more than she'd planned to. Like, *way* more than she'd planned to. She'd miscalculated. Underestimated.

Stupidly.

"Stop that."

The voice surprised her. It also surprised Millie, judging by the way she woke up with a start and a little yip.

"Stop what?" Jessica asked as Catherine entered her office, followed closely by Emily. Catherine carried a bottle of wine in her hand. Emily had a large paper bag.

"Stop beating yourself up for misreading things with Sydney. You've been doing that for two weeks now, and I'm sick of it."

"*We're* sick of it," Emily added, but winked to let Jessica know they said it with love.

Jessica didn't respond. She simply watched while they set up dinner on her desk. The food was from Bucky's—she could tell immediately, as she'd recognize the scent of Javier's brisket anywhere—and the wine was a deep red Zinfandel. Despite being poured into a clear plastic cup, it made Jessica's mouth water just looking at the color.

When they finally sat, food dished out, wine distributed, Jessica looked at them both, touched. "You guys. You didn't have to do this."

Catherine shrugged. "We know. We wanted to."

"Cat's been worried about you," Emily said.

Jessica's gaze turned to Catherine. "She calls you Cat now?" she asked in surprise, knowing Catherine hated the nickname.

Catherine's eyebrow was already arched. "No. She does not."

Jessica chuckled as Emily leaned over and kissed Catherine on the cheek.

"How'd you get food from Bucky's?" Jessica asked, biting into the brisket and humming with pleasure, which was not an atypical reaction in the slightest. The stuff was like heaven on a plate.

"I stopped home to take care of the boys," Emily said, referring to her and Catherine's two dogs. "Catherine decided we were having dinner with you." Her grin, as always, was infectious. It was hard not to like Emily Breckenridge, even when you tried.

"Well, thank you." She lifted her little plastic cup and touched it to the other two. "I appreciate it. You guys are the best."

"I knew you would've either eaten alone or not at all." Catherine said it so matter-of-factly that it actually made Jessica pause with her food halfway to her lips and experience a moment of self-pity. Because she was right. "Speaking of you not eating alone, we have a proposition for you."

"Uh-oh." They were the first words Jessica could think of and they surprised nobody, given the tandem grins on both the faces before her.

"We want you to come to dinner with us and some friends tomorrow night."

Jessica studied Catherine's face as she chewed. She swallowed and took a sip of wine before saying, "One of whom is single, and you want me to meet her."

"So close," Catherine said, holding her thumb and forefinger millimeters apart. "You *almost* got it. One of whom is single and *she* wants to meet you."

"Oh." Jessica sat back in her chair. "Well, that's new."

"I've talked about you before," Emily said, "but she saw you on the telethon and was all about how I needed to introduce you."

"Is she nice?" Jessica did her best to appear interested. And she was. A little. And while her initial reaction was to decline, part of her thought maybe this would be a good way to get a certain television reporter out of her head. Or at least shove her to the back and up on a high shelf.

"She is. She's in advertising. Really smart. Hard worker. Cute."

"And she's single why?" Jessica asked, her red flags rising.

"Her partner died a couple years ago. Cancer." Catherine sipped her wine and watched Jessica over the rim as if daring her to push further.

"Oh. That's terrible."

"So, you'll go then?" Emily was noticeably excited. "I've known Trish for a while. I think you'll like her."

Two facts triggered Jessica's positive reply. One was that there really wasn't any way she could say no, not after these two had brought her dinner and were doing so much to keep her smiling. And two: maybe going on a date, even one that she knew already would go nowhere, would keep her from dwelling on Sydney. She was getting better. At first, her mind had been occupied with Sydney nearly the entire time she was awake—and some of her sleeping time as well. But after two weeks, that had dwindled a bit. Focusing on making Millie a part of her family had helped take some of the focus. Maybe this would, too.

"Sure. But I'm meeting you guys so I can escape if I need to."

Catherine turned to Emily. "See? She laid down the law."

"Just like you said she would," Emily replied, and they fist-bumped.

"Oh, you two are hilarious." Jessica shook her head and continued with dinner as Catherine changed the subject to a couple of the senior cats that had been adopted this week. She listened to her friends, thanked God she had them to keep her from drowning, to help her stay social. Catherine knew Jessica had the propensity to lock herself away at the shelter and barely deal with the outside world at all, so as her friend, she saw it as her duty to prevent that from happening. Jessica was lucky and she knew it.

It was time to let Sydney, any hopes of being with Sydney, and any memories of Sydney go.

A date would surely help.

*

Sydney flopped back onto her couch and surveyed her handiwork. It was amazing what a little pop of color could do for a room. The light blue scarf valances twisted around the wrought iron rods she'd installed above the living room windows really changed the entire look. The color was a few shades lighter than that of the couch, but in the same family, and Sydney finally understood what it meant to "tie a room together."

"Looks nice in here, doesn't it, Marge?" The fish ignored her, choosing instead to swim in circles. "Well, I think it looks nice." The painting on the wall was also new. Sydney hadn't planned on purchasing it. It was in the display window of a furniture store in the mall, and when she'd walked by it, it had pulled her. It was the image of a serene landscape, a clear blue lake in the distance, trees and grass and wildflowers. Something about it brought her…peace, was the only word she could come up with, corny as that sounded. The painting brought her peace, so she'd marched right into the store, forked over more than she'd have expected, and now it hung on her living room wall helping to further "tie the room together" with its blues and greens and bringing her a warm sense of relaxation.

Pushing out a lungful of air, she stood up and got herself a Diet Coke from the fridge, then grabbed her laptop. When she sat back down and signed onto her e-mail account, a photo of a dog showed up in her news feed and her thoughts immediately veered toward Jessica. Which was nothing new.

It had been more than three weeks since their last encounter. Sydney had fought the urge to call her, text her, e-mail her dozens of times because she'd always come to the same conclusion: that Jessica was probably better off—for now, at least—if Sydney just left well enough alone. The fact that Jessica hadn't contacted her either simply solidified the decision.

She felt different. Sydney knew this for a fact. Since spending time with Jessica, she'd changed. Something inside her had...altered, she guessed was the right word. Shifted. She couldn't put her finger on exactly what. She simply knew it to be true, felt it in her heart. It was a good thing, despite the vagueness of it, so Sydney simply accepted it and did her best to live her life.

Her inbox was fuller than she liked, but that's what happened when you weren't online every other minute of the day. That's what happened when you spent your Saturday shopping for, then installing, curtain rods and window dressings. That's what happened when you had somewhat of a life outside of work. She grinned as she sifted through junk, answered a couple of e-mails from Connor about the interviews they were doing next week, looked at photos of three separate pairs of earrings Zack had sent, asking her which ones Laura would like best. Then she stopped. First at one e-mail, then a second e-mail. Two. On the same day.

The first was from the TV station in Austin, Texas.

The second was from a TV station in Raleigh, North Carolina.

She read each one. Then she read each one a second time. Then a third.

She took a moment to breathe. Just breathe.

Carefully, she sat forward and set her laptop on the coffee table. Then she slowly stood up and walked around to the middle of the room.

She was reasonably sure Dr. Green could hear the whoop of excitement from inside her own apartment.

꙾

Two days later, Sydney found herself knocking on the door of Vivian Green's apartment, pizza in one hand, bottle of Merlot under her arm.

"I have got to be crazy," she muttered with a shake of her head, closing her eyes and wondering what in the world had gotten into her. She was not a winger. Sydney Taylor did not fly by the seat of her pants. Yet here she was, standing at the door of her elderly neighbor who had no idea she was coming, hoping against hope that she'd let her in.

The door opened and Dr. Green took in the sight before her, letting her gaze travel from Sydney's hands up to her face. "Is there pepperoni on that pizza?"

"Yes, ma'am."

Dr. Green opened the door wider. "By all means, then, come in. Come in."

Sydney entered the apartment, again loving how warm and full it felt. At the small table, she set down the pizza and held up the wine. "Corkscrew?"

Without a word, Dr. Green walked past her into the kitchen. Sydney followed, took the offered corkscrew, and went to work opening the wine. Dr. Green took two wine glasses out of a cupboard, then two plates. They worked in silence. Comfortable silence, which was oddly wonderful for Sydney.

Once they were seated, each had a glass of wine and a slice of pizza in front of them, Dr. Green met Sydney's gaze with her rheumy blue eyes. "Spit it out."

Sydney looked at her, confused. "I'm sorry?"

"Not that I don't love a surprise visit now and then, especially one that includes dinner and wine, but I spent my entire career reading people and you look like you've got something on your mind. Want to talk about it?" She took a bite of her pizza and waited.

Sydney inhaled a large breath and let it out slowly. "Do you mind?"

"If I did, I wouldn't have let you in." Vivian winked and Sydney knew she was teasing.

"I just...I could use the opinion of somebody who doesn't know me so well. Somebody who can be objective. You know?"

Dr. Green nodded, took a sip of wine, and waited.

"I have a problem." Sydney took a sip of her own wine, not sure why she felt nervous about talking to Vivian Green. The woman seemed wiser than most people Sydney knew and she'd been a therapist. God knew Sydney could use a little therapy. When Vivian said nothing, simply continued to eat, Sydney grinned. "Do they teach you that in psychology school? To stay silent so the other person feels the need to fill it?"

Vivian smiled and still said nothing.

"Well, it works." Sydney laughed, took another deep breath, and poured her heart out to this woman she barely knew. She gave her background, filled her in on her career up to now, her goals, her current job and how well it had been going. "I mean, my intention has always been to keep moving, to keep stepping upward. That's always what I've wanted. And a couple days ago,

I got not one, but two jobs offers, both from bigger markets than this one. That's totally what I've been shooting for, been working so hard for since I graduated from college. And they're here. Right now. Tossed in my lap. I mean, I have actual *options*!" She stopped, the wind suddenly leaving her sails. "But now…"

"You want something different," Vivian said after a beat. She'd watched her face the entire time Sydney talked and it was like she was hearing more than the things Sydney said out loud.

"I might. Yes."

"Different how?"

Sydney swallowed, studied that lovely painting on the wall as she thought. "Different in that…maybe I want to stop constantly moving so much?"

"Are you asking me?" Dr. Green grinned at her.

Sydney chuckled back. "No. No, I'm telling you that I think I might want to…stay still for a while." Laura's words came back at her then, telling her she never stayed still for long.

"And what precipitated this change in goals?"

Sydney caught her bottom lip between her teeth and turned back to the painting.

"That pretty girl from the animal shelter, perhaps?"

Sydney's eyes widened in shock. "How did you know that?"

It was Vivian's turn to chuckle. "Oh, honey, I've seen more clients in my career than you can possibly imagine. You don't think any of them were homosexual?"

Realizing she'd been silly worrying about coming out to a professional therapist, Sydney nodded. "Yes. The pretty girl from the animal shelter. Jessica." And then came more pouring out of her heart. She told Vivian everything, from their initial meeting to the last time they'd slept together; she left nothing out. "She's got me all twisted up inside. I can't get her out of my head, no matter how hard I try. And believe me, I have *tried*."

"And it's been, what? A few weeks now?"

"Since I've seen her? About that. Yeah." *Three weeks, two days, and thirteen hours, to be exact.*

"No phone calls? No texting? Nothing at all?"

Sydney shook her head, suddenly feeling miserable.

Vivian took a deep breath and gazed off into the middle distance as if collecting her thoughts. Sydney sipped her wine, chewed her pizza, waited.

"The bottom line is pretty simple." Vivian finished her wine, refilled her glass from the bottle, folded her hands on the table in front of her, and gave a shrug of nonchalance. "The only one who knows what you really want is you. Career, location, living arrangement, love life. Only you. Nobody can tell you what makes the most sense or the least. Nobody can tell you your wants or goals are silly or perfect or anything in between. Only you. You are in charge of your own destiny, my dear. Just you."

"Me."

"You."

Sydney dropped her shoulders and pressed her lips together in a tight line, took some time to absorb what had been said. After a moment or two of contemplation, she helped herself to a second slice of pizza. Maybe this had been a dumb idea. "You know," she said finally, then took a bite. After she'd chewed and swallowed, she said, "Not that I don't appreciate your help, but…is it bad that I sort of hoped for some…clearer advice?"

"You don't think that was clear?" Vivian showed no signs of irritation or even surprise. In fact, if Sydney wasn't mistaken, she was smiling slightly as she simply sat there, ate her dinner, and watched her neighbor.

"Not really." Sydney tried to lift one corner of her mouth and keep any hint of dejection from her voice.

"Huh. Maybe I've grown rusty in my old age."

Something about her tone told Sydney that Vivian was saying exactly the opposite. "Oh, I'm sure that's not it. I just think you didn't really tell me anything I didn't already know."

"Now *that*, I agree with." Vivian cocked her head, sipped her wine, and smiled.

CHAPTER TWENTY

THE SUMMER AFTERNOON WAS blazing hot, which Jessica hated. She was not good with humidity. She didn't like that it made her sweat. She didn't like that it frizzed her hair. She didn't like that it made her cranky.

She was a little less cranky lately, though. That was true. Millie nuzzled her hand as she sat at her desk in her office, and Jessica stroked the short, silky fur absently. "Hi, sweetheart." She smiled at the dog when she lifted her head to look into Jessica's eyes and it was, not for the first time, something that amazed her about Millie. Touched her deep inside. Millie looked right at her. Often. Like, direct eye contact. And more than once, Jessica had seen a glimpse of something almost…human in that gaze. It warmed her heart and reminded her yet again that she and Millie were meant to be together. Adopting her was one of the smartest moves Jessica had ever made and Millie, in turn, had filled her heart with so much love, she felt almost peaceful. Almost.

Her phone beeped, telling her she had a text, so she pulled out her phone.

Trish.

Got an extra ticket to the game tonight. Come with me?

Jessica smiled. Though she and Trish had figured out immediately that they had no chemistry during their "date" more than a month ago, they ended up liking each other anyway and decided together that it was impossible to have too many friends. As two single women, having each other was a plus if they were invited to a party or gathering of some sort where they didn't want to show up alone. Trish got baseball tickets through her work, so she and Jessica had attended a couple games so far, and Jessica'd been surprised to enjoy herself. She was ambivalent about baseball, but learned quickly that going to the stadium to watch a game live (and stuff herself with tons of junk food she wouldn't normally eat) was infinitely more fun than trying to watch on television and wanting to blow your own brains out.

Let me see how the afternoon goes, okay? she texted back.

Though things had died down at Junebug a little, it was still bustling. Adoptions had been steady, but unfortunately, so had their intake. When she'd first started to learn the ins and outs of shelter business, one of the hardest things for Jessica to learn was that even if the shelter was doing well re-homing animals, they would never stop coming. There would always be abuse cases. There would always be underground dogfighting rings. There would always be careless owners.

She was also in the process of interviewing for a new head of public relations. The day after the telethon, a very coolly worded resignation e-mail from Anna arrived. It was addressed to Jessica, but also CC'd the rest of the board. Jessica, David, Catherine, Maggie, and three other members of the shelter's staff got a blow-by-blow of exactly why Anna was resigning. Unprofessional, to say the least, but a big part of Jessica knew she'd deserved it. So she'd sucked it up, taken her medicine, apologized to her staff, and moved on. She'd been painfully embarrassed for the next week or two, but she'd pushed through and her staff was finally beginning to look at her like normal again.

Tossing her phone to her desk, she forced herself back to the e-mail she'd been responding to. She was just finishing up when Regina buzzed her on the intercom.

"Excuse me, Jessica?"

"Yes?"

"There's a customer here to adopt a cat. They asked if they could have your help choosing."

Jessica sighed and pinched the bridge of her nose. This was not uncommon and had actually increased since the most recent telethon. People saw her on TV and felt like they knew her, like they trusted her. So often, they asked for her guidance when they adopted an animal. Jessica glanced at the stack of papers in her inbox and gave a small groan.

"Lisa can't help them?" she asked hopefully.

"They specifically asked for you." Regina's voice was apologetic and Jessica didn't want to put her in an uncomfortable position.

"Okay. Ask them to give me five minutes and I'll be out."

She hung up the phone, finished her e-mail, and hit Send. Then she looked down at Millie. "Want to come with me? We can get one of your cat buddies a new home. What do you say?" Millie's nub of a tail started wagging and Jessica leashed her up.

It wasn't long after the lunch hour, so the lobby was fairly busy. A summer camp was visiting as a field trip, so about a dozen five-year-olds were buzzing around like bees, three camp workers—easily designated by their neon green T-shirts—tried their best to wrangle. The gift shop had three people waiting in line to pay for their purchases.

As always was the case, Millie was a draw, especially for the kids. The process was always the same. First, they'd do a double take. Second, an expression that was a combination of slight fear and deep curiosity would land on their faces. Third, they'd look up at Jessica. As soon as eye contact was made, she'd ask if they wanted to pet Millie. The answer was almost always unanimously yes.

She was squatting in the middle of the lobby as four members of the field trip gently ran their hands over Millie's body when Jessica glanced in the direction of the cat wall and felt her breath stick in her lungs.

Sydney Taylor stood there watching her, a hesitant smile on her face.

Oh, my God.

They were the only coherent words that would enter her brain. She'd done her best to wipe Sydney from her memory banks (impossible). She avoided the Channel Six news at all costs, but she honestly thought Sydney would be long gone by now. Off to Austin. Or Raleigh. Or Tallahassee. Or someplace—anyplace—other than here. And yet, there she stood, looking annoyingly beautiful in black dress slacks and a pale yellow silk tank top. Her hair seemed a bit shorter and it swooped to the opposite side as Jessica remembered. The eyes hadn't changed, though, and neither had Sydney's ability to make Jessica blush from across the room. She cursed her pale skin as she felt her cheeks warm, and turned her attention back to the kids for a bit longer, asking them questions about their own pets or pets they wished they had.

She needed time. At least a few minutes. To steel herself. Brace for impact. Prepare. All this time, she'd shaken it off, joked about it even. No big deal. She'd told that to her friends. She'd said it to herself. And yet, there stood Sydney Taylor, not fifteen feet away, in Jessica's lobby, and all she could do was feel the butterflies in her stomach like she was a teenager about to talk to her crush.

"Okay, Millie and I have some work to do," she said to the kids as she stood, simultaneously excited to talk to Sydney and dreading it. "But thank you guys for being so nice to her." The kids waved as Jessica led Millie away and they walked toward Sydney.

"Hey," Sydney said, meeting Jessica's eyes with obvious uncertainty. She squatted down to lavish attention on Millie. "You did it?" she asked Jessica without looking up. "You adopted her? I'm so glad."

"Yeah, I decided I had to. We were meant to be together." Millie looked up at Jessica with utter devotion in her eyes and Jessica made a mental note to give her an extra treat later for that performance. "So. You're looking for a cat?"

Sydney stood and the way she wet her lips and her still stunning eyes darted around made it clear to Jessica that she was nervous.

Good. That makes two of us.

"I decided I'd like to give it a shot. I've got the goldfish, but…" She let her voice trail off.

"A cat's gonna need a bit more care than a goldfish does. You know that, right?" Jessica sounded a little snippier than she'd meant to, and she grimaced in reaction.

"I do." Sydney nodded with enthusiasm, apparently unoffended. "I do. Yeah. I'm ready."

Jessica stepped toward the cat wall and scanned. "Do you think you want an older cat or a kitten? We have both."

"What do you suggest?"

"Well…" Jessica shifted into work mode. *She's just a client. She's just a client. She's just a client.* "It depends, really. First—obviously—you'll have a kitten longer. That being said, there is also training and the kitten phase to go through. Eating things that aren't food, finding little nooks and crannies you didn't know your apartment had, litter training—though that's usually pretty easy—getting to know their personality as they grow with you. With an adult cat, you have different features all together. You'll get to know them, but they already have a fully developed personality. An adult cat will most likely be a bit lower key than a kitten. Most of the time, they are incredibly loving, especially the ones from here." Jessica touched her fingertip to the glass on the cube currently occupied by Ella, a six-year-old cat whose elderly owner had passed away, leaving her with no place to live. She was gorgeous, ash-gray fur and enormous green eyes that seemed to see everything, but also had a small tinge of sadness in them. "I believe that the adult cats we have know exactly where they are and long for somebody to adopt them. When that happens, they tend to bond with their new owners very quickly and very tightly."

"She's beautiful," Sydney said quietly of Ella as she leaned closer to the glass. "What's her story?"

Jessica told her the details. Tried hard not to feel Sydney's eyes on her. Failed.

"Can I sit with her in the Visiting Room?" Sydney asked.

With a nod, Jessica led her to a room off the dog wing where people got to sit with potential adoptees to see how they got along, see if they clicked. Sydney took a seat and Jessica handed over Millie's leash. "Hold her, please, while I get Ella."

Closing the door behind her, Jessica locked eyes with Lisa down the hall. "I need a cat," Jessica said, then went through the door that took her to the back of the cat wall.

"Is that Sydney?" Lisa asked quietly as she entered with the keys.

"It is."

"What's she doing here?"

"Apparently, she wants to adopt a cat."

"You okay?" Lisa's voice was matter-of-fact rather than sympathetic, and for that, Jessica was grateful.

"Fine."

"Good."

Together, they got Ella out and Jessica murmured to her as she cradled the soft, warm body close. "Okay, m'lady. Somebody wants to get to know you a bit. You all right with that?" Ella immediately started to purr in her arms. "'Atta girl. Get that motor running. Make an impression." Back in the Visiting Room, Sydney sat in one of the orange plastic chairs, bent forward and talking quietly to Millie, who seemed for all intents and purposes to be listening very carefully. "Ella," Jessica said. "This is my friend, Sydney. Sydney, this is Miss Ella." She gently handed the cat over to Sydney, who very carefully set her in her lap and looked the tiniest bit terrified.

Sydney looked up at Jessica. "I've never had a cat before and I haven't had a pet in eight years."

"You have fish," Jessica reminded her.

"Yeah, well." Sydney made a sheepish expression. "I'm on my third Marge and my fifth Homer. What if I'm a terrible cat mom?"

Jessica gestured at Ella, who looked all kinds of comfy on Sydney's black-clad legs and had turned up the volume on her purring. "She seems to be doing all right with you."

Sydney ran her hand down Ella's back, scratched behind her ears. "She does, doesn't she?" And when she looked up at Jessica, her face showed such childlike happiness, it squeezed Jessica's heart.

"I never expected to see you again," Jessica blurted before she could stop herself.

"Never?"

Jessica shook her head. "I figured you were in Austin by now. Or somewhere…"

"Nope. Still here. And I *always* expected to see you again, for the record. Just…after I took care of some things."

"What things?" Jessica eyed her, not sure what to do with this information.

Sydney shrugged, grinned, looked a little less nervous, but still seeming to tread carefully. "Things. Lots of things. I'd like to tell you about them some time. Maybe over dinner?"

Jessica's eyebrows shot up in disbelief. "You're asking me to dinner? Now? After a month and a half of no contact whatsoever?"

Sydney's nod was full of confidence, if that was something that was even possible. Her nervousness had evaporated, as if this was the very reason she'd come, the cat only being secondary. "Yes," she said with surety. "I am asking you to have dinner with me. And last time I checked, phone lines and Internet connections ran both ways." She gave a pointed arch of an eyebrow to Jessica before she looked down at Ella and let those words sink in. Jessica swallowed, watched as Sydney continued to stroke the cat's fur. "Look, Jessica, I'd really like to talk to you. I have a lot to share, but I'd rather not do it at your work." She looked back up, made eye contact with Jessica. Intense eye contact. "Have dinner with me. Please."

Jessica bit her bottom lip, torn. She was still angry with Sydney. Angry that she'd never bothered to call her or text her or anything her after their last time together. She'd spent quite some time stewing over it, ignoring her own passive-aggressiveness because, of course, Sydney was right. Jessica had made no effort at contact, so she was as much to blame for the radio silence. She had to shoulder some of the responsibility; it was only fair. And damn Sydney if she didn't still look positively edible.

Jessica blew out a frustrated breath. "Do you want the cat or not?"

Sydney held her gaze for another beat before glancing down at Ella. "I do."

"Fine. She has to go through a checkup and you need to fill out an application. Once both of those things are done, you can take her home, so"—she shook her head—"I can't believe I'm saying this, but how about if I bring her by your place tomorrow? We can talk then."

The grin that split Sydney's face was so wide, it was almost comical. "I like that idea. I like that idea a lot."

"Okay," Jessica said, forcing herself not to mirror the smile. "Do you want more time with Ella?"

Sydney kissed the cat's head. "No, you can take her for now. I need to go buy cat stuff." Her excitement sounded almost childlike and Jessica couldn't smother her own grin this time as she took Ella from Sydney's lap.

Jerking her chin toward Sydney's clothes, Jessica commented, "You'd better get used to that."

Sydney looked down at her lap, her black dress slacks now covered with soft, gray fur. And she laughed. "Perfect. I love it. It's perfect."

Jessica furrowed her brow at the sound. "Regina at the front desk can give you an application. Just fill it out and give it back to her. I'll see you tomorrow at…seven?"

"Excellent." Sydney practically skipped out of the room, but not before stopping to nuzzle Ella one more time on her way. Jessica took a moment to watch her face, subtly smell the citrus scent of Sydney's hair so near her nose, remember what it was like to be this close to her. Sydney looked up, said softly, "Thanks, Jessica. See you tomorrow." And she was off.

Jessica stood in the Visiting Room for a moment, trying to get her bearings, right her world, which had tilted strangely and ever so slightly on its axis today. And as she took Ella back to her cubby, congratulated her on a job well done, and closed her safely inside, only one thought echoed through her head on a continuous loop: *what the hell have I gotten myself into?*

CHAPTER TWENTY-ONE

WHEN THE BUZZER RANG, Sydney jumped. Literally jumped. Like, out of her skin.

"God, tense much?" she said to the empty apartment as she twirled in a circle and gave it all a final once-over. She'd cleaned like crazy from the second she'd gotten home from work, going so far as to scrub the tiny kitchen floor and entryway on her hands and knees. She'd dusted, dust mopped, and scoured until the entire place shimmered like the sunlight on water.

In the corner was a cat tower…one of those climbing things covered with carpet that had a bed-like platform at the top so Ella could lie on it and gaze out the window. A set of bowls sat on a paw-print placemat on the kitchen floor. In the bathroom was a litter box, tucked sensibly in a corner. The couch was neat, its afghan folded over the back, the throw pillows lined up tastefully. A bottle of Pinot Noir sat on the counter, two empty glasses next to it.

With one nod to the room, Sydney hit the button on the intercom. "Yes?"

"Cat delivery," came Jessica's voice, and Sydney couldn't help but grin.

"Come on up." She pushed the button to the door for a full three seconds, then opened the door to her apartment and went out into the hall to peer over the banister.

The sun was shining through the leaded glass windows in the lobby and it bounced off Jessica's copper-colored hair in sparkles. She held a carrier in one hand, her purse over her shoulder with papers sticking out, and a leash attached to Millie in the other. When she looked up, her blue eyes met Sydney's and held for a beat before she smiled hesitantly and said, "Hey."

The wave of pure…happy, there was no other way to describe it, that washed through Sydney at the sight was something she didn't quite understand and didn't have the opportunity to analyze right now. Instead, she met Jessica halfway down the staircase and took the carrier from her hand.

"Hi," she said, meeting Jessica's gaze. "I'm glad you're here." She turned and went back up the stairs, and she could feel Jessica behind her, making her nerves kick into overdrive like a teenager on a first date.

"I hope it's okay I brought Millie. Ella likes her. I thought maybe she'd help her settle in just by being here."

"I don't mind at all. I think it's great." Sydney gave Millie's big head a pat. Inside the apartment, Sydney set the carrier down on the floor and deferred to Jessica. "What's the best way to do this for her?"

"Let me take a look around first. Make sure there's no place she can get hurt. Is that okay?"

Sydney held her arm out in a *go ahead* gesture, then watched as Jessica wandered the apartment she already knew fairly well. Her gaze hovered on the curtains, the wall art. "You've made some changes."

"I have." Sydney bounced slightly on the balls of her feet, the nervous energy needing to go somewhere.

"I like it. It looks…inviting now." She stood in front of the painting, seemed to take it in.

Unable to keep her eyes from wandering Jessica's body, Sydney decided not to fight it. The jeans were light and worn and looked super soft, especially the white spot near the back pocket that was almost worn through. Her navy blue button-down tank left her arms bare, and for that, Sydney thanked her lucky stars as her eyes roamed over the creamy pale skin, lightly freckled shoulders. Jessica moved out of her line of sight, presumably into the bathroom and bedroom and the idea of her in Sydney's bedroom gave her a quick shiver of pleasure.

Stop it, she told herself. *Let's not get ahead of the game. Okay? Just chill.*

"Looks good," Jessica pronounced as she returned to the living room and pulled Sydney out of her own head. The cat tower caught her eye and she pointed at it. "That's a nice touch. She'll love it."

"Good." Sydney squatted down so she could look into the carrier. "Hi there, Ella. You ready to see your new home?" The cat blinked at her with those enormous green eyes and yawned, her pink tongue curling out like a New Year's Eve party horn. With a chuckle, Sydney glanced up at Jessica. "Is it okay?"

"Go for it."

Sydney opened the door to the carrier. She took her sweet time about it, but Ella finally stepped out, took a look around. "What do you think?" Sydney asked the cat quietly.

She wandered the apartment as both women watched, sniffing here and there, poking her head into corners. Nose to nose, she stood in front of Millie, almost like they were having some sort of telepathic conversation. Then she went into the bedroom and Sydney and Jessica looked at each other, Sydney in slight panic.

"It's fine," Jessica said. "Give her a minute."

In less than that, she was back out, not walking so much as strolling. She stopped at the cat tower, gave it a sniff, looked up at the top platform. Then she leapt up, turned in one circle, settled in and made herself comfortable in the evening sunshine. Her purr could be heard across the room. Millie settled down on the floor at the base of the tower, put her head down, and closed her eyes. Sydney and Jessica looked at each other for a beat before they both laughed, their relief obvious. Before either could utter a word, the doorbell buzzed.

"That's dinner," Sydney said. "I hope you like Chinese." She'd taken a chance, as she didn't know anybody who didn't like Chinese.

"I do."

"Be right back." Sydney grabbed her wallet and treated the trip down the stairs as an opportunity to find her footing, take a breath. Jessica was here; that's all Sydney needed. Next up, be honest. Be open. Be transparent. She opened the door, paid the delivery guy, and took the two bags back up. In the apartment, she was surprised to find Jessica pouring the wine.

That seems like a good sign.

Sydney put the bags on the counter, got plates, and pulled things out. They worked together in companionable silence, sharing the rice, the cashew chicken, the vegetable lo mein, the egg rolls. Once their plates were loaded up and they each had a glass of wine, they moved by unspoken agreement to the couch and set their dishes on the coffee table.

"To Ella's new home," Jessica said, as she held up her glass. "And don't let me forget that I have some paperwork for you. Just some basic information about owning a cat, things to look out for, her medical records, that kind of thing."

Sydney gave a nod and said, "To you being here. To us being here together. To you not tossing me out of the shelter on my ass." She partnered her words with her best crooked, self-deprecating grin.

"Yeah, well, it was touch and go for a minute there." But Jessica was softly smiling.

They touched glasses and sipped.

The food was excellent, which they both mentioned. Finally, Jessica asked the question that opened up the subject once and for all. "So…what brought you back to the shelter?"

"You did." It was a simple answer. And the truth.

Jessica squinted at her. "What does that mean, Sydney?"

Sydney took a deep breath. "I've done a lot of soul searching over the past six or so weeks. A lot of soul searching."

"Yeah? How come?"

"Because I needed to. Because it was about time." Sydney took a sip of wine. "Do you know what a self-fulfilling prophecy is?"

"Of course."

"Well, I think that's what I was creating for myself."

Jessica chewed her egg roll and studied Sydney's face. Sydney did her best not to shift and squirm under such scrutiny. Especially from this woman. "How so?"

Another deep breath. Who knew you needed so much air to have a deep conversation? "I know I've mentioned it before, but my parents are…less than present in my life. It's been that way since I was old enough to stay home alone, so it's normal for me. I'm used to being alone and I'm fine with it. I can take care of myself. I've never needed anybody."

Jessica nodded, put a forkful of rice in her mouth, her eyes steadily on Sydney's.

"I've created not only a solitary life for myself, but a…nomadic one, for lack of a better phrase. And that never gave me pause until I was here."

"Really?"

Sydney shook her head. "Never. It was always just…who I am. And then I met you and I assumed you'd just be a fun distraction for a bit." She looked sheepishly at Jessica. "No offense."

Jessica shrugged.

"But when you left here that night…"

Jessica grimaced and nodded once.

"It really made me stop in my tracks."

"But you never called. You didn't come after me. You didn't even ask me to stay. You just…let me go."

"I know." Sydney looked down at her plate, set down her fork, her appetite waning a bit. "I know, and I am so sorry about that. That was a big mistake. Big. Huge."

Jessica squinted at her. "Are you quoting *Pretty Woman* at me in the middle of a serious conversation?"

"I am." Sydney grimaced. "I'm sorry. Just trying to lighten the mood."

Jessica set her fork down and shifted so they were face to face on the couch. "How about you just talk to me?"

"I can do that."

"Good. Where were we? Oh, right. You didn't come after me, didn't text, didn't call. For weeks. We were there."

"Right." *Okay, so she's a little bitter. That's to be expected.* Sydney swallowed. "I got to thinking about things after I talked to Laura. I told her what had happened between us and she pointed out some fairly obvious things about my life that I never really paid attention to. Most importantly, that I am always looking for a place to belong, yet I never let myself stay in that place long enough for it to feel that way. And I'd like to change that." She blew out a breath. "There. I said it."

She waited.

A beat passed.

Two.

Jessica took a sip of her wine, her eyes on Ella, still lounging in her tower. "That was hard for you to say," she said matter-of-factly.

"Yeah. I've never actually said it out loud before."

Another beat passed.

"So now what?" Jessica's eyes were on her now, intently. She sipped her wine, never looking away. "Why am I here?" It was a valid question, but she seemed less…angry? And that was good. Sydney would take that. "And when are you headed to Austin? Or wherever the next place happens to be?"

"I passed on Austin."

Jessica blinked at her. "You what?"

"They offered me a job and I said thank you, but no thank you."

Jessica blinked some more, wine glass stopped halfway to her lips. "But…why? You were so anxious to get the hell out of here."

"I was. But then…" Sydney grinned at her. "I took your advice."

Brow furrowed, Jessica asked, "What advice was that?"

"I have spent the past three weekends exploring your city." The fact that Jessica's eyebrows shot up in surprise made Sydney laugh out loud. "It's true."

"What did you see?"

"I went to the museum. The art gallery. The falls. I hit a baseball game. I've tried six restaurants in the past two weeks. I did a wine tour. I saw a play in the new theatre downtown."

Jessica's jaw had dropped open.

"You know what?" Sydney asked. "You were right. Your city has a lot to offer. There's an LGBT film festival here in the fall, isn't there?"

Jessica nodded, words seeming to have left her for the moment.

"I want to do a story on it. I've already talked to Brad about it."

There was more silence, but this time, it wasn't uncomfortable. In fact, it was kind of awesome. Sydney bit into an egg roll, smiled at Jessica as she chewed.

"I...I don't even know what to say," Jessica finally told her. "I'm...shocked. Amazed. Impressed."

"You're a lot of things."

"I am." Jessica sat back against the couch and just studied her. "So...you're staying? For a while at least?"

"Yeah." Sydney nodded. "I like it here."

"That's..." Jessica stared off into space for a moment. "That's good to hear. It's good." She nodded, turned a tender smile toward Sydney.

"Yeah? Well good. Because I wanted to talk to you about one more thing." Sydney swallowed hard, did her best not to show how nervous she really was about this particular subject.

"What's that?"

"Us."

"Us?"

Sydney nodded. And waited.

"Is there an us?" Jessica asked quietly.

"I think there could be." Sydney cleared her throat. "I mean, I'd like there to be."

Jessica gave a slow nod, as if she was absorbing the idea.

Sydney shifted in her seat so she was a bit closer to Jessica, close enough to lay a warm, gentle hand on her thigh. She drew nervous circles on the denim with her thumb. "Look. I know we've had a couple of rough patches. My fault."

"Not completely your fault," Jessica interjected.

"But like I said," Sydney continued, undeterred. "I've been doing a lot of soul searching, and even though I've figured so much out about myself and I've made some adjustments, it still feels like there's *something* missing." She looked up at Jessica's face. "I think that something is you."

Jessica returned the gaze with those big, beautiful blue eyes, her expression a combination of hopeful and guarded.

"I just feel like we could have something. If we gave it a real chance." When Jessica still didn't answer, Sydney gave it one last try. "I've missed you."

Jessica looked down into her lap and when she raised her eyes again, they were watery. "I've missed you, too."

Sydney hadn't really known what to expect out of tonight. She hadn't known what Jessica would say, how she'd react. She didn't even know what she wanted her to say, but this? This right here? This was perfect. *I've missed you, too*, was absolutely the best thing she could have hoped for her to say.

"We can go slow," Sydney said softly, leaning in closer. "We can take our time. There's no hurry at all." She pressed her lips tenderly to Jessica's, so elatedly happy, she could hardly believe it. Her thoughts were cut short, though, when Jessica's hands came up, grasped her face, and *kissed* her. Really kissed her, deeply and with tremendous passion.

Sydney had no idea how much time had passed when Jessica finally pulled back, but she didn't care. Her head was swimming and she was so achingly turned on she wasn't sure what planet she was on at the moment.

"What if I don't want to go slow?" Jessica whispered.

"If you kiss me like that again, you can have anything you want," Sydney said breathlessly.

"Anything?"

Sydney nodded.

"Take me to your bedroom."

Sydney's eyebrows flew up. "Seriously?"

"Yes, seriously."

"You're sure? I mean, we can talk more if you want."

"Sydney. Do you need to talk more? You said you think we have something. I agree, and think it's worth exploring. I'm in my thirties. I don't need to analyze something I know I want."

The idea of Jessica not only wanting her, but saying so, made Sydney's core tense up—in a good way. She nodded again and stood up. She held out a hand. Jessica grasped it and Sydney led her to the bedroom door.

Where Jessica stopped them dead. "Wait."

Sydney turned to look, almost afraid to, almost expecting her to change her mind, back out, say goodbye, tell her she was just kidding.

"I need you to know something."

"Okay." Sydney braced.

"I need you to know that I'm not leaving tonight. If we do this, there's no running off when we're done like some one-night stand. Okay? I don't work like that."

Sydney felt her own smile form and grow. "Good." She glanced over Jessica's shoulder at Millie, snoring softly, still at the base of Ella's cat tower. With a suspicious squint, she looked back at Jessica and said, "Wait a minute. Is that the real reason you brought Millie?" Her eyes widened. "Did you *know* you'd end up staying?"

For the first time since she'd arrived, Jessica looked slightly uncertain, gazed down at her feet, but didn't let go of Sydney's hand. "Is it bad that I hoped?" she asked with hesitation, her voice small.

"Not even a little bit," Sydney said, more certain than she'd ever been about anything in her life. She kissed Jessica softly on the mouth, and led her into the bedroom. "I plan on holding you all night long. I hope you're ready for that."

"I've been ready for that since I first laid eyes on you." Jessica seemed surprised by her own words, but then smiled. "True story."

"Then come with me," Sydney said, and led her into the bedroom.

The End

By Georgia Beers

www.georgiabeers.com